LOVE LETTERS TO POE

VOLUME 1: A TOAST TO EDGAR ALLAN POE

JEREMY MEGARGEE   J. L. ROYCE

ELEANOR SCIOLISTEIN   TROY SEATE

RENEE CRONLEY   MELANIE COSSEY

NATASHA C. CALDER   KARL LYKKEN

HAILEY PIPER   JELENA DUNATO

RICHARD M. ANKERS   RHONDA EIKAMP

AVRA MARGARITI   ROBERT FRANK

JACKSON KUHL   EMELINE MARIE BEAUCHÊNE

T. E. STURK   ETHAN NAHTÉ   AERYN RUDEL

LIAM HOGAN   H. R. OWEN

M. ALAN VREELAND   KATIE DIBENEDETTO

MALDA MARLYS   CODY MOWER   MARK TOWSE

R. LEIGH HENNIG   ROBIN POND

T. C. GRASSMAN   J.E.M. WILDFIRE

RICHARD ZWICKER   SHARMON GAZAWAY

EVAN BAUGHFMAN   SHAWNA BORMAN

EMMA BROCATO   WADE NEWHOUSE

SARAH HANS   CLIO VELENTZA

JESSICA ANN YORK   ELLEN HUANG

JARED BAKER   COLLEEN ANDERSON

LENA NG   NEMMA WOLLENFANG

ANNA OJINNAKA   A. A. RUBIN

NANCY BREWKA-CLARK   ROB FRANCIS

AVITAL MALENKY   ELLEN DENTON

TRISTIN DEVEAU   KEVIN HOLLAWAY

JENNIFER WONDERLY   JUDE MATULICH-HALL

SAM KNIGHT

Edited by
SARA CROCOLL SMITH

Love Letters to Poe
Volume 1: A Toast to Edgar Allan Poe

ISSN 2693-8804 (online)

ISSN 2769-1578 (print)

ISBN 978-1-956546-00-2 (ebook)

ISBN 978-1-956546-01-9 (print)

❀ Created with Vellum

CONTENTS

Free Offer   xi
The Masque of the Red Death Artwork

A Year of Love Letters to Poe   xiii
Sara Crocoll Smith

ISSUE 1: A TOAST TO EDGAR ALLAN POE

THE ROWHOUSE   3
Jeremy Megargee

THE SONG OF HELAINE   7
J.L. Royce

THE HEART OF ALDERMAN KANE   14
Eleanor Sciolistein

KINGDOM BY THE SEA   20
Troy Seate

THIEF OF ETERNAL DELIGHTS   24
Renee Cronley

MIDNIGHT RIDER   29
Melanie Cossey

ISSUE 2: BLOOD IS THICKER

IN THE ALDER GLADE   37
Natasha C. Calder

WHERE THE HEART IS   43
Karl Lykken

THE INHERITANCE THREAD 48
Hailey Piper

THE DISAPPEARANCE OF ALICE 54
HARPER
Jelena Dunato

ISSUE 3: DISCIPLINES & DARKNESS

THE HUMAN IN ME 63
Richard M. Ankers

THE SPEAKING SKULLS 71
Rhonda Eikamp

FOSSIL FEVER 78
Avra Margariti

RESURRECTIONIST 80
Robert Frank

AN INCIDENT ON MULBERRY STREET 86
Jackson Kuhl

ISSUE 4: EVERLASTING LIFE

EMBER'S LAST LIGHT, REFLECTED 95
Emeline Marie Beauchêne

HIS EMBRACE 100
T.E. Sturk

ROSE & THORNS 104
Ethan Nahté

THE NIGHT, FOREVER, AND US 107
by Aeryn Rudel

ISSUE 5: MEMENTO AMORI

MOURNING POST 113
Liam Hogan

TEMPLE 117
H.R. Owen

SARAH   120
M. Alan Vreeland

FORGET ME NOT   123
by Katie DiBenedetto

ISSUE 6: MODERN GOTHIC

DEATH LOVES FROGS   129
Malda Marlys

ANNA   134
Cody Mower

THE TASTE OF BOURBON   138
Mark Towse

PIANO MAN   143
by R. Leigh Hennig

ISSUE 7: POE REIMAGINED

CORPORATE CULTURE   153
Robin Pond

A LINE OF CROWS   161
TC Grassman

THE HEART TELLS THE TALE   168
J.E.M. Wildfire

THE BIRD WHISPERER   173
Richard Zwicker

TO HAVE AND TO HOLD   179
Sharmon Gazaway

THE FALL OF THE HOUSE OF POE   185
by Evan Baughfman

ISSUE 8: MIDWESTERN & SOUTHERN GOTHIC

POISONED HONEY AND PICKLED PIGS' FEET   193
Shawna Borman

THE WALKING WIDOW   197
Emma Brocato

THE WOUNDED AND THE DEAD   202
Wade Newhouse

TAKE THE FIRE FROM HER   208
by Sarah Hans

ISSUE 9: YOUR BODY IS A CANVAS

SMUDGE   215
Clio Velentza

TARANTISM   221
Jessica Ann York

SOUL INTENTIONALLY SOLD   225
Ellen Huang

HER FONDEST WISH   227
by Jared Baker

ISSUE 10: WEEP FOR ME

LADY OF THE BLEEDING HEART   235
Colleen Anderson

THE HYPNOTIST   239
Lena Ng

ROUTES BEST LEFT UNTAKEN   241
Nemma Wollenfang

DANCING DELILAH   243
Anna Ojinnaka

THE WIDOW'S WALK   247
by A.A. Rubin

ISSUE 11: PARENTHOOD

FAMILY PORTRAIT   253
Nancy Brewka-Clark

DUST TO DUST   258
Rob Francis

MRS. ANNA ENGLISH   263
Avital Malenky

DEAD MAN TALKING   270
by Ellen Denton

ISSUE 12: DON'T LOOK
BEHIND YOU

DECAY   279
Tristin Deveau

THE HOUSE REGARDS   285
Kevin Hollaway

A FAMILY HEIRLOOM   288
Jennifer Wonderly

LIKE ANY OTHER NIGHT   294
Jude Matulich-Hall

THE DARKEST THOUGHTS   297
Sam Knight

Free Offer   303
The Masque of the Red Death Artwork

Let Us Know You Want More!   305
About the Editor   307

A YEAR OF LOVE LETTERS TO POE

SARA CROCOLL SMITH

Over 170 years beyond his death, Edgar Allan Poe
continues to inspire a fervent adoration for short gothic
fiction. Through his stories and poems, we hear his voice in
our heads, feel his passion in our hearts. His works spur
writers to weave their own gothic threads in a beautiful
tangle of words influenced by those who have gone before,
mingled with gothic worlds born anew.

Love Letters to Poe is a haven to celebrate the works of
Poe and encourage the creation of gothic fiction tapped
from the vein of Poe—a love letter to the man himself, if
you will. And yet, after a year of having the honor of
publishing short stories and poems by incredibly talented
authors and poets, as well as joining this thriving gothic
community, I'd like to propose that these gothic tales are
also a love letter to each other.

While we raise a glass in a toast to Edgar Allan Poe, let
us also raise a glass to each other. For through us, our
reading and writing, our discussions and analysis, our art
and other devotions, we're keeping the spirit of Poe alive.
Several hundred writers and poets submitted their works to

Love Letters to Poe in its inaugural year. Within this anthology are 12 themed issues that contain 48 short stories and 7 poems from 55 masterful weavers of gothic fiction.

I'm delighted to share that two stories within this collection are award nominated. "The Heart of Alderman Kane" by Eleanor Sciolistein and "Midnight Rider" by Melanie Cossey are nominees for Poe Baltimore's *Saturday 'Visiter' Awards* in the category of "Original Works Inspired by E.A. Poe's Life and Writing."

These awards recognize Edgar Allan Poe's continuing legacy in the arts and literature around the world. The prizes honor media, art, performance and writing that adapts or is inspired by Poe's life and works. Official winners will be revealed, and prize medals presented, at The Black Cat Ball, the Official Party of the *International Edgar Allan Poe Festival & Awards* on October 2, 2021. Regardless of the outcome, I'm extremely proud of these authors and all the authors and poets published in *Love Letters to Poe*. They've written accomplished pieces that do Poe justice and I sincerely hope you enjoy their haunting tales.

Cheers to you and to hopefully many more years of *Love Letters to Poe*!

Sincerely,
    Sara Crocoll Smith
    Publisher / Editor-in-Chief
    Love Letters to Poe

ISSUE 1: A TOAST TO EDGAR ALLAN POE

LOVE LETTERS TO POE

MEGARGEE | ROYCE | SCIOLISTEIN
SEATE | CRONLEY | COSSEY

Volume 1, Issue 1 | October 2020
Edited by Sara Crocoll Smith

THE ROWHOUSE

JEREMY MEGARGEE

The rowhouse is small, the rooms cramped, and there's a vague sense of claustrophobia when moving through miniscule hallways and climbing narrow stairs. When it's daylight and Baltimore is alive, it's a modest museum, and people crowd into the tiny rooms to get a sense of who he was, why he was, and what lived in his haunted heart. You can buy keepsakes, candles, leather journals, t-shirts, and talismanic objects, purchased from within the walls where he once breathed and labored. That's the surface of the rowhouse, a skimming of shallow water, but there are depths that remain unseen, a caul that breaks open when the hour grows dark and the museum closes for business. Midnight oil burns in rooms of memory, and there are sights and sounds to be heard. The past tends to stain, and the rowhouse is no different.

There's an infinitesimal attic, emaciated rafters and a lonely window. There's a mountain of bird bones here, a brittle Everest. Ulnas, femurs, carpometacarpus gleaming beneath weak moonlight, once-feathered wings, and skulls polished clean by mice and insects, beaks no longer able to caw…

Ravens shatter the window every few months, drawn inward as though by magnetism, and they die gasping in the attic, their insides equally shattered. The window is frequently replaced, but the bones are never touched, for it would be unlucky to desecrate the graveyard that the ravens have chosen for themselves.

We won't linger, for the bird skulls resent being watched, and it's not polite to stare. Down through the ceiling, the walls pressing inward, making you feel like you must bend and contort to navigate from room to room. There's a bedroom, and a feverish scratching from inside, quill on paper, desk rattling, ink pooling and bleeding blacker than sin. The sound represents desperation, a yearning to rise above the station he was born into. There's a smooth, fruity flavor overhanging the room, the smell of brandy hitting the belly and lighting fires there, fuel for ideas after dark, literature being born. A tugging, a rattling, like a wounded heart beneath floorboards. Some writers give birth over and over again in their lifetimes, sending their beautifully repulsive children out into the world to be admired or disdained. It takes a toll, those mental exertions, and sometimes it drives one to drink and drink until death is almost blissfully certain…

We creep on, and mind the wooden planks, they're sensitive, they squeal, and splinters are a constant gift. The next bedroom is smaller, closer to that aforementioned attic, and it feels crooked, never quite solid, a nest for bent angles and walls that were never taught to remain straight. During daylight it's the quietest room, but at night it's the loudest, a nocturnal element in play, for every tortured soul finds a voice that's been lost in the witching hour.

Sporadic noises, ragged coughs full of viscous liquid

and infinite suffering. It's hot in here, a taste of Hell's precipice, and the sauna-like temperatures make the invisible cougher even more vocal. It brings to mind images of a brow with skin thin like parchment, beaded with sweat, and a pallid literary man's hand wiping at it hour after hour with a wet rag, hoping to give her just a sliver of comfort…

Sometimes the coughs come with a splatter, and a red mist will stain the hardwood floor, blooms of blood from nowhere, roses that never last, disappearing with the dawn. It was called consumption because it *consumed*. The disease made one as frail as a cadaver, lips forcibly crimson from the coughing, and a human in such a state was a pitiful thing to see, clutching at blankets in hopes of warding off a cold so deep it chilled the marrow.

If the rowhouse has a soul—and I believe that it does—surely that soul wasn't born with a lust for the macabre. It was imprinted, *stamped* into the architecture of the place, as inevitable as a wound never allowed to close as a knife keeps splitting it open and refusing it the chance to heal. A cloud lorded over the life of the man who lived and wrote here, and he was so accustomed to the shadow of it that he never expected it to leave him be. If history teaches us anything, it never did…

If the rowhouse is a part of him, the streets of Baltimore are as well. His last steps, his final mysterious delirium, his fall, skull cracking cobblestone, and all the stories and poems yet to be told draining from him as his life approached the lesser portion of the hourglass. The insult of an obituary written by an enemy, a life lived destitute, a path almost predestined to glorify tragedy. A servant of sorrow to the bitter end, and isn't sorrow one of the most inspiring emotions of all?

So the next time you're strolling through Baltimore,

that special pocket of gloom where the streets are dark and might have teeth, stop to admire the rowhouse, and let your gaze drift up to a window. If the night is right and the stars shine phantasmorgically, you might see a face looking down at you. Pale, drooping, a broken moonflower of a face, and hair as black and wild as the circumstances of his life. You'll meet his eyes, and behind them is a murderous orangutan, a black cat, a heart pounding under floorboards, and a legendary raven that perches and speaks from a familiar chamber door…

All that he is, all that he was, all that ever lived and lurked inside of him. Lift a glass of cognac, and hold tight to a rose until the thorns pierce your palms. The monsters that were in him are in us all, and it just takes a little push to get them out…

It'll all make sense in time…

The rowhouse will show you.

Jeremy Megargee has been writing horror fiction for several years now, and most of his stories delve into a dark Poe-esque direction. You can follow his work on Facebook (JMHorrorFiction) and on Instagram (xbadmoonrising).

THE SONG OF HELAINE

J.L. ROYCE

Je veux dormir! dormir plutôt que vivre!
Dans un sommeil aussi doux que la mort…

— C.B.

S hunned by family and friends, rejected by my class, reduced to frequenting the low establishments still willing to take my coin: I visit public houses slopping wretched ale, their *filles de joie* offering the most desultory of embraces. Life had become a desperate search, a stultifying circuit from that gloomy mansion where once our laughter reigned, to those scabrous beds, and back: to weep at the ivy-bound tomb where my Helaine sleeps.

Yet, this wretched half-life soon may end!

My carriage slows to turn—we pass through wrought-iron gates to wend our way along the drive to reach the columned portico. I sense excitement in the woman huddled next to me, though nothing like my own—to hear your dulcet voice again, my sweet Helaine!

Helaine! The brightest butterfly to dance among Spring's flowers, where we as lissome youths wandered, innocent of love. Would that we had died then, in that natural, supple state of grace! But we matured, and scales fell from our eyes; and when we knew each other to be clothed, we craved to tear those clothes away.

We wed, but only to ordain the amatory joy we'd already tasted in each other's arms. With power and wealth, accoutered lavishly, we swept society into our train without a thought beyond the latest titillation we might find, in wine, in opium, in Passion's house. Season after season passed this way, the world beyond us burning in wars and revolutions, while nightly we consumed each other in the human flame.

Helaine! In full flower, voluptuous and daring, flaunting everything—but yielding to none but me!— teasing and denying all who dared to plead for her caress, her laughter bright as knives…

~❦~

Entwined in passionate embrace one evening, fingers wandering her raven waves, I chanced upon a streak of brilliant white, emerging at her brow and sweeping sinistral. In days, a lush ivory coil graced her midnight mane. Had we known the meaning of this portent, would anything have changed? Would penitence and prayer have followed, with remission from above?

Then came the fateful night when, late for some debauch, I burst into our chamber unannounced to chastise my Helaine. She stood before her cheval mirror, in knickers and perfume, closing down her lamp as I

approached—I thought, in feigned modesty. I clasped
Helaine to my chest, our plans forgotten; and bending to
her mane, murmured at her ear:

"Je plongerai ma tête amoureuse d'ivresse
Dans ce noir océan où l'autre est enfermé…"

Leading me to our canopied retreat, Helaine took me
with a fearsome appetite, seeking respite from her nascent
fears. My eyes had not perceived the subtle transformation
of her flesh my hands revealed: as half her tresses faded, so
the left side of her perfect form *regressed*.

We dismissed her maid, to keep the secret through the
sun-kissed summer. I helped Helaine rouge her pallid
cheek, stuff half a *soutien gorge* within her corset to pad her
thinning breast. She wore long sleeves despite the heat, to
hide her wasting limbs. Her now-crooked smile was forced;
insisting our nightly revels continue unabated, we danced,
though less and less. But when her left eye's cornflower
blue darkened to the zaffre of a winter dusk, we could no
longer conceal her transformation from a voyeuristic
world. For a time Helaine appeared masked, defiant,
flaunting a braid of black and white. As her left side with-
ered, she lost the will to move her right. Her speech, once
voluble, faltered into silence. No physician could restore
Helaine to her health.

As autumn painted the landscape in splendid decay, we
withdrew to our estate, then our manse, our chambers…
our bed: our first and final pleasure. Albeit speechless,
Helaine still could *sing*, regaling me with songs sweet and
sensual, expressing all the emotions she could not utter.
She drew her strength from our impassioned coupling, and
found her only peace exhausted in my arms.

We could not deny the looming end. My ardor fed her

spirit, yet bound her to her half-dead flesh, this world of suffering and decay. My selfishness brought me nightly to her side, expending myself, renewing her imprisonment.

I cleared the mausoleum, long-ignored, preparing for our last repose. I drove the workmen with Pharaonic cruelty, evicted its moldering occupants, and sumptuously refurbished it: this temple to great Thanatos! The finest artisans crafted a marble sarcophagus of double width, crowned with a divided lid of burnished bronze. Beneath its pedestal, a cunning clockwork drive would raise this roof. Its single chamber was readied for our occupancy with down-filled pillows and duvet, covered in finest crimson satin. In death, as in life, I meant us to remain entwined forever: for I would take my life when hers had lapsed.

My health was near collapse. On our last night, I passed into a drugged, sedated sleep, resigned to Death, Helaine curled within my arms.

Of the days that followed I have no recollection; and when I did awake, it was to find Helaine gone—*gone*!

Retainers said that my beloved wife was being borne to her final rest. I struggled to my feet, and throwing on great-coat and boots, tottered out across the field to where the granite house of Death crouched against the blank October sky. I received no sympathy from her family, but hate-filled glances, muttered imprecations. I collapsed upon her bier, only to be rudely pulled away. I would have joined her within the vault even then! Restrained by rough hands I watched, helpless, as she was brought inside, the massive outer door closed, the tomb sealed. My Helaine— immured, alone!

~❧~

Where lies the border between life and death? After her demise, and my exile from society, I obsessed upon Helaine's fate. Might gentle Thanatos abide a *truce*—accept Helaine's sinistral half-death and permit *half-life* to recommence? Did she yet linger at his threshold, waiting in an undead trance? The frozen Earth Herself rose every Spring from Winter death, surrendering to Sol's fiery embrace—

Helaine! My thoughts hearkened back to our last week, and how her strength and color seemed restored in our couplings. The notion possessed me: that sufficient passion could raise her to *life* once again! I set out to restore my health, consulting physicians, foreswearing the tincture that had become my crutch. I groomed, and set a wholesome diet, and walked in Autumn's watery sun to build my strength. My lingering guilt—that my waning ardor had spelt her doom—drove me on. Clearly, my youth had fled, and could not be restored.

Could I supplement my passion with *another's*? Foolishly I sought out wantons in public houses and *maisons de passé*, searching… I found lost creatures little healthier than I had been, lacking the heated spirit of arousal. Near despair, I sat one night in a distant inn, alone, when *she* flounced up to me.

What's your pleasure, sirrah? came a buoyant voice. Raising my gaze, I regarded the serving girl: a flower fresh-blossomed, inviting as a Spring day. Blonde curls framed an open face, flushed in the fire-lit room. I placed my bejeweled hand upon hers—she did not withdraw!—for her eyes revealed a hunger I knew all too well.

A coin secured her companionship for the night. I rushed her to my coach and thence to home, ushered my young guest within and made her wait, still cloaked, listening to the fading sound of hooves. Then with torches lit I brought her back into the night, across the fallow field, beneath mute stars, to your resting place, Helaine!

~❧~

Helaine! Not once since that devastating day have I dared look upon you, though I had secured—stolen—the key from your jealous kin. I turn it in the lock, swing the heavy door aside, and urge my companion forward. I light the candles in their sconces, as she wonders at the luxury surrounding us.

Fumbling at strings and stays we loose our clothes, embrace unfettered, my kisses hungrily returned.

She gestures at our crypt and asks, *Shall I put my cloak upon't, m'Lord?*

No, I reply, and bend to my task, rotating the ornate wheel that works the massive lid. Protesting, the clockwork advances, the halves retract, revealing our consecrated bed. She peers about, catching but a glimpse of that altar profane.

Faintly from within, *a sentimental lyric floats*: is it my insane imagination? No—for the girl beside me laughs, exclaiming, *Not unlike a music box!*

The sacrament of life is nigh! Helaine feels it, as do I! Enflamed, I kiss my young guest's face, her neck; release her hair from bondage—and secure the ribbon round her eyes.

A surprise, my poppet, I assure her; then usher my trembling acolyte up the marble steps, led by the seductive voice—the song—of my Helaine!

~❧~

Quotes from *Le Léthé* and *La Chevelure* by Charles Baudelaire, who translated the work of Edgar Allan Poe and brought it to the attention of the French public.

J**.L. Royce** is a published author, primarily writing science fiction and macabre tales, though also noir, crime, romance, humor, non-genre…whatever else strikes him. He lives and works in the northern reaches of the American Midwest.

He's had pieces accepted at *Allegory*, *Ghostlight*, *Sci Phi*, *Stupefying Stories*, and *Utopia*. Anthologized stories may be found at www.amazon.com/author/jlroyce. Find him on Facebook at (AuthorJLRoyce) and Twitter (Author-JLRoyce).

THE HEART OF ALDERMAN KANE

ELEANOR SCIOLISTEIN

That this tale will be met with disbelief, I have little doubt. Yet, I am forced, by conscience and duty to recount, as best I can, the details of my downfall and my lurid descent into infamy.

My hope, is that by making this confession I may find some measure of forgiveness for my transgressions. For I assure you, dear reader, that though they may test the bounds of credulity, the things I have written are in all regards faithful to the truth.

I was there, I did do these things and I am, as penance for my sins, cursed forever, to remember.

It was in a small, Baltimore Inn, a dive of the species often frequented by those for whom intemperance is a habit and alcohol a close, but capricious friend, that I first met Albert Wynne. Having handed over any measure of self-control with the dollar I used to purchase my ale, I had become the worst type of raucous and loose-lipped drunk and was complaining loudly of a lover by whom I felt I had been hard done, she having accepted the affections of another and left me unceremoniously bereft.

I swore revenge on the man who had left me a cuckold. This sermon was not directed to anyone in particular, but was rather a cathartic lament addressed to everyone and no one in equal measure. Only Albert was listening.

He sidled up beside me with the slithering ease of a serpent and with a sly smile every bit as reptilian. In appearance, he was toad-like, squat, with a head like a misshapen pebble. His eyes, which seemed somehow to swivel and turn as if unattached to the rest of his head, were wide and shone with an energy that was in equal measure as alluring as it was malevolent.

"If you wish to do harm or rekindle your love, those things are within your reach," he hissed. "Though you must be aware that the price of such service is high."

Initially, I thought he was offering to take action against my usurper personally, and whilst I had myself, on many occasions, considered and even dreamt of offering violence to her new lover, I had long ago rejected the notion as futile. I thanked my new friend but assured him that such an undertaking would be impossible.

"My love's new flame is none other than the *Alderman Kane*. An official of high enough status and regard as to be untouchable. Far beyond the reach of a back alley hiding or a discouraging threat." With this I turned and ordered yet another pint of ale, considering our brief conversation to be over.

Albert Wynne thought differently.

"Nobody," Wynne insisted, "is beyond reach." With this, he moved his glass, filled with green opaque liquid I instantly recognised as absinthe, into the path of the candle so that it cast a long shadow across the surface of the bar.

"Every man has a shadow. A piece of the dark from which he cannot escape, which he cannot remove nor ever cut away. It is attached as firmly as our skin to our bones, it is and always will be with him. No one is untouchable, as long as their shadow touches them. It is a pathway to his soul, for those willing to follow it." As the barman laid my drink before me, the stranger all at once, lifted it and moved it into a new position, so that this receptacle also cast a shadow.

"These objects, for now, do not touch." With the slow deliberate movements of a stage magician, he extended one bony finger and gently pushed the glass so that it slid closer to me. The shadow of my glass merged with the shadow of his own to form a single, solid black puddle. He then traced the line from my glass up the side of his own. "Now," he proclaimed, "Perhaps they don't touch, but they are, doubtless, *joined*. A bridge from one to the other, from him to you."

Over the next two hours, during which time I abandoned my fidelity to ale and joined my friend in embracing La Fée Verte, he explained his business and his intent. He could, he assured me, by means of signs and incantations scribed in lore forgotten by most, bring harm to anyone he wished, and could, if I so desired, sharpen my ill feeling toward the Alderman to a fine invisible point that would, without my ever needing to be within reach of that fellow, damage him *irrevocably*.

Much aroused by this talk of esoteric magic, if not a little by the absinthe, I loudly enthused about the possibility, declaring that I, with my new sorcerer friend, would vanquish my enemies by magical means, tear his very heart from his chest, and wielding malifice as my new weapon, bring him to his knees as I reclaimed my lost love. Oh, what folly! To have made sport of such things!

At length, Wynne extended to me an invitation, suggesting that I accompany him to his home. An invitation which I readily and drunkenly accepted. As he paced and I staggered through the chill autumn night toward his abode, I did, I blush to admit, consider for an instant the wisdom of my actions. Before I could pay more heed to my mind's warning however, I found myself outside a grim old brownstone and being led hurriedly inside.

At first, still shaking off the residues left by my moment of doubt, I was comforted when I found myself in a modest but perfectly ordinary kitchen. We shared yet another drink, after which I felt my apprehension begin to dissolve.

It was only when Wynne, seemingly far less inebriated than myself, paced toward a door on the far side of the room that I again became apprehensive. Opening the door, he beckoned me to follow and led me down the stone steps toward a small and dimly lit cellar, in which my companion had amassed an expansive library, stuffed with books on all manner of dark and unsavoury material. The floor of this room was scrawled with symbols and runes in a language I did not recognise. Surveying the scene, I again began to regret my impulsive nature. I turned, determined to make my apologies and leave, only to find that I was alone.

The room, I realised at once, had become oddly still. Not only quiet, but seemingly, undisturbed. As if the very air itself were ancient, trapped long ago, like stale breath inside a crypt. I turned again, searching for my friend, who had, so I thought, been close to my elbow. I had not heard him leave, nor seen him ascend the stairs, and yet, now I could hear and indeed sense, that I was the first to move in this stillness for days, years or centuries. Then, just as quickly as the stillness had come, it began at once to retreat and I watched in abject horror, as the shadows began to melt.

From behind every object, from upon every surface, the

shadows at once became *unstuck*, bleeding and dripping downward, seeping from the walls and across the floor in slow, syrupy movements. I cried out as the pooling dark crept toward me, forming a puddle that slowly advanced, forcing me backward toward the corner. In panic, I grabbed at the candle, thrusting it forward in a vain attempt to halt the shadow's progress, and in doing so, swung it recklessly sideward and dropped it. Terror, like frozen pins, jabbed at my insides as the light went out and the entire world was shadow. For a moment I stood, listening, only to the sound of my own breath, when, from out of the darkness, someone or something reached out and touched me. My mind, unable to cope, succumbed to the black.

When I awoke, I was in the hospital. At first, my blurred recollections and the fanciful nature of these events, led to me to consider whether they were not in fact the product of some strange dream or reverie. A fabrication, which I, wound up in a web of sin delicately spun by that fabled green fairy, had hallucinated.

Later, I was told that I had been found in the gutter, raving and bleeding and that I was brought in by some considerate soul who to this day I have never met. My only clue as to my actions after being swallowed by the darkness, was a note I found in my jacket pocket. Above a line of those same curious runes was the name 'Alderman Kane', the words 'I agree to pay the price' and my own scrawled signature.

Upon first waking however, I was less concerned with the details than with my injuries, for I could sense instantly and to my infinite horror, that my right hand had been removed.

Unbeknownst to me, a few floors below in the morgue, the body of Alderman Kane was being laid out upon the slab. I only know this now because of reports of the strange discoveries made during his autopsy.

For you see, when the cursed Alderman's chest was opened up, his breastbone was found to have been shattered, and around his very heart, clasping the organ in a vice like grip, was a perfectly formed *human hand*.

~

Eleanor Sciolistein has contributed to a number of horror and Sci-fi anthologies and hopes to have her own collection of short horror fiction available on Amazon by Halloween.

You can find her non-fiction work on horror by searching her name online. She's also on Facebook (eleanor.sciolistein.779) and Twitter (Eleanorsciolis1) if you'd like to get in touch.

KINGDOM BY THE SEA

TROY SEATE

The red boiling disc disappears, leaving only an explosion of orange above the dark abyss that is my jailer. The surf creeps onto the shore like an eyelid closing over the sand. The metronomic certainty of its cadence should be soothing, but the eerie moment of silence between slaps of water is like the silence before a scream, the waves mimicking the rhythmic beating of my heart.

It's been two weeks since arriving at this desolate island, marooned. Yet, I am not alone. There *is* Carol, my wife. The two of us paddled to this uninhabited place on a piece of our exploded boat's wreckage. The island has vegetation, but nothing edible, so it's lucky I had the fore-thought to gather a small amount of food and water into a pack and sling it over my shoulder before jumping into the water.

Carol lies on the shoreline next to me. The fact that she is dead isn't as tragic as you might think. I'd considered killing her more than once during our tumultuous marriage. After a few days here, her histrionics about our plight became more than I could endure, not to mention my diminishing supply of fresh water and consumables. I strangled the life out of her right on the beach. Who was there to see? Only the occasional bird or a creeping sea crab. Although she's a reminder of my actions, her presence helps thwart my feelings of isolation. I fear I won't be far behind her, for chance of rescue appears remote.

I turn my face toward my dearly departed while enough light remains to see her. She deteriorates evenly from exposure. Small crabs have been equally effective favoring the opportunities in and around her orifices. Her hair is loose, long strands mingling with the sand. Her skin is drawing to her skeleton. She's beginning to rot. The smell doesn't disturb me. Our relationship spoiled long ago, and somehow it's reassuring that she's dead and I'm not. She is disintegrating as I watch. Her current hairline reveals rusty green splotches as if mud and seaweed had been part of her oily make-up.

Her blind eyes eternally stare at the heavens, filled with the horror of having life choked from them by her beloved. Her breasts are becoming deflated pouches, the warm blood from her veins settled. No more throaty murmurs, or grumblings in her sleep. Little left but dead meat and the absolute loss of modesty, not that she ever had much.

As I observe what's left of my wife, something unexpected happens. Her head slowly rotates toward me, like the mechanical workings of a clock's second hand. Her body rises just as slowly to a sitting position, her eyes now moving around as if they were the counterbalanced movements of a doll's eyes. Her face begins to twist into something horrible, something *inhuman*.

A wide, clownish grin stretches her decaying cheeks. Her eyes, sightless no longer, are now the bulging, black orbs of a hungry shark, vibrant with menace, burning a hole into my soul. Her hair transforms into writhing tentacles not unlike Medusa's snakes. She's become a hideous form, transforming from a dead body into something incalculably dark and ancient. A deep, gravely sound emanates from her emaciated throat. Is she a demon, or an avenging angel? My nerves tingle with imminent peril.

I sit up. "Stop it, Carol," I stupidly say, trying to fight whatever illusion is tricking my mind into believing the impossible. "Stop it! You're *dead*!"

Her head cants to one side. The abominable grimace pulls her mouth into a death's-head grin and her jaw distends from her skull and unhinges. An obscene, elongated tongue slithers around inside the maw and then spills out revoltingly. It lolls beneath her chin and flicks its tip.

A hand darts from this monstrous changeling that was once my wife and closes tightly around my arm. I'm too astonished to react. Leathern wings unfurl. Fading sunlight shines through their partial transparency, a sight becoming exorbitantly more inhuman with each passing moment. The creature's mouth approaches mine like a dark cave of terror, the grotesque appendage within seeking me.

An unwanted kiss?

When I stop screaming, Carol is once again no more than a slimy, crab-covered husk laying on top of me, face to face with her decomposing head, the translucent wings no longer encircling my body in a hellish embrace. Near hysteria, I push the corpse away in hopes the event is a vivid hallucination due only to throes of hunger, thirst, and isolation.

But I fear something *worse*.

A king in his kingdom by the sea, lending my dear Carol the sword of Damocles?

And so, all the night-tide, I lie down by the side
Of my darling, my demon, my sins and my bride

In our sepulcher there by the sea—
Never to be dissevered from our tomb by the sea.

Troy Seate is a writer who stands on the side of the literary highway and thumbs down whatever genre comes roaring by. His storytelling runs the gamut from *Horror Novel Review's Best Short Fiction* to the *Chicken Soup for the Soul* series. His memoirs and essays report fact while his fiction incorporates fantasy, horror, or humor featuring the quirkiest of characters. Visit his website at www.troy-seateauthor.webs.com.

THIEF OF ETERNAL DELIGHTS

RENEE CRONLEY

The hour is late and the walls within the castle rise out of the darkness like black curtains hiding sinister secrets. Merry music coming from the great hall pours into my ears. The king is entertaining the lords and ladies of his court with dancing, troubadours, and wine. The jubilant noises grow faint as I approach until dissipating into silence as I peek inside to find it empty. I blink, then refocus my eyes on the desolate room, but the joy I heard a moment ago never manifests into the life it promised. I shrug my shoulders, blaming it on the whiskey.

I take a swig from my flask before stumbling through the castle, looking for something valuable to slip into the pockets of my waistcoat. The stakes are high when stealing from a king. But it makes the thrill that much more intense when the consequences are fatal. It makes my heart beat fast and I feel alive. Because when the thrill wears off, I feel empty again—dead inside. Perhaps tonight, I'll find what I'm looking for.

I stagger into a large, empty room lit with ornate candelabras. Distant whispers echo throughout the room as I stand frozen in the centre. Grotesque shadows spring from the walls and dance around me, threatening to touch me. The scent of decay invades my nostrils, conjuring images of corpses rotting in the dark. There are too many voices, growing louder and louder. They threaten my sanity. I cover my ears and shut my eyes to block the sensory chaos before I go mad.

After a few moments of suspected silence, I remove my hands from my ears and peek through half-closed eyelids. A blurred silhouette of a skull manifests on the wall, then floats toward me. Instead of running, I unsheathe my dagger and throw it at the apparition. Both the skull and wall vanish, and in its place a stone archway introduces a long corridor.

The whiskey must be taking its toll on me. I shrug and reach for my flask, taking a large gulp. The same irresistible impulse that brought me to the castle takes me down the corridor.

It's lit with flaming torches and a large stained-glass window with blue, purple, green, orange, white, and violet panes marks the end. Portraits of wealthy nobles flanked by knight's armour stretch across the length of the passage.

An icy chill nips my ear and takes me by surprise. I stumble into the metal plates of the suit of armour closest to me and the clanging echoes loudly. Heart in my throat, my eyes dart to the entrance to see if the noise alerted anyone to investigate, but there's no one… and nothing there but a solid wall.

Fear paralyzes and shackles me to the floor. This castle is a cage and I, it's rat. I'm used to steady nerves to match my hands, but they now tremble as I drink my flask dry.

Another cold nip at my ear and a feminine whisper startles me into dropping my flask. I spin around.

There's nobody there.

A portrait of a noble woman guarded by knights' armour steals my attention. Her beauty takes me aback and I forget my fear under her gaze. It is a painting for my eyes alone, hung on the wall for some time, dusty and unloved… waiting for me. With the face of an angel and a sweet, bewitching countenance, she wears a slight smile hinting that she knows something I don't. I can't help but smile back at her.

The hairs on my neck rise to attention, directing me to the stained-glass window. A woman in a long black dress stands in front of it, a rich rainbow shimmering around her like a halo. I recognize her immediately.

How could I not? She has the face of an angel—*my angel.*

Quiet whispers lace the air like a sweet perfume trying to mask another scent. It's sobering, yet I'm dizzy as I walk towards her. I need to profess my love to her, but the words come out low and slurred. She holds her finger to her lips to silence me—my words aren't necessary. She already knows. That small, secretive smile plays with the corners of my angel's mouth. Behind that smile is the secret to my eternal happiness. She stole my heart like a thief in the night prowling the castle.

Her eyes never leave mine. They are pale enough to reflect the flaming torches on the wall. The panes of glass behind her turn crimson, although I hardly notice. Goose-bumps envelop my skin, because she has that effect on me —that, and I seem to get colder the closer I get to her. I need her to warm me. These ideas would have seemed strange to me only minutes ago, but seeing her portrait planted a seed within me that sprouted deep roots and are now cascading out of control. The closer I get to her, the further behind I leave myself. But the distance between us is enough to pull my soul from my chest and render me breathless. I *need* to reach her. With my eyes on my beloved, I could almost ignore the sharp, shooting pains threatening to bring me to my knees as I close the gap between us.

Ominous whispers saturate the corridor but evade me and I am glad for it. They seem to have so much to say, like they have been waiting centuries for ears to hear their pleas. But I know that if I listen to their words, I'll beg to be deaf. They are tortured whispers of the ages, trapped in a part of the castle built of blood and bone.

The stained-glass window fades to black and is replaced by wooden double doors on hinges that curl decoratively on to the door like claws inviting me in. I can hear an orchestra playing behind them. The sound of a flute swims throughout the corridor and soothes my soul to sleep with its sweet vibrations.

In the glow of the torch light, I see that my angel's cheek has a scarlet stain. Her cryptic smile returns when she catches me noticing.

The music gets louder and louder. The ticking of a clock booms from behind the door, its pendulum swinging with a dull and heavy monotonous clang. My angel dons a black and red masquerade mask, then offers me her hand. I take it—bringing her cool and clammy hand to my lips for a kiss. I can feel the stickiness—not from her skin, but from mine. I don't have to look to know that blood is weeping from my pores. But a small price to pay for her caress.

"Come my love, the hour is almost stricken." Her voice is dry and throaty—like she hasn't spoken in ages. It makes me delirious with pleasure.

As the double doors open, my soul finally stops the search it has been on for some time. For what it couldn't find in life; it found in death. The stakes are highest in love.

The clock chime reverberates throughout my sepulchre as the music overwhelms the rhythm of my soul and disrupts the rise and fall of my chest. My angel of death may have plundered my soul, yet it is I who have stolen the pleasure to dance with her into *eternity*.

∼

Renee Cronley is a poet, writer, and nurse from southern Manitoba. She studied Psychology and English at Brandon University, and Nursing at Assiniboine Community College. Her work has appeared or will appear in *NewMyths*, *The Brandon Writers' Collective Anthology*, *The Quill*, and *The Westman Journal*.

She's part of a local writers group called the *Brandon Writers' Collective*. You can also find her on Instagram (reneecronley) and Twitter (reneecronley).

MIDNIGHT RIDER

MELANIE COSSEY

I f I could stop time, return to the singular moment when my path diverged from happiness to one of despair, I would switch my course and walk away from that cursed beast who had eyed me with contempt on our first meeting. But I cannot, and it is my greatest torment.

In the unfortunate hours during which I wake from the gift of nothingness into this new reality, I am doomed to replay the events that led to the loss of my beloved, until sleep finds me again.

When Anabelle had at last agreed to marry me, it was the happiest moment of my half-lived life. I was a malingerer, you see. My working life was spent in lowly positions: a dustman, a rat catcher, even a pure finder. It seemed fitting to look down on me, but I was single-minded in my goal to create for myself a better life than that of my father and his father before him. Nary a half-penny I misspent. I became educated in matters of investing, financing several lucrative ventures. I applied those profits towards a coal mine on the West Coast of Canada. It has since exceeded the wildest predictions of success.

I knew Anabelle favoured me. At the grand balls, her head would turn when I neared, inclining toward me rather than her dance partner. But to win her hand, I knew I must impress her father, and so I set out to succeed in the same way that I had succeeded in building my wealth.

She delighted in my declarations of adoration at her beauty, her carefree, childlike spirit, her compassion, and her tenderness. And then, she delighted in my gifts. I admit that it became as an addiction for me, to see the flush of pink rise to her cheeks and the failed suppression of a smile. Then the dip of her head as a finger moved to smooth a blonde lock behind her ear.

Such gifts proved my love for my Anabelle, but I do curse them now.

One afternoon, while strolling with Anabelle's aunt, we came upon a pasture where several Friesians grazed. Anabelle remarked that she didn't much care for these inferior Friesians, bred lighter and faster for trotting races. She'd a keen love for the power and grace the breed had once possessed as formidable war horses. So, I set upon the idea to procure for her a stallion of original stock. Such a lavish gift would surely convince her father of my means and devotion.

I'd come by the horse, not at auction—the likes of which produce questionable stock and worn-out nags—but through a trusted colleague. The stallion's pedigree was impeccable. My colleague had advised me to bring my top offer, as there were several interested parties. I hurried to Norfolk, to secure the stallion.

You never saw such a handsome creature: the lustre of his blue-black coat, gleaming in the sunlight; his muzzle, sloped in a regal incline; his eyes intelligent, taking me in with the wisdom of a decorated general surveying the battlefield. But there was something more— a look of contempt—before, with a snort, he was off for another turn around the ring.

Upon my mentioning the beast was to be a gift for my sweet Anabelle, the breeder protested. "Oh no, sir. This is not a lady's horse. This is a breeding stallion."

I swore that I would not allow Anabelle to ride him. But of what use is a man's caution when a lady is determined to do as she pleases? I offered on him, and the breeder accepted.

I created an elaborate affair of my gifting him. I had his mane decorated in purple velvet ribbons and his hide scrubbed clean to shine like satin. His tail was braided and his hooves buffed and polished.

When Anabelle hurried to the gate to greet me, she could not hide her delight, and then her exhilaration as, dressed in my finest attire, I asked for her hand. With her father's approval, we wed as soon as could be arranged.

Four months into wedded bliss the ghastly news came. I was in my study and leapt up as Thomas' shouts reached me. "Mr. Richards, come quickly. Mrs. Richard's been thrown. She's—oh god! It's dire, sir."

I jerked open my desk drawer and grabbed my pistol.

"Anabelle," I shouted, bursting out the kitchen door. The vining of terror and sorrow strangled me as I raced toward the huddle of staff near the forest's edge.

Hands reached to stop me, but I pitched myself down the embankment into the woods below where my beloved Anabelle lay, but the angle of her head and neck revealed what I'd feared. I fell before her disordered body and lifted her head, loose on her neck, to kiss her still-warm lips. Those lips that would never again utter my name. Her violet eyes had now darkened to indigo. I touched the bodice of her riding habit, her lungs lay still, forever relieved of their function. I let her slide from my grasp and

rose. The pistol's weight in my grasp galvanized me as I
blinked away tears in my determination to find the beast
that had stolen my Anabelle from me.

The damnable creature moved through the trees like a
trail of smoke after a gunshot. I followed him to a clearing
where he turned to me, muzzle pressed forward, head
lowered, ears flat against his skull. I levelled my pistol at
him, and when the evil flashed in his eyes, I fired. The
beast struck the earth, dead. My wails for Anabelle mixed
with the fresh copper of spilled devil's blood.

It's been two weeks since Anabelle was taken from me.
I am a mere outline of a once-rich painting. I sleep by day
and awaken to the subtle variances of my furnished room
cloaked in darkness, and, through the window, the silver
lawn beyond. And to something else. On the edge of the
embankment, where my Anabelle took her last ride, there
is movement. A shadow paces, weaving itself through the
trees.

Is it my love come back to me? Come to curse me for
gifting her that hellish creature who threw her to her
death? Or has she come to absolve me? To admonish me
not to despise myself, for heaven is all she's imagined and
more? I do not know which, for the shadow does not step
forward and reveal itself.

When I next awoke to the shadow moving at the
forest's edge, I summoned my courage to open the window,
and I called out, "Anabelle, my dearest." I waited, straining
my ears in the silent night. But only a foul odor, like the
taint of death, was returned to me. Choking, I slammed
the window and collapsed in tears.

It was after this night that I began to hear my name.

Hayden. It reached through the nothingness and prised apart my eyes. My gaze fell upon the open window. Had I left it so? I could not remember. As I threw the covers aside and placed my feet on the floor, an icy chill grabbed me. Then it sounded again—my name, cloaked in a kind of screech that echoed across the property. Whatever it was out there, I could avoid it no longer. It had summoned me.

With dread, I pulled on my dressing gown, ran downstairs, and thrust myself into the starless night. I raced across the lawn, through the lacy mist, toward that shadow. Toward my Anabelle? But another shriek cut through the tomb-like silence, halting my steps—the deep and urgent nicker of a horse. My mind stalled as my innards twisted, throwing me into a terror I had never known.

Then, the shadow began to take form. It loomed over me. His muscular chest once reflecting an inky sheen, was now dulled with mud and detritus. Those purple velvet ribbons lay tattered and tangled in his mane. His angular nose pressed forward into the moonlight, eyes gleaming with malice. The beast, the devil Anabelle had named Midnight, stood fully before me. Between those fearsome eyes, the bullet wound where I'd shot him, oozed blood. It trickled down his face, painting his muzzle in grisly crimson.

"Take me to her. I beg you."

The dreadful horse bobbed his head and that weeping wound splattered me with the blood of the damned. There was nothing left for me in this world. A world without my beloved, my Anabelle, was a world foreign and detestable to me, and so I bore my terror, ran at the hell-sent creature, swiped at the bedraggled rein that hung from his shoulder, and flung myself onto that cursed hide. I flayed him into action, a motion he only readily accepted as with a pump of that powerful neck he bore me away towards the embankment and towards the arms of my beloved Anabelle.

~

Melanie Cossey has enjoyed a lifelong fascination with Victorian Era culture and is especially drawn to the era's bizarre death practices, views on science, and pursuit of mental health. Her short fiction and poetry have won honorable mentions and made shortlists. Her work appears in several anthologies, including *Quoth the Raven*, and *Love Among the Thorns*, both edited by Lyn Worthen. *A Peculiar Curiosity* was published by Fitzroy Books in 2018. She's currently working on a vampire tale based on the Casket Girls of New Orleans.

Melanie is a certified editor, a member of the Horror Writer's Association, and teaches writing workshops on Vancouver Island.

You can find her blog and links to her work at www.crumblingmanor@blogspot.com.

You can learn more about her editing services at www.polishedandpreciseeditingservices.com.

ISSUE 2: BLOOD IS THICKER

LOVE LETTERS TO **POE**

CALDER | LYKKEN
PIPER | DUNATO

Volume 1, Issue 2 | November 2020
Edited by Sara Crocoll Smith

IN THE ALDER GLADE

NATASHA C. CALDER

Sorcha stands alone and raises hand to brow, her dark curls discing down over her fingers as she squints into the falling sun, her heart become so light she fears it will not withstand even the weight of her own blood for much longer. It's always like this when her sister wanders off: the lightness, the dread.

In her left hand she holds a pellet. It is one of several such that she found clustered in the dust beneath Ann's empty bed, its compacted ash slivered through and through with sucked-dry beetle shells and who can say what else. She'd known at once what it had meant, of course, known at once there must have been the usual signs as well: the words unsaid, the eyes not met, the bread uneaten. It meant—it *means*—that she has not been watching closely enough.

But then Ann had seemed much better lately.

The pellet gives way beneath the pressure of Sorcha's touch, crumbling in her hand and scattering to the ground. She drops her eyes to where the ashes fall and thinks of

Ann's feet planted where she now stands, the roots of foxglove and delphinium at her heel, the earth scratched and dry at her toe. The track stretches out beyond and into the forest. Ann's there, she's sure, in amongst the alders' looming dark. Above the trees, a shock of sparrows sudden-clouds the sky, as if startled by some unknown beast.

Sorcha frowns and touches the charmed knife belted to her waist. She tries to picture Ann returning with the dawn, unharmed, her words all knew-I-shouldn't truths, her smiles all won't-again lies. But the image slips and fades, however Sorcha tries to keep it fixed. Wishes. Prays.

Heavy-hearted, she steps onto the track and starts to trace her sister's steps into the wood. There is no need to wonder if she's chosen right; this is the way, she's sure, though she does not recall the branches being broken back like this, nor the bracken trampled down. She thumbs the handle of the knife and hurries on, pausing only at the sight of a familiar, clumpen mass that lies beside the path. Squinting, she can just make out the shards of bone and matted feathers within the clot of regurgitated ash.

When the light fails, Sorcha slows her step, picking over root and stone. She's drawing close, or so her memory says, as much as she might wish there were a hundred yards to go instead of ten.

Eight yards.

Six yards.

Four.

Glade's edge. She stops.

Draws the knife.

A pale figure crouches up ahead.

Oh, she breathes. *Angel eyes.*

Even in the gloom, she cannot ignore the mangled sparrow half-alive between the creature's teeth, nor how

the bird—feathers all at horrid angles—makes no bid to
fly. *Ann*—

The name tears from Sorcha's lips and rings
throughout the wood, loud enough to wake the marrow-
spiders. Yet the creature does not move, does not look up.

But neither does it flinch when Sorcha's fingers light
upon its shoulder.

Ann.

Her heart. Her answer and her ask.

She kneels beside her sister, picks a bloodied feather
from her hair, and gently prises the mangled fledgling
from her grip. Sorcha slides her blade across the bird's
throat and sets its dead and broken body down among the
fallen leaves, just beyond Ann's reach. She wants to
shout—

How?

Again?

This bad again?

So quick?

But, knowing better, lets her questions go unmouthed.
So she's surprised to see Ann tilt her head as if she's heard,
as if considering a response. And then she notes Ann's pale
eyes are fixed so wide they are almost lidless, tracking
something that moves amongst the trees but that Sorcha
cannot see or guard against; will or no, knife or no. She
watches helpless as Ann flinches back, rips apart her lips
and screams.

Sorcha reaches out to pull Ann from her waking
terror. *Angel eyes it's me it's safe it's only me and no one else it's just
the dark I'm here I'm here I'm here.*

She does not think that Ann can hear her rough incantation but the words are, perhaps, enough to scare away
the creeping formless shades and soon the scream dies to
silence. Then Ann just sits, staring. A husk.

Enough. Sorcha sheathes her knife and wraps her arms unfelt around her sister's frame. Lifts.

Falters.

Straightens. Grips tight.

Stumbles on with fierce, unsteady steps, not stopping to breathe or dream of end but only step and step and step till gasping, panting, she gains the open air beyond the trees. And all the while her sister hangs limp between her arms, unspeaking and unseeing.

The sun has nearly set.

Sorcha staggers through the garden and on into the house. She sets Ann down and does her best to clean away the forest; scrubs the dirt from off her sister's face and arms, takes the knife and traces each nail of each finger on each hand, lifting the caked dirt with the blade's edge. Ann whimpers a little, but does not resist.

And then Sorcha guides her into bed, takes the chair beside and sets to watch. Ann looks from corner to corner, her eyes never lighting on Sorcha for more than a moment, restless, unable to settle.

This, too, Sorcha recalls more clearly than she cares for.

She gently takes her sister's hand and brushes her fingers with kisses.

Thinks: *Please don't please don't please don't.*

Whispers: *I've got you, angel eyes.*

Ann slowly stills; her breath steadies and deepens, her pale eyes flutter closed. She murmurs something that could be 'Sorcha' or could be 'sorry' and might be both. Then, releasing Sorcha's hand, she turns onto her side and gives herself to sleep.

Sorcha pulls her chair closer still and watches as the last of the light fades. The knife lies across her lap, a guard against the shadows.

She struggles to stave off sleep herself.

Fails.

Dreams that she is flying.

Wakes sometime later to see moonlight falling across the bed. The covers are smoothed out flat and lying at the centre of the sheet is a single clotted mass of ash and bone.

Her heart understands before she does, battering violently against the inside of her ribs. Not daring to believe the warning of her blood, Sorcha slowly turns her head to inspect the room.

On the window sill perches a monstrous, pale-eyed owl. *Ann.*

Sorcha's eyes fall from the lamp-like eyes to the curled talons. The owl has the knife, grasped in its left foot. A low moan escapes Sorcha's lips. She starts and tries to stand but her legs will not obey. She falls back limp in the chair, tears streaming silently down her face.

The owl, indifferent to her plight, merely sits and watches. There is not long to wait. They both know the charmed blade cannot protect her now, cannot keep her bound from such a distance. Sorcha closes her eyes, unable to bear the sight of her body as it diminishes into its true form; the bones fluted and air-light, the feathers dusty brown.

At last, the owl lets the knife drop forgotten to the floor. Spreading its wings, it launches itself from the sill, dreadful talons outstretched to catch the fluttering sparrow.

Natasha C. Calder is a graduate of Clarion West and has co-written a novel called *The Offset* which will be published by Angry Robot next year under the alias 'Calder Szewczak.' You can find out more about Natasha at www.natashaccalder.com or follow her and her writing partner's joint account on Twitter (@calderszewczak).

WHERE THE HEART IS

KARL LYKKEN

O ur old house loomed almost mansion-like while Sheriff Buck led Charlotte and me down the over-grown front path. It struck me as funny, considering how small it had come to feel over the past few years, but I couldn't quite seem to laugh.

Father opened the door before we even reached the porch. I suppose I should've appreciated that, as so few things could pull him away from staring at our Mother's portrait. And I know the Sheriff appreciated it, as it meant he had no need to knock. He stayed on the path, a good five yards from the front steps, watching as my sister and I slunk past Father back inside.

Charlotte squeezed my hand, hard. For a such a deli-cate little girl, she was surprisingly strong. I wanted to look over into her big, emerald eyes and promise her that every-thing would be alright, but somehow I couldn't manage to lift my head. Father never spoke much anymore, but this silence was different. It seethed.

"Charlotte's nearly thirteen, and she's not spoken to a soul besides me and you in almost two years," I said, more to talk than to explain. I heard my voice rising, though I directed my words squarely toward my feet. "I'm older, and I can still remember what the world is like, but if I don't introduce her to life outside of this house soon, the world won't even take her when you finally let us go."

The silence softened. I could feel right away that Father was getting ready to speak, even though it still took him the better part of a minute. "Home is where the heart is, girls. Like to as you might, you can't run away from your heart. We can never leave here, makes no difference if the world will take us or not. I hope you understand, Bette, I'll have to start locking you in at night, too, until I can trust you again."

He walked back over to his chair and sat down, and my head finally lifted. I made no effort to hide that I was glaring at him, for I knew he wouldn't notice. He resumed his dull-eyed stare through Mother's portrait, the portrait he moved down here the day he said she'd gone away. I followed his gaze as far as the painting, which I studied for the first time in years. I suppose it captured aspects of Mother—the Sun's lingering touch on her skin and hair, the way she still smiled when trying to look serious—but I never saw her in it. It was near life-sized, but far from life-like. But that wasn't why I hated it.

"Let's go wash up for dinner, Charlotte," I said. She squeezed my hand again. I still couldn't bring myself to look at her, not after I'd promised I'd get her out. I had been so sure if we could just get to Uncle Jack's house, we'd be free. But when we'd gotten there, it was clear as day that house hadn't been Uncle Jack's—or anyone else's—for quite some time. I should've known he wouldn't have stopped visiting if he still lived but a mile away, even if everyone else did. I should've known getting away wasn't that easy.

"Charlotte," I whispered as we reached the top of the stairs, "we're leaving again tonight. This time, though, we're not the ones the Sheriff will hunt down."

"Who will he hunt down, then, Bette?" Charlotte asked.

I didn't reply.

~🕮~

Father locked my bedroom door that night, but not my window. He never fully thought things through anymore, not with his mind always on that portrait. I crept out on the roof, then through the window to Mother's sewing room, and from there into the hallway. Blind in the dark, I navigated by memory—not a difficult task in a house where nothing could be moved from where Mother used to keep it. I counted my steps until I reached Charlotte's door. I unlocked it and called her, quiet as I could, to come out.

By the dim light from her window, she looked like a little fawn, rising unsteadily to her sleepy feet. She asked no questions as I led her into the sewing room, and when I told her to come running downstairs if I called to her, all she said was, "I will, Bette."

I headed back into the hall, shutting the sewing room door behind me and even stopping to re-lock the door to Charlotte's bedroom. Should Father awaken and wander the halls, all would appear as he thought it should.

I inched my way down the stairs on my backside, careful not to make them creak. Reaching the bottom, I moved to the portrait with a good deal less caution—my nerves were getting the better of me. I forced myself to breathe before I lifted Mother's still form off the wall, and I was fortunate to have gotten that breathing out of the way. Years of suspicions and nightmares prepared me for the sight of the hole in the wall, but not for the smell of it.

Stepping over to the buffet to light a candle gave me a needed respite, but all too soon I was back before the hole, this time confronted with a sight no nightmare could match. I couldn't recognize what was left of my Mother, but even in the faint candlelight I knew her yellow dress. And Uncle Jack's coat.

The candle dropped to the floor, the flame blowing out en route, but I could still see them, even after I made it back upstairs. I couldn't tell whether my footsteps were quiet, or how long I stood inside that sewing room before I realized Charlotte wasn't in there. Once I realized it, though, my fear for my sister pushed all other terrors aside. I must've made it down the hall to Father's room faster than the sound of my screams.

I wasn't fast enough, though.

They were both there, neither one making a noise. Father lay still on the bed, and Charlotte stood beside him, holding Mother's sewing scissors. The moonlight came in through the window, making her blood-flecked face glow. She smiled up at me, affectionately.

"Are we leaving, now, Bette?"

A boy dropped our groceries on the porch stairs, grabbed the money I'd left out for him, and scampered away down that overgrown path. I thought idly of following him as I brushed Charlotte's soft hair.

"Turn around, Charlotte," I said, when I finished. "Let me take a good look at you."

She obliged, with a smile. I couldn't help but smile

back. She looked so young and innocent, even with her graying hair.

Karl Lykken's dark fiction can be found online in *Daily Science Fiction* and *Theme of Absence*. Or, if you're in the mood for some lite fare, check out his humor pieces in *The Big Jewel*.

THE INHERITANCE THREAD

HAILEY PIPER

Father never told me why he made Mother sew her lips shut. He did it before I was born, and I had to find out his reasons for myself.

Of course I asked him. I had endless questions, as if I spoke double to make up for Mother's forced silence. Often I bombarded him as he boarded a rented coach from town to take him away on business.

He would smile, and say things like, "Dear Priscilla, your mother is a banshee. She'll wail across the moors and frighten poor townsfolk to death if we unseal her lips."

"But Father, there are no moors here."

"She'll find some." He'd then shut the coach door, and the coachman and his horses would carry Father away from my questions.

While he was gone, I would turn my questions to Mother. She taught me to sign at an early age so that she could speak to me by hand, but often we sat for hours in the sewing room, not speaking one way or another. We'd mend old clothes from seemingly bottomless wooden chests, or stitch patterns into cloth over our embroidery hoops, or sometimes she would have me snip a loose end after she'd re-threaded her lips.

Our language in those hours was the tune we'd pass back and forth without a word. *Hm-hm-hm*, we'd hum, and then smile to each other.

We were quite alike, I thought. Both of us took readily to thread, needle, and shears. We enjoyed all that sewing and humming, and sometimes Mother taught me how to dance. Practice for the future, she would tell me, for when I would someday grow up, dance with men from town, and find myself a husband.

When I asked how she could live without eating or drinking, she told me her sustenance came from the sun's warmth, my laughter, Father's love, and the ocean's music. Our house sits on a cliff overlooking jagged rocks and a frothing sea, and often I'd find her staring out and listening to the waves.

"Do you want to leave us?" I asked her one day.

Mother shook her head and smiled a stitch-lipped smile. The water's rhythm gave her comfort, that was all. On nights when Father was away on business, she stayed in a small attic room at the top of the house, storage for things from her old life, where a wide window looked out on the cliffs and infinite waves. That same ocean music helped her sleep, I supposed.

I only asked her once why her lips were sealed. Her deliberate hands told me that when she was a girl, she had an ill sister. On the night that child-aunt passed away, Mother snuck into her bed, coaxed out her last words, and then ate her dreams. Mother's lips remained shut from then on, else her sister's dead wishes would surge screaming from freed jaws.

Her tale scared me so badly that I never asked her

again. Surely that was her intent. For a time, it even worked.

But in adolescence, I learned about the world and what it does to us, of childbirth's horrors. For weeks, I had constant nightmares of Mother drowning in agony, yet unable to shriek as she gave birth to me, a wailing baby who had stolen her screams.

I began to wonder exactly how alike we were. I wondered if we sat and sewed and hummed together because someday I might trade mending cloth for threading my own lips. Practice for the future.

I had to free her. If a dead child-aunt came screaming from within, then I would scream with her. No matter the price, I had to open Mother's lips. Perhaps then mine would stay unsealed.

It was only a matter of time before Father traveled on business again. He would only be gone for one night; that was my chance. I waited hours after dark for Mother to drift up to her attic room. Her cot creaked, and a long quiet followed until I was sure she was asleep.

I was never more quiet than when I climbed those worn attic steps, shifting my weight so the wood wouldn't groan. The steel of my sewing shears felt cold against my sweating palm.

The attic room was no stranger to me by daylight, but I'd never stepped inside at night. Moonlight shone through the sea-facing window and colored the walls in white lunar brilliance. I spotted a rusted flintlock pistol mounted on a wooden plaque. Behind panes of glass, I found ancient letters bearing royal insignias in strange languages, the paper worn by centuries.

Mother looked to have plundered many shipwrecks. She had given up a life of some adventure to settle with Father, and in return he'd made her sew her lips shut.

Moonlight draped her peaceful face. Her breath was soft, almost silent. One might think she was dead, but even in sleep, her familiar hum danced in my ears. *Hm-hm-hm,* we hummed together as I leaned the shears toward her lips.

The blades opened. One wayward scrape, a snip too loud, and she'd wake up. What would she do then?

The blades snapped shut, and one black thread split in two. Her ragged lips parted ever so slightly. I flinched to scuttle back and count myself lucky for getting away with this much, but I couldn't quit until finished.

Shears forward, I snipped another thread, and then another. Mother's lips drifted apart until at last I'd cut them free.

Morning was too far away to wait on hearing her voice; I needed it right then. I cupped my free hand around her chin and tugged her jaw open. My shoulders tensed.

But there was no sisterly scream. There was a song.

Beautiful, sorrowful notes swam past my Mother's lips and filled the night. Soaked in longing and splendor more powerful than any hum, it was the kind of song that made me smile and cry all at once. I clasped my hands, no longer sweating, and sat beside the bed to listen. My eyelids grew heavy. This was an old lullaby I had needed as a baby, been denied for years, at last set free by my own hand.

My drowsy reverie ended when the house shuddered. Thunder crashed through the walls, as if a giant's fist had slammed into the cliff overlooking the sea. Mother went on sleeping and singing somehow, but I heard another sound sliding between beauty and chaos. I ran to the sea-facing window.

Moonlight painted the clifftop, where figures of men darted past the house, toward the cliff—

I shut my eyes and covered my ears, but that did not shut out their screams as they plummeted to the sea. Thunder crashed again, and the house quaked.

Mother slept through it all, coaxed into dreams by her own lullaby.

I didn't count how many men had flung themselves off the cliff by Father's return the next morning. I never looked out that window again. He climbed into the attic carrying needle and thread, his ears stuffed with wax-coated cloth as if on his way back, someone had warned him what happened to men who drew too close to home. He woke Mother and helped clamp her jaw shut while she sewed her lips together once more. It had been her choice all along.

He didn't speak to me. Neither did she.

Boats soon went out on the water, rowed by townswomen who'd come looking for brothers, sons, husbands, lovers. I watched from the cliff overlooking the sea.

And I saw worse. There is neither port nor beach beneath our cliff, only jagged rocks and a sheer wall. Ships that had been sailing by moonlight would not have headed here, but when Mother's song filled the night, the sailors had steered our way, where merciless waters tore their hulls apart. The wreckage floated far out to sea, carried by the tide. I couldn't count the ships; their pieces were too small.

There were no survivors.

Mother doesn't watch the sea anymore. She sits on the cliff still, listening to the water's rhythm, but she keeps her back turned to the waves, and she no longer hums.

Some days, I think of how alike we are, and I wonder what inherited song might rise up my throat unbidden. She's made a choice, but I don't think she understands it. She hasn't given up her old life, voice, and songs so that she can live with Father and me. We're already hers. She's given up these things so that she can have what she wants but not drive anyone to drown for it.

And then I think we might not be so alike after all.

Nowadays, I'm the one who watches the sea. I scan the rocks for drowning men and driftwood draped by ship-wrecked corpses, so that I'll get used to seeing them. Practice for the future, you might say. I practice many things for the future, but I don't sew anymore.

Hm-hm-hm.

Hailey Piper has written one gothic novelette, *An Invitation to Darkness*, as well as the novellas *The Possession of Natalie Glasgow*, *Benny Rose, the Cannibal King*, and *The Worm and His Kings*. She's active on Twitter (@HaileyPiperSays) and sometimes on Instagram (@haileypiperfights). All of her publication details can be found at www.haileypiper.com.

THE DISAPPEARANCE OF ALICE HARPER

JELENA DUNATO

Trigger warning: Mental health themes

16th June

Henry sent Dr. Jones to see me today. It was a clever move; the good Doctor has known me since I was a little girl and if anyone could persuade me to act reasonably, Henry probably thought it would be him.

"Alice," he said as he entered the room, "How are you?"

The most innocent of questions.

"I am perfectly well, Doctor." I wanted to add, *as I am sure you know*, but I knew Henry was eavesdropping. He likes to linger in front of my door.

I let Dr. Jones examine me. I need him to be my ally. His stethoscope felt cold on my skin as he asked, "Are you bleeding at all?"

"Why would I bleed?" I said, and he let it go.

I wanted to ask Sarah to bring us tea and cake, but Dr. Jones said he couldn't stay.

~❧~

18th June

Not feeling well.

Henry won't let me go down to the dining room, he says I'm too sick. Sarah brings me all my meals up here. The food tastes funny and I try to eat as little as possible, but I still need nourishment if I ever want to escape this place.

I feel so dispirited. When the wave of gloom threatens to engulf me, I focus on the room. The deep teal walls, like the ocean in autumn, the stucco ceiling with its elegant curves, my rosewood desk with its mother-of-pearl inlay. My bed, my refuge, my burrow, my coffin…

My thoughts wander and I'll stop here.

~❧~

20th June

Sarah came in today with my breakfast tray, set it down and sighed, "I wish you would talk to me."

I pretended there was something very interesting happening on the empty beach outside. My sister touched my shoulder, forcing me to turn around.

"I know you didn't mean to do it, Alice. But you're sick, and if you won't let us help you…"

"I know you're fucking my husband," I told her calmly. The profanity hit her like a slap. "These walls are not thick enough to muffle your moans. And his grunts, *oh Sally, oh Sally*…"

She ran away from me and I rinsed my mouth with tea.

~☙~

21st June

I woke up to find a dark stain on my bed. It was cold and sticky and smelt like iron and earth. Why did Dr. Jones ask if I was bleeding?

Would they tell him what they were doing to me? Is he an accomplice?

~☙~

22nd June

Raised voices downstairs.

"You cannot keep her here forever!" Dr. Jones said.

"What am I supposed to do?" That was Henry, my grunting husband. "Have her locked up?"

Afterwards, as Dr. Jones examined me, he whispered, "Let me help you."

I wanted to kiss his dear old face, but I just nodded, hot tears spilling from my eyes.

"This is not good, you should have proper care," he added.

"Yes," I whispered back. "I think… I think Henry wants to be rid of me."

There. I said it.

But Dr. Jones gave me a strange look. I don't know if I can trust him completely.

~☙~

25th June

Henry doesn't come to see me at all. I hear his footsteps creaking along the corridor. I see him through the window, walking down the beach. He has taken to wearing black, probably thinks it makes him look thinner. It does, I must admit, but it also makes him look sallow and old, though it doesn't seem to bother my sister.

Brought together by common misery. A crazy lady in the attic, how tragic, how romantic.

If I were dead, they could marry and live happily ever after.

But I have other plans.

27th June

"Do you think I'm dangerous?" I asked Dr. Jones today.

"No, Alice, I don't think you are," he replied, gently.

"Then why am I locked up here? Can't you see what they're doing? They're trying to drive me mad and be rid of me. My husband refuses to come and see me."

I cried until I fell asleep, sick and exhausted.

28th June

Sarah came in with a bowl of stew.

"Alice…" She hadn't addressed me since I accused her of sleeping with Henry, so I raised my head to see what she wanted. "Dr. Jones told Henry today that fresh air would do you a world of good."

I watched her in silence, waiting to hear what she had in mind. She cleared her throat.

Unlike Henry, black becomes her. Her slim frame looks elegant, her sandy hair shiny. I can see the allure.

"I could take you to the beach," she suggested. "When Henry goes to work tomorrow. I can take you if you promise you'll be good."

I'm not a dog, I wanted to tell her. *You don't have to worry I won't be good.*

But I just nodded and said: "I would like that very much."

The stew was bitter. She's trying to poison me.

30th June

I have the key. That's all that matters.

Sarah came to take me out in the morning. When I felt the salty wind touch my skin, I wanted to spread my arms and run towards it, screaming for freedom. But I behaved. I did not want to make her suspicious.

"Do you remember when we were little girls?" she said. "We used to run through the surf and Mum would be livid when our dresses got wet."

I should have drowned her then. I wanted to ask her about Henry, it was on the tip of my tongue. Who dared to touch first, whose kiss lit the fire, all the gory details. But I watched the seagulls instead, sailing on the wind.

When we came back to the house, I pretended I had to go to the bathroom urgently. She was careless, she did not know there was a cabinet with spare keys in the hall just outside the bathroom door.

I have the key.

~❦~

3rd July

Today was Sarah's shopping day so I waited by the window until I saw her leave the house. Then I sneaked out of my room and went into the study. I searched through the drawers. Henry's envelope with the money for food and bills was in its usual place. Full. I took a few notes. Sarah is a negligent housekeeper; she won't notice.

There were other papers in the drawer, too. I snooped around to see if there was anything about my medical condition but, of course, there was nothing. It was all made up, all of it.

There was a birth certificate of one Sally Anne Harper, born on the 2nd June. I left it where I found it and went back to my room.

I'm leaving tonight.

I'll hide this diary in the boathouse. If someone finds it, I hope they'll let everybody know how my husband and sister conspired to murder me.

~❦~

Gull Island Gazette, 5th July

Missing: Alice May Harper, 26, from White Bay Cottage, Gull Island

Mrs. Harper disappeared on the night of 3rd July. The police believe she left the family cottage and took the sailboat out to the ocean.

Mrs. Harper is 5 ft 3 in, slim, with brown hair and blue eyes. She was wearing a navy-blue dress. As of this morning, the Coast Guard has found no trace of her.

This is the second tragedy to hit our prominent local entrepreneur, Mr. Henry Harper and his family. The Harpers' newborn daughter, Sally Anne, died in cot last month.

~

Jelena Dunato is working on her debut novel. You can find her on Twitter (@Jelenawrites). She also has several short stories forthcoming in various SFF magazines.

ISSUE 3: DISCIPLINES & DARKNESS

LOVE LETTERS TO POE

ANKERS | EIKAMP | MARGARITI

FRANK | KUHL

Volume 1, Issue 3 | December 2020
Edited by Sara Crocoll Smith

THE HUMAN IN ME

RICHARD M. ANKERS

I created her from the cracks in my psyche, those deepest, darkest places. She took time, craft, composure, and a spade, but since losing… I had time aplenty.

I moulded her limbs from liquid porcelain poured into such exquisite casts as to demean an angel, fired them with my heart and cooled them with my soul. Her body was of a metal alloy, the sort to never rust, never yield. But it was her face that worried others and her eyes that worried me; they were more human than my own, always had been.

She came to life at an exact moment, with a gasp from her and a grin from me. She shot bolt upright and tore the wires and cables from her breast.

Not wanting to seem anything other than a gentleman, I passed her a towel. She wrapped it about her hair.

~❦~

It took a year for Sara to walk, another to talk. By the third, the rest had fallen into place. Sara did everything a real woman could. She even had a hobby.

Sara loved flowers, adored them. Where some people nurtured gardens, she grew a rainforest, a kaleidoscopic sprawl of wondrous beauty. She applied the same unnatural sciences to them as I had to her; she was a fast learner, and they faster growers. To these falsities, these mimickers of nature, she exuded unrestrained love, and they rewarded her with spectacular displays.

People noticed, pointed and stared. Sara's plants didn't like being pointed at. When they reciprocated, things went rapidly downhill.

A policeman came by one evening. Sara answered the door and smiled.

"We've had a report that an unidentifiable plant, one allegedly owned by yourself, has eaten a certain councillor's prize Pomeranian."

"That's right," she replied.

"Well, I must say!" he huffed.

"Is this unusual, officer?"

"Extremely. Serious, too."

"If my plant had died of starvation, wouldn't it have been serious for it?"

The policeman removed his helmet and scratched at a thick mat of black hair. "It's different."

"How so?"

"It just is, ma'am."

"My name is Sara, not ma'am."

"Sorry, ma'am," he persisted, "but facts are facts and your plant has committed a heinous crime."

"Unless my plant has equal rights to that of the dog, it has not."

"Then the charge would pass to you, by which I mean, it already has."

Sara tottered. "You think my rights any more than beast or briar?"

His stammer condemned him.

Sara dragged him through the doorway quicker than a palpitating heartbeat.

I saw it all from my berth by the fireside and recoiled. I wasted no words. Sara wouldn't have listened. She tore him apart like a lion a raw steak.

Things were different after the attack. Prior to the assault, I had regarded her with a certain personal satisfaction, but no longer. For like those disturbed souls who frequented the asylums, who see neither light nor day, she remained impassive.

There were ramifications. A veritable pool of constabulary broke down our door and searched our home; Sara made them tea. They, of course, found no trace of that poor man who'd merely done his duty, so turned their attention to the garden; Sara's fingers clinked against her cup. As the first spade dug in with a schlup of displaced mud, the teacup crunched into a thousand pieces.

"Is she well?" asked a pleasant sergeant with whom I'd struck up a conversation. He'd been nothing if apologetic.

"Just a little highly strung."

The sergeant peered over to my darling girl; Sara sucked at her finger.

Clever girl, thought I.

They left us in peace after inordinate hours of blustering. We said we'd pray for his safe return.

~❧~

Our neighbours regarded us differently after that, even the coal merchant and his kin. They squinted at our dwelling, crossed the street, whispered sly words like *it* and *inhuman*. We had attained notoriety, and so I deemed it necessary to move. Sara disagreed.

~❧~

I picked my moment with the care afforded the finest cut crystal.

It was early Spring. The flowers in the garden sighed each morning with relief and expectancy for the Summer to come. Sara, in her stilettos as always, click-clacked her way from paving to lawn. She held a watering can in one hand and a selection of chocolates in the other; she applied both to all. My moment had come.

"Sara?"

"My sweetest darling," she replied.

"I have been considering our future."

"As have I," she interjected.

I coughed.

"Yes," she said, "I will marry you."

The deafening silence affected her not one jot.

My plans for a holiday now quashed, I had no choice but to smile a faked delight.

~❧~

I convinced Sara to marry in a chapel not too far away, but far enough. There was us and the vicar.

Sara wore a diamond-white dress fit to blind the sun. I wore black. She had donned her usual stilettos. I wore shoes conducive to speed.

The end of the ceremony went something like this.

"…and do you, Sara?"

"Just Sara," said she.

"…take…"

I was out of the door and running for my life. I leapt the stone wall, for I'd locked the wrought iron gates, and headed for a dense wood about a mile away.

The vicar's scream foreshadowed splintering wood and smashed stone. Sara's footsteps made maracas of the pathway.

My plan reached fruition when she attained the meadow beyond the church limits. I smiled a cunning weasel.

During the winter, the area was a wetland reserve interspersed with trees, untouched by man, wild and ragged. I knew it like the back of my hand, having lived my formative years just a few miles away.

When I came to a dell of Hawthorne and Cedar, dappled by flowers of citrine and royal blue beauty, I collapsed and wept. Through joy or relief, who knew? But I was as free as the proverbial bird and ready to migrate. I just needed to catch my breath.

I settled back on a hillock and closed tired eyes in peace for the first time in an age. My breaths proved as meditative as the sunlight did rejuvenating.

~❧~

I woke to a feeling of complete asphyxiation, or, more

exactly, its possibility. Unyielding chords strangulated my entire body, tight like steel cables. What's more, I was on the move.

A slick wet had long since chilled my spine, my shirt having ridden up to my shoulders. A star-speckled sky gleamed above in all its celestial finery. There were no sounds: no birds, no insects, nothing.

Sara was there. A changed Sara, anyway.

Her blouse streamed from her like a cat-o'-nine-tails, her dress, worse. As for her footwear, one heel was broken and the other lost. She tottered more than ever. Her hair sparked a mania. The slits in her clothing revealed milk-white arms, unnatural in the moonlight. Only when my forward propulsion stopped, my legs released and fallen to the ground, did my once dear Sara turn. Her one remaining eye dealt murder.

"Release him," she said, in a devastating whisper.

My binding of ivy withdrew.

"Why?"

"Because you are mad." What choice had I other than honesty?

"I am human," her flat response.

"Less so than earlier." I pointed to her face.

She touched to her eye and dipped her head.

"I... am... human."

"You are inhuman."

"Because I have a human in me?"

She craved for a yes, but got nothing.

"Was I born?"

"In a way."

"In a way?"

"The wrong way."

Sara's one good eye flashed a serpent's glare. "You made me."

I raised myself to my knees, which sunk into the marsh. "Yes, badly,"

"But I care."

"And you kill."

"Because I am human."

"Because you like it."

"But I have given life, as did you. My children are many and varied."

"They, too, are wrong."

"Science made me wrong."

"No, my dear, I did. And ever shall you remain unchanged."

Sara looked to the night sky, then to her hands. "Inhuman is wrong?"

"Very."

"Can I die?"

I shrugged.

"Can I drown?"

I shrugged again.

"Can you?"

She fell forward and wrapped her weight about me. She kissed me, though it felt like a peck, nuzzled me, though it felt like a filing.

I deserved my penance.

The grasses and weeds of the place licked her like a mother cat her kittens. Sara remained becalmed. But as the marsh water rose higher, and we sank ever more, she struggled with a question for which she'd long desired an answer. As the water tickled our chins, she asked it.

"Did your first wife look like me?"

"Yes, Sara, you have her eyes."

~

Richard M. Ankers is currently working on a trilogy of books titled *The Bohemia Chronicles*, a Victorian-based dark fantasy of love and loss. Richard's personal website is richardankers.com and you can find Richard on Twitter (Richard_Ankers).

THE SPEAKING SKULLS

RHONDA EIKAMP

Confined afterwards to my room in that house of light turned evil darkness, terror gripped me. Had I killed my uncle? What rage had lifted the heavy candlestick? I touched my skull beneath my curls – was there not a bump of decency there, beside the perverse bump? Was I this bone only….He'd had no right to say it.

Escape my sole hope, I set to picking the bedroom lock. I was a woman, depraved; this would prove it. The hallway shadows confounded my resolve. There were others in this moldering house and they had ears: the servant called Moth, more an elephant from his size, who had locked me in before returning to see to Uncle Henry. There was the guest newly down from the capitol, the illustrious name I recalled – Senator Nathan Beattie. With silvered hair, body sleek as a mountain lion, standing straight as if in invisible uniform as Uncle Henry presented me to him so deferentially that first evening. *My niece Talitha, Sir*.

The hall conjured my uncle's image and I moaned. The blood had seeped from beneath his head like a living thing.

A door slammed in the house's nether regions. *Hide*, my imperfect skull screamed.

Into the nearest room I slipped, but it was not deserted. A man I had never seen turned to stare.

From that lowly physiognomy, I knew my error.

"You're the niece," he growled.

"You're the murderer."

My uncle, renowned physician Henry Wortham, was a childhood memory become a stranger. On his doorstep that first evening, aghast at the decrepit state of the house I'd loved as a child, I thought him happy to take me in. I had nowhere, nothing. A wife fleeing fists. His guest, Senator Beattie, seemed understanding. It was over dinner that the shadow rose and grinned.

"But phrenology reveals the soul's *prima mobilia*, Talitha. Every faculty, every tendency is shown in those protrusions. The skulls speak." The fire flickered. My uncle was obsessed with this new science of skulls, the Senator more so. Some scheme to identify criminals *before* their crime, refashion the penal system. The wrongness of it had chilled my blood and I argued with them. A man's head was not his soul. "Phrenology is our future, dear niece, the way to betterment."

"You really must be measured," Senator Beattie remarked. Uncle Henry nodded, eyes hooded.

Thus it was on that next evening that I found myself led by giant Moth to a dim laboratory where my uncle proceeded to lift my curls aside and determine by tapes and strange implements the hidden nature of my soul.

"Enlarged audacity." Cold iron against my scalp startled me. "As I thought."

The dinner conversation haunted me. "Surely, Uncle, you cannot charge men with crimes before the commission? That imp is in all of us. It takes the circumstance."

More measurements. "Irascible, *selfish* – yes, we have before us a woman who would desert her lawful husband." I no longer knew his voice. Was it the influence of that obsessed senator, some miasma of the house?

"Charles is a monster, Uncle."

He appeared oblivious. "To answer your question, Dr. Gall's researches in phrenology find a faculty of perverseness in those who have killed, which betrays itself above the *os frontis.* The bullety forehead. We presently harbor a murderer here in the house in fact, his skull misshapen from birth. Strangled a man in rage."

Moth, my senses whispered. Yet the servant had no bullet forehead. At my wide – my *audacious* – glance, Moth tweaked his collar to hide bruises on his neck I hadn't before noticed. Attacked by the murderer? What beast it must be that could lay hand on Moth.

I started up, determined to be rid of it all, but Moth pressed me down.

Uncle Henry spoke. "We dispose of them, you see. Remove them, for the good of society." He could not mean what I thought. It was evil too great to bear; my mind could not birth it. "Beattie's very keen on it. Brings me those he can commandeer. When the measurements prove out – and they do – Moth takes care of them for us." *Flee*, my every nerve cried. "Just one more measurement, dear."

Oh then his gasp confirmed my pounding fear, as iron brushed the back of my head. "Not...*that* bump. On *you?*" When he came round to confront me, his gaze was dead. The shadows of this house – of his horrid science – had his soul, for it was not there. "The bump of *utter depravity*..."

"First do no harm," I pleaded, praying to wake that oath in him.

He clucked. "I'm sorry, Talitha. Society must be bettered."

As he turned to Moth, my hands found the brass candlestick and swung.

The shock of his copious blood rendered me horrified long enough for frantic Moth to lock me away.

"Yes, I killed a man."

And here before me now, the bullety forehead…yet I felt nothing but cool calm. Malformed of skull he was, this murderer, but the eyes bespoke kindness.

"Reuben Nye," he introduced himself.

"I'm afraid I'm a member of your club, Mr. Nye."

"Not a genteel club."

"I've assuredly killed my uncle."

"Good." He smiled wryly, which did wonders for his face. "Justified, I presume. Mine was. The man I killed had mistreated a woman of the night – a good woman – and she died. My rage was justified. The jury didn't see it that way. Beattie promised to save me from hanging if I would commit myself to his scientific endeavors."

More shouts ascended from below, Moth or the senator. Minds obsessed.

Through the moonlit window past Nye, I glimpsed the morose hills, gray bumps of vegetation that should have been green. Some execration held this place in its maw and shook it. Upon occasion, the house would shudder; I'd noticed it several times. We stood atop a great skull, those rough bumps testament to its evil. "They plan to execute us."

"I know."

"Incomprehensible. This house was full of light once. I cannot believe what *I've* done. Did some evil move my hand?"

I'd asked the dark only, but Nye answered. "Vitativeness. Love of life. The *good* doctor explained it to me. Sounds immanently desirable, but it's animalistic, causes a rage for survival." He touched the back of his head near the neck. "Here, somewhere."

The door flew open. Of course they'd found us.

Vitativeness was not my first thought when Moth wheeled in Uncle Henry. Henry's bandaged head held a concave spot, still oozing red, gumming the wheelchair's rim, his face gray as the hills.

"I'm not so easily done in, niece." Behind him came Beattie, with a glinting staghorn knife he handed to Moth. "Ah, Senator. As you see–" Henry touched his bandage – "I've discovered another disposable. My niece, unfortunately. I always said my brother married a woman lacking in our faculties."

"Your presumption of immunity amazes me, Wortham." Beattie indicated the bandage. "Look to your own faculties." I began to grasp the depth of the senator's perverse convictions. "There, the faculty of ideality, wholly crushed."

"Don't be ridiculous. I still have the idea of myself." Upon Henry's uncomprehending gaze, pity gripped me in spite of myself.

Beattie shrugged. "The skull speaks. You are reduced to an animal, Wortham." At his nonchalant gesture Moth stepped to my uncle.

"*No!*"

The demise of hope is a terrible thing to witness.

Henry's scream just before Moth slit his neck drove me past all sense.

Beattie deigned to notice my terror. "His small science was just a start, you know. I've discovered one much more admirable. More…*powerful*. How do the two of you like my handiwork?" He indicated Moth. I recalled the marks on the servant's neck. "He was hanged for his crime, but I brought him back." *From the dead?*…. Beattie was insane, delusional. "When I've enough for an army, I'll wake them." He gestured and Moth advanced on me.

"You cannot do this," Nye shouted.

"They can, Mr. Nye. I am nothing." Yet he understood my glance. Rapport – it has ever been so, with my beloved Reuben, since that fateful night. Not surrender. A signal.

We attacked together, Reuben wresting the knife from Moth with alarming skill and applying it to his ribs at the same moment I hurled myself at Beattie. All Beattie's cunning hadn't prepared him for a woman's vitativeness. My fingernails found his eyes, then I was fleeing, Reuben close behind.

Downward, into shadow. All outer doors locked, we ended at a root cellar, stumbling blind across rock-strewn ground until Reuben struck a match. *Skeletons!* – skulls, the lovely and misshapen there together – *we walked on the bones of those they'd executed*! Reuben's face mirrored abhorrence equal to mine.

The match went out.

Above, Beattie emitted a lupine howl, an incantation. I felt then in those bones that slippage that had oft caused the house to shudder.

They were *waking.* And they were ever so angry, but not at us.

Ahead lay light, dawn through the chinks of an outer

door, escape from that hell-house, and we scrambled toward it.

Rhonda Eikamp is an accomplished short fiction writer. Her next story coming out is "The Eyedom" in C.M. Muller's anthology *Oculus Sinister*. You can find more of her work at *Writing in the Strange Loop* and on her ISFDB (Internet Speculative Fiction Database) listing.

FOSSIL FEVER

AVRA MARGARITI

I have not slept a wink since I found you
my brain filled with primeval scales of terrible
    lizards.
Am I hatter-mad to say I want to break
into museums and excavation sites to be with you?
Am I Bedlam-bound to admit I would incinerate
all my books and white coats if it meant spending
a day or an eternity by your sempiternal side?
I would bleach my skin off my bones
to be alike you
would let my eardrums bleed and burst
to hear the roaring secrets of your kind.

I brushed you clean of grit and soil after I
    unearthed you
so tender in the sunlight.
Since then, my forehead has been hot and clammy,
my body burning–fossil fever.
My wife blanches when I tell her of the creature
remains deep underground.

She clutches her pearls, reaches for the fainting
    couch.
This is the Lord's reckoning, she says,
and what if those beasts I speak of ever awaken
and find their way back to me, the one who
disturbed their bony slumber
and unveiled them to the world?
What if their giant jaws close around me
and carry me back to their dirt-and-root realm?

Oh, what if, indeed?

~

A**vra Margariti** is a queer Social Work undergrad from Greece. She enjoys storytelling in all its forms and writes about diverse identities and experiences. Her work has appeared or is forthcoming in *Vastarien, Asimov's, Mirror Dance, Frozen Wavelets, Liminality, Glittership, Space and Time, Star*Line, Eye to the Telescope, Arsenika,* and other venues. You can find her on Twitter (avramargariti).

RESURRECTIONIST

ROBERT FRANK

You must understand, the exhumation and sale of
fresh corpses is simply a necessity of the times.
Nearing the turn of the nineteenth century, the availability
of corpses for medical research and training is scarce at the
absolute best, and nonexistent at its worst. In Philadelphia,
some in the trade refer to themselves, albeit romantically,
as "resurrectionists"; but I find the need for poetry rather
indecorous. We are what we are: thieves of corpses.

Being a woman in this foul practice presents certain
undeniable advantages over my male cohorts. The croc-
odile tears of young, pretty women are usually sufficient to
assuage the doubts of suspicious eyes where the clumsiness
of men oft fails. I've found that little more is required to
convince onlookers at funerals that I am the banker's long-
lost niece twice removed, or the wealthy aristocrat's child
of affair. Regardless, I sincerely hope you don't mistake my
confidence for pride in my dubious career; while it is
extremely lucrative, it is also undoubtedly profane.

I was introduced to this lifestyle through my cousin. His

father, my uncle, is a doctor and professor at a medical college wherein he is a student. In correspondence with him I revealed that I was struggling financially, and he enticed me into moving to his hometown in pursuit of opportunity to make money working with the college. Of course, he neglected to inform me of the task's sinister nature until I had already left my life behind and found a home in his city, otherwise I would have never agreed.

Unfortunately, I was out of options and had no choice but to oblige and join him for his grim operation. I was faint and ill to my stomach the first time we exhumed a corpse. However, after I saw the money afforded to me, I grew to steady my nerves in the presence of such morbid sights and ghastly smells. The rest from there is history and I have been working alongside him for several months. He handled most of the moving of the bodies while I primarily scouted out funerals to make note of where fresh earth was ripe for the plundering.

Truth be told, we made a spectacular team. Our efficiency kept us out of reach from the law, and the college made sure our pockets were well and full. I mention my experience not to regale you with tales of gruesome thrill, but to elaborate the fact that I am well acquainted with the grisly reality of what becomes of a person postmortem. However, I now find my imagination and unconscious thoughts vexed by what I witnessed on our most recent pilgrimage.

My cousin and I set up to embark on another night-veiled expedition to a neighboring town, following up on a recent interaction with an informant working at the town cemetery with whom we are well acquainted. He told us that there was recently a tragic house fire that left the entire family of four dead; yet strangely at the funeral, none of the corpses appeared to be burnt. Even stranger still, he claimed that at the procession, there were several people he had never seen in town in all his forty-odd years there.

Apparently, these strangers came to the funeral in normal attire save for a peculiar symbol they all wore around their necks. One by one, they removed their ornaments and placed them in the caskets with the deceased family members. We paid little attention to this, writing it off as simply strange traditions of superstitious country folk.

That night, with the help of local ruffians who didn't mind dirty work for dirty money, we exhumed all four of the caskets and loaded them into our cart and we were summarily on route to our destination.

During the ride however, I had an extremely uneasy feeling and could not help but keep my eyes over my shoulder pinned to the caskets. My cousin made several crude remarks asking me if I was feeling up to the task or if I'd lost the stomach for this kind of work. I know he was only trying to lighten the mood, but I could hear in his voice that he was similarly anxious, though he'd never admit it himself.

We were roughly an hour outside of that town when I began hearing sounds coming from the boxes. Instantly my hairs all stood on end, and a lump formed in my throat. I sat there for what felt like hours staring at the caskets, never taking a single breath for fear of what would happen if I did. My cousin asked what I was doing and when I questioned him on whether he heard any noise, he denied it. However, he was unable to deny the thumping we heard from the boxes immediately after.

Chills ran down my spine and I resisted the urge to

jump off the cart and make a mad dash away from the terrible sounds. In a frenzy, I pushed and prodded my cousin to stop the horses and investigate the caskets. After some deliberation, he finally agreed and stepped off the cart to get to the back. I kept my eyes fixed to the casket nearest me.

What happened next will haunt me to my very last breath.

My cousin returned to the driver's side looking as white as a shade, and without a single word, he presented his clasped hands to me. In them, he held four strange medallions. He stammered out that he was sure they were not in the cart when he loaded the caskets; I tried to rationalize that perhaps they simply fell out during our bumpy ride, but he insisted that all the caskets remained shut tight.

The medallions were flat and made of some lightweight metal, but something about them felt otherworldly. Despite their smooth surface, the center of the symbol had depth, as if one could put their finger deeply into them. Their strange symmetry was like nothing I had ever seen; the longer I looked the more unsettled I became. In a rush of panic, I took them and put them on the floor of the cart in front of us and begged him to keep going. He reluctantly agreed. The noises had ceased, and I held onto nervous hope that there was a rational explanation that merely evaded our perception. After all, we were both well aware that gases could escape from corpses, and that phenomena had been the culprit for bizarre sounds we'd heard on previous expeditions.

Close to another hour passed in silence, with my cousin and I too shaken to make conversation for fear of any other strange happenings taking place while we sat idle and unaware. Then I heard my name being called. I could not make out the voice as it was quiet like the whispers from an empty house.

I looked feverishly around but saw nothing. I asked if my cousin had just said my name but before he could answer I heard it again. This time slightly louder, but still little more than a whisper. Though, I was sure that it was coming from behind me. Slowly, I turned my head and the thing that caught my glance sent my senses into retreat.

A young girl was peering out from the casket nearest me. Her hair was pale like straw and thin enough to see her scalp, her skin was near transparent enough that her veins looked like ink run down her body, and she had sullen, mirror-like eyes that were sunken so far back into her head that she appeared to have twin abysses on her face. She once again whispered my name, then slowly sank back into her casket.

In a break of sanity, I leapt over into the back and lifted the top off her coffin. What I saw in her casket was a swirling vortex spiraling down, down into pitch-blackness. I saw the girl and several similar looking beings, who I could only assume were the other three family members, twisting downwards into that darkness, waving up at me as if beckoning me to join them. I believe the thing that terrified me most, was the overwhelming feeling that I was supposed to join them. The symbol of the medallions burned into my mind and I felt my body moving. Yet as I nearly plunged into that nightmare, I felt my cousin's hands pulling me back. He was howling at me in a fright, but I could not make out the words, I simply glanced back and saw the casket door just as it closed with fearsome thud.

The rest of that night was a blur; we eventually made it back to the college where the bodies were to be collected. Unfortunately, we did not receive payment for our delivery.

After all, the college was not in the business of buying empty caskets.

Robert Frank is working on his debut novel and is a freelance writer. You can find him on on Fiverr (fiendishlyrob).

AN INCIDENT ON MULBERRY STREET

JACKSON KUHL

The phenomenon of phantom limbs is a common occurrence for survivors of amputation, and as a physician to more than a few men who returned home from the last war less whole than when they rode off, one with which I was well acquainted. Patients would report attempting to pick up a jar of jam with a hand they'd left at Gettysburg, or describe trying to scratch a knee last seen before Chancellorsville. One old farmer, an empty shirt sleeve pinned to his shoulder, even swore he could feel the hairs on his arm whenever a breeze blew through his yard. Most of these cases tended to resolve themselves eventually, with either the sensations evaporating over time, or, as in the case of the plowman, the survivor learning to live with his invisible appendage. In the latter examples, often the patient reported no pain associated with the injury — the only burden, besides the obvious, was a continual and conscious stifling of any impulse to *use* the limb.

Being a country doctor who served a number of towns in the eastern part of the state, mine was a wide-ranging practice with a large clientele. Yet not all cases of phantom limbs were benign — there were some, I found, in which the patient suffered pain from it. Perceptions of heat or burning were prevalent or the feeling that the limb was twisted or bent in some awkward position. These sensations I attributed to damage to the nerves located at the site of amputation, known as the neuroma, and beyond my capabilities to remedy. Instead I referred these gentlemen to a specialist in New Haven, and in every circumstance, they returned from the visit to his office free of discomfort.

Dr. Coffman had been an instructor of mine at the medical college. Much older, he'd served as a surgeon during the war; and from the grim anecdotes shared with his protégés, we understood that he'd performed a significant amount of amputations himself, often under very poor and harrowing conditions. After my degree was conferred, we kept in touch, although less so as the years passed. Still, we remained friendly to each other and in my rare sojourns into the city, I never failed to meet him for a brandy.

It was therefore a little peculiar when yesterday evening, upon arriving at my house after completing my latest circumlocution through the countryside, I found a telegram from Coffman waiting for me. It was very brief, as telegrams usually are, hinting at some astonishing breakthrough and asking that I visit him in New Haven as soon as possible. While I'd been gladly anticipating some rest, its urgent tone made ignoring the invitation out of the question. So the following morning I pecked my wife on the cheek, told her I'd be gone for the day, and boarded the Shore Line into the city.

Having achieved emeritus status at the college, Coffman had retired into private practice, and he kept an office in a row house along Mulberry Street near the hospital. When he met me at the door I was taken aback by his appearance; he'd lost weight since our last meeting, and all color had left his hair and beard, leaving it a silvery white. I told myself these were natural signs of aging and that I hardly looked the same as when I was a student: I have become very self-aware of the gray spreading at my own temples. He invited me to lunch at a nearby café, where I observed he ate very little, and after some small gossip about the whereabouts and careers of shared acquaintances, Coffman began hinting at the source of what I could tell was barely concealed excitement.

He asked me if I knew how he relieved the suffering of those patients I sent to him. I confessed that I didn't. The patients themselves gave few details, suggesting the technique was beyond their understanding, and I assumed it involved some relaxation, if not outright removal, of the nerves closest to the neuroma. Coffman only shook his head and leaned closer to me across the table, concerned we would be overheard.

In low tones he explained his process did not involve nerves at all. Years ago, while working with saw and tourniquet in a blood-soaked Union tent, Coffman formed a notion that amputation only removed the physical extremity. What remained, he believed, was an ethereal limb that couldn't be sliced away with steel. As the material body was composed of cells, likewise it had an ephemeral counterpart fashioned from an unseen essence. This substance existed alongside our cells, imperceptible to our senses but detectable by certain instruments of his own invention.

In the intervening span, Coffman had enlarged his theory to the extent he could operate on this invisible aspect of the human body. His technique with my patients, he told me, had been merely to excise the ghostly remnant from the neuroma, just as the physical limb had been cut away before. The discomfort they felt was real because the

ethereal limb was real, even if it couldn't be perceived by
ordinary methods. By removing the phantom limb, he
removed the source of their pain.

As I sat listening to him, I was awash with embarrass-
ment and an almost elegiac sadness. Coffman, once my
instructor and even my idol, my *friend*, had clearly slipped
into dementia. His results with my patients were undeniable, yet clearly whatever procedure he employed was now
subsumed by this hogwash about wraithlike substances. I
knew I could never refer another patient to him.

Absurd though his beliefs were, I still felt cordial
toward him, so having paid the bill I agreed to accompany
him back to his office, where he wanted to show me something. Coffman could hardly contain himself as we walked
from the café. The ethereal limbs he amputated, he said,
were not inert tissue; just as they weren't composed of flesh
or muscle, their quintessence eluded definitions of life or
death. They were still viable. For the past several years,
Coffman had been engaged in a project to salvage these
loose parts, but his final objective was stymied by locating a
phantom *head*. After all, no one can survive having his
braincase amputated, he said; and such a thing as a disem-
bodied head was therefore a rarity. As fortune would have
it this difficulty had been solved nearly a week prior, when
Coffman was able to secure what he needed following a
gruesome construction accident. Hearing this disclosure, I
resolved immediately to contact a colleague I knew at the
asylum in Middletown, where my friend Coffman could
live out his remaining years in comfort and safety.

Entering his office, we passed through to Coffman's
laboratory, filled with strange mechanisms and dominated
in the center by a stout but bare table. A bedsheet lay on
the floor beside it.

Coffman, leading the way, stopped very suddenly, and

when I looked toward him to gauge the reason, I observed his stare lay exclusively upon the crumpled sheet. As I watched, an expression of panic convulsed across Coffman's face. His features rippled in contortions so overwhelming that I found myself infected, and in surging dread I glanced around the room, terrified of some danger. But beyond the furniture and machines and that simple square of white cotton, I saw nothing.

Suddenly and inexplicably, Coffman jerked upwards onto his toes. I asked him what the matter was, but in reply he uttered only a strangled gasp. Thinking he'd been stricken by a stroke or fit, I sprang forward to aid him. Without warning I too was struck — struck by something swung heavily at my jaw. A combustion of lights exploded before me, then my vision collapsed and I remember only darkness as I sprawled to the floorboards.

When I came to, I found Coffman lying before the open doorway. On the far side of the office, the door onto the street also hung unlatched, but more than an hour passed before I realized the strangeness of that — for I distinctly recalled shutting it behind me when we entered from lunch. I crawled to Coffman to check his pulse. I found none, and my pocket mirror placed before his lips likewise failed to produce any fog on the glass. His eyes bulged in fright, his tongue curled in his mouth like a shriveled black worm. Thinking his heart had seized, my gaze fell lower along his body. It was then that I recoiled from my old friend, shuffling backwards on palms and feet to escape, halted only when I struck a heavy leg of the table behind me.

The distance wasn't great enough to obscure the horror of what lay across Coffman's neck. Striping both sides of his throat were two sets of purple contusions, imprinted on the skin like ink. I counted ten of them.

Jackson Kuhl is the author of *A Season of Whispers*, a gothic novel set in a haunted 19th-century transcendentalist commune, and *Samuel Smedley, Connecticut Privateer*, a biography of the American Revolution's most daring sea captain. His short fiction has appeared in *Black Static*, *Weirdbook*, and several anthologies, and some of his stories have been collected in *The Dead Ride Fast*. You can find him online at Twitter (jacksonkuhl) or at jacksonkuhl.com.

ISSUE 4: EVERLASTING LIFE

LOVE LETTERS TO POE

BEAUCHÊNE | STURK
NAHTÉ | RUDEL

Volume 1, Issue 4 | January 2021
Edited by Sara Crocoll Smith

EMBER'S LAST LIGHT, REFLECTED

EMELINE MARIE BEAUCHÊNE

There, in the dark corner it rests, covered in linen as if wrapped in grave cloth. Mocking, scornful and hateful. Billowing tattered ends of the faded cover dance from a breeze of uncertain origin – all windows tightly shuttered against night's howling wind.

The movement of the cloth beckons, silent yet screaming nonetheless. The bronze mirror underneath gazes through the sheet as if to the bottom of a shallow pond. It knows I have returned. Patient. Awaiting my waning constraint. I have already set logs ablaze in the fireplace. A slippery slope.

Therein lies a struggle as old as the garden. Knowledge. Knowledge of good and evil. Distinction. I have seen the fluttering shades of lightness and dark and suspect the difference. Like most, I dwell in the gloam of ambient twilight without true comprehension. The mirror, however, shows absolute truth. I cannot hide in its reflection.

Questions asked to the mirror under precise conditions yield clarity. The knowledge I yearn for my troubled soul to abate the pain. Answers to questions dared not asked anyone, save the reflection of my weary visage.

Three sounds fill the chamber, subtle yet strong. First is the crackling of flame consuming wood. Second are the machinations of the grandfather clock behind me. Lastly, the cacophonous tattoo of my heart thumping wildly in my chest like that of a frightened rabbit.

I remove the sheet over the mirror like a magician revealing a trick, theatrics lost on all but the cold stone bricks of the inglenook walls. Firelight languidly twinkles in the sullied surface of the bronze mirror. The once stately artifact now merely glimmers under a thick patina; its once proud luster reserved for kings and queens now tarnished to my morbid desire.

I move the mirror in position, its legs shrieking with contempt as it is dragged across the marble floor. I place it facing the fire as a weary traveler drying out from an unexpected downpour. The metal surface is cold like the mortician's slab.

My heart's desire, addressed. The promise of it dries my mouth and flutters my stomach. Would that I know the truth?

It is growing close. The logs crumble and the flare diminishes. I walk to the window, opening the panes and pulling apart the shutters. Moonlight pours through the angulate window and falls across the floor like a large silver door.

I have to turn away, if only for a moment. I consider the blustery night swaying the garden of the estate. Wispy clouds veil the moon for a transitory moment as they sail through the vast heavenly sea.

The glowing coin in the sky makes me wince until my eyes adjust to the harsh light. Then, I can see the imperfections on the lunar sphere. I see his face in the mottled surface. Nathaniel.

My long white hair flows as if I have taken flight. The nightgown pushes taught against my chest. A mournful wail from the trees tries to warn me against such blasphemous action. Yet the fire and clock conspire behind me, urging that time is nigh.

I turn again, this time aided by the wind to proceed. I glide towards the mirror as if in a dream. I place my hands on the curved frame like upon the shoulders of my beloved.

Though the phrase is etched on my very soul, I read the inscribed words again as if to glean something that previously eluded my grasp. The incantation is carved into the back of the flat surface. The mirror's words echo from my cracked, crimson lips.

Upon fireplace gaze I will gloat,
*   then burning questions I can explain.*
Unlit, reflections are ill of note,
*   and by flame questions asked are in vain.*
Embers last light with time's final smote
*   reveal heart's desire in truth and so plain.*
Three questions revealed — no more to quote
*   'til harvest moon brings midnight again.*

I glance behind me to see the arms in the clock-face pointed skyward, both nearly aligned. I round the mirror, seating myself on the warm hearth. In the large oval reflective eye, I am just to the side so that the fireplace still takes center stage.

I can feel the last heat of the dying embers on my back. The pendulum lyre swings, its bob swaying back and forth. The first chime of midnight begins.

The reflection fogs briefly. A shadowy shape takes form.

It is the horrific deed that haunts my nightmares. In the mirror's realm, I straddle Nathaniel as he lies on the ground. My black hair pours over his dying face. In that reflected surface, I drop the dagger that had pierced his faithful heart, clattering to the marble floor. Oh, that fateful night since past!

Nathaniel looks through my reflected doppelganger beyond to the real me seated on the hearth of the fireplace. His terrified gaze falls full into my eyes. It is time for my first question.

"Please, Nathaniel, tell me. When I plunged the dagger into your chest, were you without pain, my love?"

Nathaniel shook his head. "No," he gasped.

The fourth gong of the clock echoes through the inglenook and through the vestibule beyond. Time for the next question. I lick my lips.

"Nathaniel," I ask, "can you please forgive me?"

Nathaniel's eyes grow wider, knowing his demise imminent. "No," he croaks.

A tear betrays my gaze, spilling down a wrinkled cheek. I wait four more bells of the hour. The last question.

I whisper, "Nathaniel, do you still love me?"

His reply comes as his countenance fades with the last chime of midnight. "No," he says.

I sob as his reflection yields to the scene of the cold, dark embers. At long last, I know my transgression. The fatal error I made was in dispatching my love in a manner that allowed him time to reconsider. I should have taken him in his sleep so that he would love me forever.

I push the mirror back into the corner where it will rest beneath its shroud for another year. Until the harvest moon in the midnight sky shines upon dying embers, reflected in the mirror. As I have done so now for many, many autumns. Now, I wait. I wait for the answers to change. I wait for embers' last light, reflected.

Emeline Marie Beauchêne is a second generation American with strong cultural and genealogical ties to France. Along with her love of all things French, she also inherited an adoration for horror stories. This was most likely a genetic trait as her grandmother, Tante Estelle, was a huge fan of Guy de Maupassant. Emeline, however, preferred Edgar Allan Poe. She is still perfecting her craft, currently branching out into a cozy mystery series.

HIS EMBRACE

T.E. STURK

Sitting at her vanity, Eleonore fingered her cold earlobe, working by touch to insert the gold-and-ruby earring he had given her. There was a mirror that she might have used–a smallish, beautiful Italian thing at least two centuries old–but she had covered it, for him. In any case, she did not like to see herself these days.

The earring pin pierced through the tender skin, and she let out a small, involuntary moan. The merest pinprick was a pain these days; the merest cut or bruise sent agonies through-out her over-sensitive pale flesh. Except, of course, the two small spots upon her throat, barely even scars. . . She touched them gingerly and felt a shiver down her spine, as if a lover's breath caressed her neck.

Between two heartbeats, his dark, alluring presence filled the room.

Though he had made no sound in coming, she knew he had appeared. His very scent enveloped her, musky and warm like an intoxicating drink. She shut her eyes, surrendering herself to his embrace.

'My love,' he whispered in her ear. It set her head to

spinning. His voice was velvet-smooth and sweet, and filled her like a fine red wine.

'Take me.' The words forced their way out of her lips. He did not wait for further invitation. His cool lips touched her neck, kissing it gently. She held her breath, not opening her eyes, waiting for the pain-and-pleasure sting. He held that back at first, drawing the moment out until she almost spoke again; before she found her voice, his needle teeth descended deep into her flesh.

She moaned, hot blood fleeing her neck. At once his lips grew warm against her skin. They did not leave a single gap, through which even the tiniest droplet of blood might spill.

As the moment drew out into a minute, she reached out, involuntarily, her twitching fingers seeking to grasp something—anything—to anchor her before she lost herself into his overwhelming touch. Her right hand closed upon a corner of the satin shawl with which she'd covered up the mirror.

He tore away his mouth, blood streaks splattering her neck and dress like shameful, scalding brands.

'None of that now,' he said, his voice commanding underneath its sweetness. He put a warning hand upon her arm, the fingers digging harshly into her all-too tender flesh. She gasped with pain, and he relaxed his grip.

'I'm sorry,' she whispered. 'I did not mean to—' She trailed off as she met his eyes. Dark and deep, they swallowed her, drowning her words.

'Hush.' The corners of his mouth curled in amusement. 'All is forgiven.' He leaned forward to kiss her, his lips still tasting of her blood.

Her eyes closed yet again, and for a time she had no thoughts at all, her mind consumed by the intense aura of *him*. His scent invaded her: an intricately rich perfume of coppery blood and wine and spices; of hazy, smoke-filled rooms by candle-light, and private, intimate affairs between good friends; of night-long gentle love, and flesh pressed into flesh, the unconditional surrender of two lovers into one.

An incongruent scent intruded on her bliss—a sliver of a smell, riding a soft breeze through the open window.

In sensing it, Eleonore recalled, more as a deep impression than a thought, her childhood days; picking the fragile white flowers of the stingless sugar-nettles that sometimes grew in patches near countryside paths. Sucking on them, extracting droplets of nectar, sugary and sweet. . . This scent was like that taste; a tiny trace of pure childhood delight.

At odds with the man's perfume, it had no place in his embrace. As he drew back, she turned her face into the breeze and sniffed. But it was almost gone.

The flower-scent evaporated on the air. With it went the memories, vanishing just beyond the reach of thought, their absence hanging like an afterimage on her eyelids; still holding their shape but nothing more, and fading slowly.

She sighed, releasing the final phantom shadow of the scent upon her breath.

Though it was gone, it had nevertheless changed her mood. Like one who's half asleep, she blinked around, robbed of a precious dream.

Her eyes fell on the mirror, where the shawl had slipped—not much, but just enough that she could see a corner of her face, haggard and pale; a single, baggy eye stared back, feverishly glistening. And though she knew he stood behind her, there was no-one there.

Of course, she'd always known there wouldn't be.

Before he could react—indeed, before she herself could

even think—she grabbed the mirror in an aching hand, swinging it around with all her strength. The shawl slipped off as the silvered glass crashed into his skull, splintering into a dozen shards. The broken mirror clattered to the floor.

He howled, and in a flash, she saw his face, boiling and raw as if his very skin had been set aflame. Furious eyes—filled with pain and shock and deep betrayal—bore into her before he spun away, shielding his face. In two long, leaping strides, he transformed into a leathery black mass of wings and claws, and vanished through her open window.

Then he was gone. The room was still and silent. No trace of his scent remained, nor any sign of him at all; except a shattered mirror and a blood stain on her neck. And on her lips. And tongue.

She fell out of her chair and wept, knowing, finally, that she was free.

∿

T.E. Sturk often writes of ghosts and everlasting life —its allure and its costs. They're currently querying a historical dark fantasy novel, set in the West Indies during the late 16th century. You can find them online at www.emmasturk.com and on Twitter (TE_Sturk).

ROSE & THORNS

ETHAN NAHTÉ

There she sat upon a bench,
a pale rose in full bloom —
with skin soft as petals
standing out against the gloom.

Eyes that glisten like dewdrops
upon a vivid green leaf.
This beauty I must have to hold
to stir me from my grief.

To garner her interest,
A soft-spoken word here.
To gain her sympathy,
A generous gesture there.

To my humble abode
she doth discreetly follow,
filling the space within my breast
which has long been dark and hollow.

Her tender kisses,
moist upon my lips.
The scent of her long hair
stroked by my fingertips.

Her eyes so hypnotic
tugging at emotions and my mind.
The coolness of her embrace
slows down the hands of time.

Candlelight flickers, casting shadows.
I can feel her mouth's caress.
Tantalizing nibbles upon my neck
as I unzip the back of her dress.

My breath sweet and warm
blows softly in her ear.
She wraps her arms around me
and holds me, oh, so dear.

The hold becomes a clutch.
Her eyes set ablaze.
I'm lost in a fog.
My mind, like a maze.

Her head moves forward.
I see her raven hair.
The prick of the rose's thorns,
I yield... I do not care.

Her pale, chilled skin
grows fervent and blush.
The essence of my life
flows away with a rush.

The thorns dig deeper
and my beauty has her hold.
I sought her for my passion
but the hunt was two-fold.

A victim I was
of a sordid heart
and, to the rose with thorns,
I am simply *a la* cart.

Ethan Nahté writes speculative fiction and has over three dozen published stories and poems, two story collections, and three novellas. With his Beagle Mountain Publishing company, he released the anthology *Island Terrors & Sea Horrors* (2020). He was the recipient of the National Quill & Scroll Award, 1st Place in the John L. Balderston competition, and three-time Writers of the Future Honorable Mention recipient. He resides in the mountains of Arkansas, where he enjoys hiking, camping, and fishing.

His books can be found at www.NahteWords.com More information can be found at www.livenloud.net. He's on Facebook (EthanNahteCreative) and Twitter (EthanNaht1).

THE NIGHT, FOREVER, AND US

BY AERYN RUDEL

I slip through the window of my wife's room, the mingled smell of sickness and disinfectant sharp in my nose. The only sound is the low susurrus of hospital machines monitoring the failing systems of Lucy's body, charting their inevitable collapse. She is a shadow within a shadow in the corner, a tiny, wasted thing beneath a white hospital blanket.

They put her in hospice care two weeks ago. I am almost too late.

I approach her bed, despair and the bright urgency of my discovery warring for control of my emotions. It's been six months since the diagnosis and two since I left. I still remember Dr. Wagner's face, his eyes, how hopeless they were. He delivered the news gently, but we knew a death sentence when we heard one.

We tried everything, borrowed and spent money for experimental treatments with a one-in-a-thousand chance of working. None of them did, of course, and Lucy accepted the inevitable, made peace with it. I couldn't. I searched for other remedies, grew desperate, and it led me away from her. It led me into the dark, and, finally, to the ruins of an ancient monastery on the border between Armenia and Azerbaijan. Within the crumbling edifice of black stone, I encountered a stooped monk, a pale creature who had not glimpsed the light for decades, maybe longer.

There, in the dark and quiet, I made a bargain that seemed inconsequential for what was offered. Maybe that decision will damn me, but I seized upon it and carried it with me back across the ocean.

I sit on the edge of my wife's deathbed and whisper, "Lucy. I'm here."

She turns her head, and her eyes flutter open. Her face is sunken, and her cheekbones stand out jaggedly against paper-thin skin. She wears the pink bandana I gave her months ago to cover the ravages of chemo. Only her eyes belong to her, cloudy blue but still clinging to life.

"Danielle?" she gasps. Tears slide down her face, each one an accusation I can barely stand. I left her alone when she needed me most. Neither of us had any family. Hers passed away when she was a child. I was a product of the foster care system. We had one another and nothing else. Two desperate souls who came together in the chaos of a world that should have twisted us both into human wreck-age. No matter what happens tonight, my decision to leave will haunt me forever.

If Lucy could've summoned the strength, she might've struck me or raged at my selfishness. I would've accepted it, welcomed it for my sins. But she is long past such things, and she reaches up to touch my face. My own tears come, and I am thankful she cannot see their color in the dark.

"I'm so sorry I had to go. Nothing could help you here, but . . ." I nod at the night beyond her window. "I found something to make you well again."

A sad, tired smile overtakes her face. "Danielle, you

ran. . . because you couldn't accept it, and I hated you."
She chokes back a sob, grimacing with the effort it takes.
Her eyes cloud with pain. "But I don't care anymore. I just
want you with me."

I take her hand and kiss it. "What if there is no end?
What if there doesn't have to be one?"

She sighs and turns away. I can tell even these small
movements tax her. "No more treatments. I want to rest."

"Lucy, look at me. Really look at me."

I gently turn her head and lean forward into the moonlight streaming through the window. Lucy's eyes widen.
The bottomless fatigue remains, but something new takes
hold: fear. "What did you do?"

"Don't be afraid. I did it for us, for you."

"Your eyes," she says.

My eyes were blue before my trip to the Caucuses, like
a winter sky. They are the color of the fading sun now.

"I know it's strange, but I don't feel pain. I don't fear
sickness. All that's missing is you."

"What . . . what are you saying?

"Be with me." I touch her cheek. She flinch-
es, maybe noticing for the first time how cool my skin is.

She reaches up and grasps my hand with surprising
strength. "I'm so scared, Dani."

I want so much to soothe her. "I love you, Lucy, more
than life, more than death. Trust me. Please."

She shudders. Her face contorts and her mouth trembles. "It hurts. Can you make it stop?"

"I can." I gather her into my embrace and kiss away
the pain.

~•~

Thirty minutes later, Lucy rises from her death bed.

She stands in the moonlight, a pale specter so lovely my soul aches to look at her. Her hair has returned, falling around her shoulders in a cascade of liquid black. Her body has regained its flesh, her face its proper contours, and her eyes burn a soft red, like mine. She doesn't appear sick anymore, she glows with dark purity, stark and beautiful.

I hold out my hand. Our cold fingers intertwine, and I kiss the top of her head, like I used to do and will do for a thousand years to come.

"What's out there?" she asks, excitement and wonder in her voice. I push open the window and smile in the dark. "The night, forever, and us."

∽

Aeryn Rudel is a freelance writer from Seattle, Washington. He is the author of the Acts of War novels published by Privateer Press, and his short fiction has appeared in *The Arcanist*, *On Spec*, and *Pseudopod*, among others. Aeryn is a notorious dinosaur nerd, a baseball fanatic, and knows more about swords than is healthy or socially acceptable. He occasionally offers dubious advice on the subjects of writing and rejection (mostly rejection) at www.rejectomancy.com or Twitter (Aeryn_Rudel).

ISSUE 5: MEMENTO AMORI

LOVE LETTERS TO POE

HOGAN | OWEN
VREELAND | DIBENEDETTO

Volume 1, Issue 5 | February 2021
Edited by Sara Crocoll Smith

MOURNING POST

LIAM HOGAN

I wooed my beloved from afar, as she wooed me.

We met at a funeral. The dreary weather matched
the mourners' mood and attire, making for a particularly
sombre affair, enlivened only by her luminous presence. A
second cousin, once removed, upon the recently deceased
matriarch's side. We spent a couple of hours on the fringes:
the back pews of the chapel, then beneath a shared
umbrella as we huddled around the open grave, before
finding a quiet spot on a landing when the wake retired to
the grand old house whose windows and mirrors were
shrouded in black.

Our obedient presence was the only thing required of
us, too old to be indulged as children, too young to be of
much interest to the assembled aunts and uncles. As our
brief time together came to an end, I handed her my card
and she scribed her address on the paper with which my
funeral biscuit was wrapped. And then we were unceremoniously returned to our former lives, two hundred miles
and a world of duty and expectation apart.

Our first communication was tentative, uncertain. Had

I read too much into our quiet conversation, into her intense but tender gaze? The writing of my black-bordered letter was fraught with such doubts. I steeled myself for the cruel blow of a cold and formal reply, or worse, no reply at all. But I knew that I would forever regret it if I did not brave the hazard.

Our letters, so coy and yet so full of hope, overlapped; hers arriving before my entreaty could possibly have found its way into her fine-boned hands. The cold sun shone a little brighter that day; our interests were indeed aligned, our curiosities equal, our passions kindled.

In a fit of unparalleled joy, I sought out an artist friend of mine, begged of him some of the materials he uses to dress each scene. A bouquet of dried, black tulips, deliciously fragile, as temporary and fleeting as life itself, accompanied my very next letter.

I received a rare volume of poetry, the melancholy verses cut like the November wind through my soul. There was no recognition of my flowers in her note, just as there was none of her carefully chosen gift in mine. Again, our exchange had crossed somewhere in the cruel miles that separated us.

The letters were secondary, always playing catch up. It was the gifts that came to matter most. Usually memento mori of one kind or another, they tended towards the macabre, some might even claim ghoulish. That the family was still in mourning might have been part of it, but I think it spoke of how our souls were entwined not only through this but through other, unseen realms.

A raven, the work of a skilled taxidermist, arrived one morning to perch on my desk, frightening the cleaning lady into a fit of vapours. An antique looking glass, the aged silver having the peculiar effect of making even the most youthful of faces appear ancient, travelled in the opposite direction for her delight and amusement.

A lock of black hair, tightly coiled, arrived hidden behind the casement of a pocket watch that ticked a most doleful tick. A crystal vial of my own blood formed the centrepiece of a necklace shaped like a creeping, strangling vine…

But what had begun as an enchanting hunt for exotic peculiarities soon became a chore. A tiresome burden, distracting me from my employment, cutting deep into my savings until I was forced to borrow heavily from friends and relatives. A mania, all consuming.

It wouldn't have been so bad if our correspondence had followed a normal pattern, so that each response could be thoughtfully weighed, the growth as slow and natural as the season. Instead, our simultaneous courtship had become a contest neither of us was willing to lose, the bids blind, the rules obscure.

The search for gifts worthy of my distant love became utterly exhausting. And so, in a pit of black despair, I sent an exquisite silk shawl, laced with tuberculosis spores. She dispatched a puzzle box, full of small, black, venomous spiders whose bite turned my pale skin necrotic. Had we hoped, perhaps, to poison a relative sharing the same address, leading to another family funeral, one where we could be reunited?

Perhaps. Though it doesn't truly matter. Our gambits were both far too successful.

Our final exchange was a pair of headstones, our names and the year of our deaths carved deep and implacable into the marble. They'll stand together; our grieving families have decided that, in the same cemetery where first we met.

And though I am loathe to admit it, the one she sent to

adorn my grave was far more elegant than the one I sent her. So she scores the ultimate victory. When future generations wander past the spot where we two lie and compare our headstones, they'll never guess that it is *I* that lost.

Liam Hogan is a short fiction writer. You can find links to all his published pieces, many of which can be read for free at *Happy Ending Not Guaranteed*.

In addition to the writing, he helps host *Liars' League London* and volunteers at the creative writing charity *Ministry of Stories*.

TEMPLE

H.R. OWEN

She finds herself staring, unable to look away even though her heart twists in her chest at the sight. Every part of the body before her is familiar; playground scars memorised like Bible verses, freckles and errant hairs like the Stations of the Cross.

Light bleeds through the curtains as the world outside edges tentatively towards morning. A blade of fragile sun illuminating in gold each narrow curl of the hair on the pillow, finding soft bronze in the sweeping shoulders and rose quartz in the fullness of the lips. She sighs and turns to the figure standing beside her.

I never thought it would be so colourful, she thinks.

The figure's head tilts almost imperceptibly under the sweep of their hood. They hear her.

Forget it. I'm being melodramatic. The universe has survived worse than this, I know.

Staring a little longer, her fingers twitching as she fights the desire to reach out and touch. Such a simple want, something she'd taken for granted – the ability to touch whenever she'd wanted, take whenever she'd needed. It

had never eluded her before, but now it was everything –
all those tiny brushes of self against self, skin against skin,
breath against lips.

She closes her eyes.

*I should have told him. I should have…Whatever. You know all
this.*

Tell me.

Two syllables echo in her mind, sand in the wind, but
she can feel the need in them. The ancient loneliness.

She chews her lip and frowns, crossing her arms over
her chest with a shrug. The figure waits for her to speak.
They won't hurry her. They don't know the meaning of
the word.

He's got this real funny way of talking, she thinks at last. *Like
you can practically hear him dotting the Is and crossing the Ts. Real
precise.*

Shifting her weight, she considers this. Grey eyes watch
her, implacable, reminding her of a poem about horses in
the hour-before-dawn dark. The horses had frightened
her too.

Bambi, she smiles. *Big brown Bambi eyes like tar pits, they just
pull you right in. Got a brain like a whip-crack, and I swear he's got
no idea how funny he is – spits these jokes out totally deadpan and
then when you laugh, he jumps out his skin and looks at you with this
sweet blushy smile that's all eyes more than mouth because he's so
surprised…*

She looks up, grinning and flushed, falters, and falls
silent. A century passes, or maybe only a minute. The
person in grey moves and she's surprised their skin doesn't
rustle. The meaning is clear. It's time to go.

I should have…

She turns to look at the body on the bed, still hogging
the covers, still warm. She closes her eyes against the sight,
so familiar and yet so grotesquely wrong.

"I thought I had time," she whispers.

The hand that closes round her wrist is altar-stone cold.

Everybody does.

∾

H.R. Owen frequently writes about isolation and connection. They run a weekly fiction podcast called *Monstrous Agonies,* a radio advice show for monsters and creatures of the night. You can find them on Twitter (callmehagar).

SARAH

M. ALAN VREELAND

Trigger warning: Self-harm

Sarah knew not of the depths
my love had lately plumbed,
nor could she fathom countless steps
that left my heart succumbed.

Sad the man whose mistress' eyes
are nothing like the sun;
for Sarah's eyes were yond the skies,
a universe of one.

Her raven hair, so sleek and soft
caressed her slender neck;
once a visage so aloft,
has left my heart a wreck.

This cursed plague descended
on her lovely graceful frame;
her bloom could not be mended;

Death has a soul to claim.

Insatiate Reaper will not win!
My Sarah stays with me
beneath the rosebush safe therein
— nature's thorny filigree.

Circling buzzards overhead,
osmatic — they betray;
why can't they smell instead
the balm of love's bouquet?

Damn fever now flows through my veins;
Oh, Death, perhaps you see;
do pity me my heartfelt pains —
to Sarah, please send me!

But why presume that Death will call;
could torment be his game?
Must I wait in shadowed pall
to find my soul unclaimed?

No! I will ensure my fate
and lie among the roses;
a helpful blade to consummate;
my placid clay reposes.

As life drains in a pulsing flow,
I fade and close my eyes;
How well will scarlet roses grow
with blood to fertilize.

I do believe our spirits merge;
Sarah's soul to mine does call.

Weep not for us, nor play a dirge;
for Sarah, love is all.

～

M. **Alan Vreeland** is a poet and teacher. As a middle school language arts teacher, he often writes humorous rhyming poetry to get reluctant students interested in poetry. Lately, he's branched out into other poetic forms, including gothic and horror. His poem "Fixer Upper" is published in *Putrescent Poems* anthology. You can find him on Facebook (M. Alan Vreeland).

FORGET ME NOT

BY KATIE DIBENEDETTO

My white porcelain teacup rattles against its saucer in my lap as I shiver awake. Dim light from the waning moon outside the window provides minimal aid as I glance around. I sense it again, that presence lurking. The phenomenon where my mouth goes dry, my heart stops, and my stomach capsizes.

"It is purely in your head," I whisper to myself, "Calm down," I run my fingers through my tangled black curls and get up from the chair.

The shiny silver hands of the grandfather clock say I should get on to bed and go back to sleep, but I cannot help myself, it is not that simple. Slinking quietly across the cottage, I peak in every room and throw back every dusty curtain to assure myself I am, in fact, alone.

When I reach my wooden bed, I fold the faded green quilt over uncovering my side and a heavy metallic crack sounds down the hall.

I flinch, knowing in my head it is only the shifting temperature causing the wooden front door to creek and rattle the iron lock, but I cannot help it and I scamper back to check the door again. Short little inhales are all I can manage as terrifying scenes creep their way into my imagination.

"Breathe, you are safe, end this nonsense," I tell myself, as I go to the fireplace and attempt to warm away the trembling with the glistening garnet coals. I breathe deeper, slowly, one…two… three times.

'*Clang*,' sounds from a few feet away, which my ears register as a reverberating wail while my eyes can clearly see the black metal stoker has fallen over.

"It is only the fireplace poker, you have got to calm down," I say, but the immediate thought of '*what knocked it over*' hastens after. I scour the room for any glimmer of a trespassing shadow.

Breathing deeply again, I return to the bedroom. While double checking the closet, my fingers trail down the sleeve of a tweed jacket. Warm, cedar wood scent plays at my nose as I slip into the cool sheets. Slowly twisting the brass knob of the oil lamp on my bedside table, I ease the room into darkness.

Every minuscule sound the house makes, from the tick of the clock to the creaking of the roof, echoes through my head. I try to block it out, sing a song in my mind, but nothing can ease this anxious panic.

A spring rainstorm blows in, demanding attention as it patters on the roof and windowsill. Eventually it transforms into a plinking sound in the tin bucket in the corner where the roof leaks.

My skin is crawling and I cannot get comfortable. Why are the nights so unbearable? What is this presence that infiltrates my brain and causes me to feel like I am under attack?

With a whiff of the pillow beside me, a vision blazes in my mind. Rain drums on the grave marker in the family cemetery. Tiny blue flower blossoms droop under the weight of the raindrops. Tears flood my eyes, my breathing becomes jagged and harsh, a lump forms in my throat, and I swear I hear footsteps plodding down the hall.

I spiral out of control, my stomach clenches and I grip at the sheets as the bottom drops out of the mattress and I sink forever deeper and deeper. My breath turns shallow and labored. The ever-expanding hole fills with water, piercing cold as it penetrates the flannel fabric of my night gown and numbs my toes. Time swirls by and the longer I go, the brighter it gets as a new day breaches. Suddenly I am expelled onto sun-warmed grass and reality stares me in the face with her sharp, biting nature.

I reach out to touch a lingering raindrop on a tiny forget-me-not bud and look up at my husband's name, freshly carved into that grey stone. With quivering hands, I trace the letters, as yet again I must ingrain the truth into my mind.

"Breathe, this is real, and you have to keep breathing."

∼

Katie DiBenedetto is working on a fantasy novel trilogy with medieval heroic quest vibes. She lives in Ohio with her husband and their adorable kitty, Nimbus. Katie graduated from Ohio University with a degree in creative writing. Her hobbies include crafting, reading, and tea. You can find her on Instagram (tea_fueled_writer).

ISSUE 6: MODERN GOTHIC

LOVE LETTERS TO POE

POE

MARLYS | MOWER
TOWSE | HENNIG

Volume 1, Issue 6 | March 2021
Edited by Sara Crocoll Smith

DEATH LOVES FROGS

MALDA MARLYS

Death paged through a *National Geographic* between a vending machine and a potted palm.

Jessie had only seen Death twice before. She'd watched from her parents' porch as Death arrived at an elderly neighbor's door a minute before the paramedics. She'd been about five, so the memory was as much the smell of sidewalk chalk and sunscreen as it was billowing black robes. The second time was in college, part of a gawking crowd outside a fraternity house about to be shut down.

Death seemed embarrassed to be caught, if the soft cough from a fleshless throat and rustle of paper was anything to go by. She hesitated in the empty doorway, swallowed, and decided not to turn around.

Her feet knew every step. She'd walked this way every hour or two for days, just to have a destination. There were gardens around the hospital, a fountain in the foyer, a jarringly garish gift shop. She knew all those like the blur inside her eyelids, but they were for less fraught moments. Jessie could look at flowers while she waited on a scheduled procedure, not day three of the latest vigil.

Her debit card shook its way out of her hands. Not a caffeinated option this time, then. She pinched the bridge of her nose with a faint groan and looked down at her shoes, hoping it hadn't bounced far.

Jessie had time to glare at the empty expanse of beige carpet before the card reappeared between two bits of speckled gray bone. "Here," said a voice like her dead grandmother's, like distant summer thunder, like the sharp anxieties of student loans and romantic failure that kept you awake at night.

She tried to be casual while not touching the skeletal fingers even a little bit. "Thank you."

"Sorry. I should know better," Death said. Jessie fitted her best noncommittal noise with an upward inflection by way of polite answer. "No, I know I upset people. It's alright."

Jessie made a point to assume everyone else was also trying their best. "I'm sure it's been a long night for you, too."

She recalled recently reading a half-decent think piece about Death. It compared fictional depictions of Death's emotional expression over time (and a sprinkling of memes and uncredited tweets). Yet she'd never imagined that Death might laugh with ironic detachment, an exhausted huff that mocked mirth without meaning it any ill will. "Know when they built this hospital?" Death asked her.

Jessie finally remembered to buy her drink, listening intently to the tumble of the bottle on its way to freedom. "It's pretty old, right?"

"1943. Places like this, I'm always needed sooner or later. No point in leaving just to come back."

"Damn." She leaned against the soda machine, its faint vibrations sharp against her sleep deprived skull, and made her best approximation of conversational eye contact.

Difficult to do to a black shroud with void beneath, but her eyes weren't focusing great anyway.

"Tonight's been quiet, and, well, it *is* four in the morning," Death shrugged, shoulders more like a vulture's wings than was quite comfortable. "I thought I was in the clear for a break."

"Couldn't they give you an office or something?" Being existentially upsetting wasn't Death's fault. No one else had to restrict to the cold comfort of a plastic chair and an article about frogs to the deepest part of the witching hour.

"Hasn't been in fashion for a while," Death said with a majestic shake of their head.

The injustice of it struck Jessie with the weight only a distraction from ongoing misery can. She'd taken a few anthropology courses before she'd settled on her English major. Death's Chambers appeared across cultures in the Bronze Age, and the decline was usually attributed to different patterns in urbanization and other stuff she didn't remember from fifteen years ago. Surely a post-scarcity society could manage Death's Break Room? "This place is huge. They've got space for that ugly fountain in the foyer."

"I could sit *in* the ugly fountain. It wouldn't bother me."

"You totally should."

"Hard on the magazine, though."

"Yeah." She looked down at the unopened bottle in her hand and blinked a few times. "Is my mom—" She cut herself off. The silence thickened for a moment, cut only by the hum of the soda machine and her own heartbeat in her ears.

"I don't know any more than you do," Death said, their beautiful, terrible voice even.

"Yeah, that makes sense, sorry."

"It's alright."

Questions like spooked squirrels scrambled through the molasses of her thoughts. Mrs. Ramirez and the fraternity kid. The cold hand of capitalism and its exclusion of humanity's first ally. Picklesauce, the ancient cat she'd said goodbye to last fall as if she didn't have enough to mourn. Eons of living and dying. For all the history of grief, an empty doorway and a maple leaf.

What she said was, "Want a soda?"

"Yes, actually, thank you."

"It might be a little warm by now." Her sense of time was shot. She handed it over and didn't trouble herself to avoid the bones this time. They were painfully cold, but she didn't mind. It was something to feel. "Thanks for the company."

"Any time." That not-laugh again. "But you'd probably rather not."

"No, really, it's cool." Maybe it was the sleep deprivation talking, but– "I'll stop in tomorrow night if we're still here."

"I'd like that."

"Enjoy the frogs."

"Absolutely."

Did you know Death likes frogs? What do I do with this information, her modestly viral tweet might say. She didn't think they'd mind. Maybe after a little sleep. Jessie let her feet pick their accustomed way back to her mother's room, accompanied by only the sound of a turning page.

Malda Marlys teaches science just outside Chicago and writes the sort of speculative fiction that requires too many qualifiers for the normal flow of conversation. Fortunately, the SFFH umbrella is wide (and kind of spooky and full of brass fittings and snakes). Her debut story, "Mayday," appeared in Issue #3 of *Fusion Fragment*. Find Malda at www.aardwyrm.wixsite.com/maldamarlys.

ANNA

CODY MOWER

A voice woke Jonah from a shallow sleep. It crept through the grey haze as quiet as the footfalls of a cat. Rubbing his eyes, the shadow of his room came into focus. Right away he noticed the familiar silhouette of a woman at the end of his bed.

"Jonah?" she said.

"Yes, Anna?" he asked, sitting up. He knew it was her. It was always her.

"Can I ask you a question?" she whispered, facing away from him.

"Yeah, sure, what's up?" Jonah propped himself against the headboard. He noticed a thin ribbon of light slashing its way underneath the door, only to be swallowed up by the hungry dark inches into the room.

"Today, in chemistry, I saw you talking to that girl. You don't…like her, do you?" Her words echoed through the silence.

Jonah shook his head and sighed. She was always doing this. This is why he couldn't just have a normal, boring, high school existence.

"Did you wake me up for that? I told you this morning, no, I don't like her. She's just a friend."

"Okay," she said, not even bothering to look back at him.

"I promise." Jonah sank back down into his sheets and closed his eyes. Anna had been getting worse over the last few weeks. Following him. Sneaking up on him during the night like this. It was overwhelming, but he knew she wouldn't leave him alone. Even if he asked her too.

"Sorry, Jonah, I won't ask again. I don't want to fight," she said.

"Good."

"Jonah?"

"What?"

"Can I stay with you tonight?"

"Yeah," he whispered. It's not like he had a choice.

"You know, I—"

In an instant the sliver of light from under the door erupted, spilling into the room, filling it with an amber glow. Jonah barely had time to think before his mother walked in.

"Honey?" He could tell from the tone in her voice she was worried again.

"I'm fine, mom."

"I heard you talking to someone," she said, looking around the room before taking a seat on the end of his bed.

"Nope, just trying to memorize formulas for Mr.Beher's test next week. You know how much I suck at math."

His mother sighed; she always knew when he wasn't telling the whole truth, "Are you taking your medication, baby?" she said, rubbing his arm.

Jonah smiled and squeezed her hand. "Yeah, I've been

taking it, I promise. I think Dr. Avery said that insomnia could be a side-effect or something, which is why I'm up."

She gave a weak smile and touched his face with a soft hand. "Okay. Goodnight, sweetheart. I love you."

"Goodnight, I love you too," he said, closing his eyes.

Before shutting the door, she looked back at him one last time. "You know, if the prescription isn't working, we can always try something else, but you're going to have to be honest with us."

"Mom, I told you, it's working. I'm just tired."

"Okay, sweetie, I believe you." She nodded. "See you in the morning."

As the door shut, Jonah was once again in the dark of his room. His heart sank. He hated lying to his mom, but the medication hadn't been working anyway. If anything, it had only made things worse, especially between him and Anna.

"You're going to get me in trouble," he whispered into his pillow.

"I'm sorry, babe." Anna's fragile voice swept in from behind him. Her words crawled up his neck like static.

"It's fine."

"Can I ask you just one last thing," she said.

He could feel the cold shadows of her fingers played with his hair. He hated it when she kept him up like this, but it was always worse if he ignored her until the morning.

"What is it?" he grunted, closing his eyes.

"Do you want to go back to taking the medication?" Her voice was a thin razor of hurt, brushing its way along his body.

"No, Anna. I don't."

"Okay," she whispered. "I don't want to lose you."

"You won't." The warmth of his blankets weighed him

down as he broke effortlessly back through the veil of sleep.

As his mind carried him far away, he heard Anna one last time. "I love you, Jonah. You're the best thing that has ever been mine."

≈

Cody Mower is a writer based in the woods of Maine. After medically retiring from the Marine Corps in 2016 with a Post-Traumatic Brain Injury, he came home to sort his shattered life out. In 2019, Cody graduated cum laude from the University of Southern Maine with his B.A. in English with a minor in Writing. He was accepted into the Stonecoast MFA Program the same year as a Creative Non-Fiction writer. He writes and works passionately about post-military life and recovery to raise awareness on veteran's issues.

His piece "Ghosts" won an Honorable Mention in the premier veteran anthology *Proud to Be Vol.9*.

Other non-fiction work has published in *Moxy Magazine*, *Entropy Magazine*, Up Portland, and a small travel blog called *Eventually Everything* about life on a traveling bookmobile.

His fiction work has appeared in *Love Letters to Poe* and *Ghost Orchid Press's The Crypt and Home Anthology*.

Upcoming work to appear in *The Dread Machine*, and *The Society of Misfit Stories*.

Currently, he works with the Maine Humanities Council as a Humanities Coordinator/Facilitator for Veteran's Book and Writing Group.

THE TASTE OF BOURBON

MARK TOWSE

There are fewer things I can imagine would be crueller in life than launching yourself from a structure with the intent of death but only succeeding in a debilitating injury. As if one wasn't broken enough already.

You're eighty floors high, Frank. Stop the crap.

As I stand perched on the edge of the building, I can only just make out the streets below through the eerie coverage of morning mist. Blood pounds in my ears, and I feel nothing from the waist up. I've got to jump before I chicken out.

I close my eyes. This is it.

The wind wraps around me, and suddenly I'm falling, stomach tumbling and braced for an impact I can't imagine I'll feel.

"Gets windy up here."

Startled, I snap my head towards the voice. A burly man dressed in a fine three-piece suit boasts a smile that is almost disguised by his thick turned-down moustache. In contrast, there's not a hair on his head. I can imagine this man ushering lions into a cage.

"Name's John. It's a pleasure to meet you," he offers.

My stomach still lurches as I take a small step back on wobbly legs. There's a passing thought that this man has been sent to talk me down, but the suit implies he's dressed for a different type of negotiation.

"I didn't mean to alarm you, my friend. I've been there, though, standing on that same edge. I know what you are going through."

"What are you doing up here?" I ask.

"Again, apologies for catching you at a bad time," he replies with a wink. "I often come here—to think, clear my head. I've seen you here before, too."

"I don't mean to be rude, but will you please fuck off." I'm taken aback by my abruptness.

"Divorce? Ex-wife and kids want nothing to do with you? Retrenched? Money problems?"

"I didn't come here to make friends," I assert.

"Me neither. But we're here now. What's your name?"

I think about lying, but there seems little point. "Frank."

"You drink, Frank?"

"Yeah, but not before 8 a.m."

He laughs. "I wasn't inviting you. Double malt Scottish whisky—ah, I can taste it now. I went there once, The Highlands—beautiful, so full of history and culture, not like this Godforsaken place."

This is insane, and I'm not going to be dissuaded. I edge across, so my shoes are once again poking over the edge.

The occasional honk of a car punctures the monotonous thrum of traffic below, and the faint sound of music adds to the haunting effect of the now-thinning mist. Tyres squeal on tarmac, and from somewhere not too far away, sirens ring out. These city notes will be a fitting soundtrack for my death.

"What was she like? Your wife, I mean—when you first met."

We danced and howled with laughter. By the end of the night, her mascara left a stream of black that ran down to her chin. She was stunning, still is. We were so bloody free back then, ready for anything. We made a deal that we would always be open and honest, cleaning wounds before allowing them to heal. How did we let ourselves get so shackled, buried alive in the concrete jungle? I was going to be a writer. Amy had dreams of opening her own interior design business.

"How many kids? One? Two? Three?"

We had a boy and a girl together. Tom and Jenna. They're adults now, of course. Both hate me. We were such a close family, sticklers for traditions—game night, movie night, even the bake-off and God-awful talent nights that Jenna used to organise. Christ. I'm thinking about the house now, the one we swore we'd never leave. Full of happiness and warmth in the earlier years, but a battleground of disappointment and resentment as our dreams were eroded by the inevitable wave of conformity. Sadness washes over me as I grieve for those lost days.

Fuck! Come on, Frank. Get a grip.

"What are your favourite smells?"

Forests. The smell of pine, petrichor, and adventure. We used to go with the kids—had a favourite spot off the trail where we often would hide, spying on people as they walked by, making loud farting noises that Tom thought was hysterical. The smells of Sunday afternoon baking, too, that filled every room of the house with wholesomeness. You could smell it for days afterwards. Tears form, but I refuse to let them roll.

Come on, Frank!

"Three," I say out loud.

"Favourite food?"

Steak with mushroom sauce. "Two."

"Can you remember the first time you made love?"

Vanessa Adams. Her parents were out of town for the weekend. "One."

"What will you miss most, Frank?" he asks.

I can't do it. I don't want to die.

As I take a step back and double over, a million thoughts and memories invade my head. Filling me with hope this time rather than emptiness, I sit down on the ground and contemplate the future.

"I mean aside from your estranged family. Will it be the smells? The feel of the wind? The taste of bourbon?"

I'll make changes. I'll make it work.

The last wisps of mist float across, but I can no longer feel the breeze that escorts them. There's a small crowd of ant-sized people gathering around red flashing lights.

I turn back to the circus master, and he offers the same smile as before.

"It's a strange feeling for sure," he says nonchalantly. "A kind of disconnect."

"Did I—jump?"

"It wasn't much of a jump. Two out of ten from me."

"No, that can't be! Please, I—"

"Tad late for regrets, my new friend."

I feel dizzy, light-headed. "So, I'm—"

"Part of the gang now, Frank."

I turn my attention back to the streets below where life carries on, and its music still plays. There's an overwhelming urge to hug my children.

"There are six of us sorry souls, and you'll meet them

all soon. We spend a lot of time here with our thoughts, chewing the fat, talking through old memories."

～

Mark Towse is an Englishman living in Australia. He would sell his soul to the devil or anyone buying if it meant he could write full-time. Alas, he left it very late to begin this journey, penning his first story since primary school at the ripe old age of 45. Since then, he's been published in the likes of *Flash Fiction Magazine*, *Cosmic Horror*, *Suspense Magazine*, *ParABnormal*, *Raconteur*, and his work has also appeared three times on *The No Sleep Podcast* and many other excellent productions. His first collection, *Face the Music*, has just been released by All Things That Matter Press and is available via Amazon, Dymocks, B&N, etc.

PIANO MAN

BY R. LEIGH HENNIG

Marin began to worry he'd done something wrong
the night he first brought a man home from the
bar. One hundred and sixteen miles from his quiet Cape
Cod along the coast of Maine, the bar wasn't one he'd ever
been to before. No one to recognize him, to pick him out
from a crowd. He couldn't remember the man's name, and
bound at the wrists and ankles, with tape over his mouth,
the man wasn't going to be giving it anytime soon, either.

He turned onto the unpaved road that curved along
the sound, his aging, rusted Lincoln bouncing on broken
shocks. A thud came from the trunk as the man within it
whacked against something hard. Marin rolled his
windows down and let the salty air flood the cabin. Waist-
high sea grass on other side of the road swayed with the
sighing of the ocean, the sound of the rolling waves against
the rocky shore a constant, soothing roar, like a television
forever tuned to static.

This far up the coast, there was no one. Marin shut the
engine off in the driveway, not bothering to pull into the

garage. He pulled an animal control stick from the back seat and popped the trunk, looping the metal hoop around the man's neck and hauling him onto the ground.

"Terry, right?"

The man grunted, blood flowing freely onto the gravel from a broken nose.

"Terry it is, then. In we go," Marin said, jerking on the long metal pole. Terry moaned as he was pulled to his feet. Marin shoved him in the direction of the front door and Terry stumbled forward, his feet struggling to catch up. Veins and cords of tendons stuck out from his purpling neck.

The setting and fixtures inside the house were archaic. Appliances rusted from the salt air and broken granite surfaces dominated throughout. Maple book-shelves and mahogany tables, polished to a sheen, reflected light from a steely ocean and slate-gray sky. A wall of floor-to-ceiling windows faced the expanse of the foaming ocean.

The piano—a Whurlitzer that Marin had dragged across the country since his mother's passing—stood upright in a far corner of the open living room. Above it was a hook, and here Marin secured the end of the pole, shoving Terry onto the piano's bench beneath.

"Drink?"

Terry said nothing. He slumped forward, but the wire of the pole constricted, and he started to choke.

"Oh, right," Marin said, ripping the tape off Terry's mouth. "I'll make it a double." He went to the kitchen, and there, pulled a pair of glasses from the cabinet and poured a dram of Bruichladdich for them each.

Marin set a glass on the piano before the younger man, who had begun to weep.

"Take a sip," Marin said, taking a knife from his

pocket. He cut the tape binding Terry's wrists tightly together behind his back. "You look like you could use it."

Terry pushed himself upright to relieve the tension from the restraint around his neck. "What do you want?" he choked.

"I should think that would be obvious." Marin nodded toward the sheet music spread out before him.

"I...I can't," Terry sobbed.

"What are you talking about? Sure you can. You said you played in a band, remember?"

"I know sets, okay? Pieces I've practiced. I can read a staff. I can't just sit down and...and...play like *this!*"

"You sounded pretty convincing at the bar." Marin gestured toward the piano before reaching forward to position Terry's limp and shaking hands atop the keys. "Clair de Lune. Debussy. Do you know it?"

Terry, his face swollen, bloody, streaked with tears, nodded.

"Not exactly an easy piece, I admit, but I have faith in you. Now play."

"Are you going to kill me?" Terry asked, his voice a throaty whisper.

Marin placed his hand on the piano and tilted his head, eyes closed, as if taking from it silent instruction.

From the piano came low, bassy chords, loud, as if a fist had been struck against the keys. Marin snapped from his thoughts and looked at Terry.

"Don't do that," he said.

Terry looked up, eyes wide, palms out in defense. "I didn't touch it."

Marin slapped him across the face. "Don't lie to me, Terry. This was my mother's. Show some respect."

Terry stammered. Spittle flew from his lips, his words an incomprehensible babble.

Marin squeezed his eyes shut, pinching the bridge of his nose while Terry rattled on. He sobbed about his brother, his sister, his parents. It was all noise to Marin, a string of nonsense that only furthered him from hearing his mother's piano once again. He rubbed his temples before resting his glass of whiskey on the edge of the piano.

"Stop," he said, raising his palm against the panicked flood of noise that flowed from the other man. Terry ignored him.

Marin suddenly stood and withdrew the pocket knife, flicking the blade open with one hand and taking a fist full of Terry's dirty-blonde hair with the other. Marin jerked Terry's head back against the restraint of the pole and slipped the blade of the knife against Terry's cheek, who promptly fainted, falling limp against his restraint.

Marin sighed, unclipped the end of the pole from the ceiling hook, and eased his prisoner to the floor. He went to the kitchen for another drink, and it was there that he again heard the clang of notes from the piano. He stopped, jerking his head from the cabinet to peer into the living room. Terry was still unconscious.

"Hello?" he asked, carefully approaching the piano. "Mother?"

A single note, soft and long, emanated from the piano.

Wide eyed, Marin approached the piano bench and sat. She'd never spoken to him like this before—directly, the piano an extension of her voice. Always her instruction had been a thing *felt*, intuited, like the way the wind smelled before a storm even when the sky was still clear. It was why no one believed him when he insisted she lived on. Her voice was a silent one, speaking only to him, but it was there, nonetheless. Had he done something wrong, then? Was this not what she wanted?

"You said to…to bring you…"

He placed his hands above the keys, unsure of what to do next. He could play, if she allowed it, if he'd done as she demanded. But it had been a long time since then, as if disgusted by who he was, what he'd failed to become. The dropout from Juliard. The failure who should've been an extension of his mother's legacy, her brilliance nearly a household name in the world of concert pianists. When he decided he would play for himself instead of the world, that was when she'd cut him off. All that mattered to Marin was the music, and that had always been the problem. He recalled the last time they'd spoken, some days before her death.

If only you were a disappointment, Marin. I could live with that. Then what am I?

A mockery.

He wanted to believe it was the dementia behind the wheel of her hatred, but her eyes had been more clear and alert than they'd been in months. He'd been unable to play since, desperate though he was to try. If the piano was to be played, it would be through the hands of others, Marin only allowed to watch, not to touch, as it had been when he was a boy.

But now a note song forth, then another. His hands remained fixed, his fingers hovering over the keys.

Terry stirred, groaned. Shivered. A fifth note came from the piano. Marin understood. Terry had been a mistake, then. Not what his mother wanted.

"I'm sorry," Marin said, taking up the pocket knife he had left on the piano. He reached across the bench and to the floor, thrusting the knife into Terry's throat and slashing savagely. Warm blood doused his hands and spread outward while Terry spasmed, gurgled, and fell silent. Carefully, his nerves wired and tense, Marin resumed his position at the keyboard, waiting for what would come next.

Silence.

He pressed a key tentatively. When there was no rebuke, no discordant slamming of furious notes in rejection of his touch, he pressed another. But that's all it was — individual notes — and he wondered what it would take for something more to come forth.

Tears fell against the keys, though he didn't know why. He tried to wipe his eyes with the back of his hands, but he couldn't. They were covered in blood.

"Please," he whimpered, urging her to let him do more, to once again make the piano sing. "Please. I just want to play."

R. Leigh Hennig is a writer, editor, and horror enthusiast living with his beautiful wife and three awesome kids north of Portland, Maine. Previously he taught a series of classes on horror in literature with the King County Library System in Seattle, has written numerous essays on disability in speculative fiction (along with the usual slew of science fiction, fantasy, and horror short stories), was the editor-in-chief of *Bastion Science Fiction Magazine*, a volunteer compiler for the Horror Writer's Association, and a panelist at StokerCon in Grand Rapids, MI. For a time he pursued his MFA in Creative Writing & Poetics from the University of Washington Bothell.

His fiction is upcoming (in hardcover print!) in *Flame Tree Press'* Strange Lands anthology and *Crystal Lake Publishing*'s Shallow Waters anthology. His nonfiction has appeared at SFSignal.

He fits these things around his day job in Boston, where he is the principal network architect for the largest datacenter in New England.

Follow him on Twitter (BastionSF).

ISSUE 7: POE REIMAGINED

LOVE LETTERS TO POE

POND | GRASSMAN | WILDFIRE
ZWICKER | GAZAWAY | BAUGHFMAN

Volume 1, Issue 7 | April 2021
Edited by Sara Crocoll Smith

CORPORATE CULTURE

ROBIN POND

In an office dingy dreary, stand two workers battle
    weary,
In the grip of righteous anger, feeling a need to
    intervene.
    Pouring coffee into mugs with apologetic shrugs,
Grinding up their poisonous drugs, planning action
    most obscene.
Heartless, psychopathic, deadly, and clearly most of
    all obscene,
    Brewing murder yet unseen.

Raven Corp. is now de-hiring. Faced with almost
    certain firing,
Which they find quite inspiring, they are led to
    stage this scene.
    Taking action out of fear to save their pitiful
    career
Neither even sheds a tear for Jim, the man they
    now demean,

Knowing well his usual habits, his desire to imbibe
    caffeine,
  Brewing murder yet unseen.

"Our friend Jim is always working, while the threat
    of change is lurking,
Never for a moment shirking," smirks Stan, the
    man, who's tall and lean.
  "Always here by eight or nine, making sure the
    books are fine,
Carefully crafted bottom line, he knows what the
    numbers mean.
Upright, neat and clean, work and life are both
    pristine.
  Hardest worker ever seen.

"He attacks his every duty like it were a thing of
    beauty,
Keenly performing every duty, dealing with well-
    worn routine,
  And his life he is arranging while the world
    around keeps changing,
Oblivious to looks we're exchanging, corporate
    intrigue unforeseen."
Stan observes contemptuously and with
    considerable spleen,
  "Hardest worker ever seen.

"How the time relentlessly passes. Love's the opiate
    of the masses.
Never wondering if the glass is empty, full, or in-
    between.
  Always feeling the need to share even though we
    clearly don't care,

Every vacation, when and where, with his kid and
    his wife, Kathleen,
Boring us with numerous pictures of his kid and his
    wife, Kathleen,
  Even pictures of their cuisine.

"He may have the best intent, but it's hard not to
    resent
How the man remains so content with his castle
    and his queen.
  Lacking in imagination, crying out for
  exploitation,
Given all this provocation, we'll just have to
    intervene."
Carrie adds while scrubbing the counter, bringing it
    to a glistening sheen.
  "At the risk of seeming mean."

Ready now to hatch their plot with the poison they
    have brought,
They have polished off the pot, thoroughly rinsing
    'til it's clean.
  Sour-faced Carrie snorts and sits, having ground
  the cherry pits,
Eager to see them give Jim fits and seeming just a
    bit too keen.
"We can certainly always count on Jim's
    predictable routine.
  He will come for his caffeine."

Stan then takes another sip as the brew begins to
    drip.
Smiling Carrie licks her lip while looking terribly
    serene.

"When it's either him or you, it is clear what you
    must do.
Murder might be quite taboo, but this is neither
    evil nor mean."
Stan says, waiting for Jim's arrival, "Regular as he's
    always been,
    He will come for his caffeine."

Carrie sighs and drains her drink, putting her mug
    down in the sink,
Trying hard to not overthink, her attitude quite
    sanguine.
    "Though the task at hand might chafe, it's the
    way to keep us safe.
Knowing we will only be safe when no choice exists
    between
Both of us and our friend Jim, when he's no longer
    to be seen,
    Gone and never to be seen."

They're not able to say more. Jim's now standing at
    the door,
Standing just inside the door of the Raven Corp.
    canteen.
    "Come right in, our good friend," says Carrie,
    sensing the planned-for end,
Unseen attack he can't defend. "We acknowledge
    you've always been
Hardest working member of our team, motivated
    and madly keen,
    Best damn worker ever seen."

Stan says, "We've just brewed a pot. Drink it
    quickly while it's hot."

But replies Jim, "I think not. I was here earlier, at
   two-fifteen.
   I arrived a bit before, knowing what you had in
   store
Having hacked your monitor. I slipped in here
   without being seen.
What you're drinking I brewed then, a mixture of
   coffee with ground codeine,
   Fifty tablets of codeine.

"From the emails I've been scanning it's been clear
   what you've been planning,
With the flames of doubt you're fanning, fanning
   and pouring on gasoline.
   Frankly you both make me sick with your actions
   politic,
Your self-serving rhetoric, I know what you really
   mean.
Dog eats dog here on this team since Raven Corp.
   must now be lean.
   Corporate intrigue unforeseen."

Carrie proclaims with a struggling gasp, her voice
   reduced to a scratchy rasp,
"I'm not sure I fully grasp what it is you actually
   mean."
   Then though she vomits in the sink, remnants of
   coffee she's had to drink,
Too confused to even think, muttering words and
   retching between,
Retching as if to expel her stomach, intestine and
   spleen,
   Feeling like she's turning green.

Jim replies, "I'm deep in debt, burdened by things
we had to get:
House, two cars, the internet, my line of credit's
obscene."
Trying not to appear too smug as he watches the
effects of the drug,
Adding with an apologetic shrug, "I discussed it
with Kathleen,
Beautiful wife, soulmate and queen, my lovely
lifetime partner Kathleen,
Love of my life and truly my queen.

"Since we have a gorgeous daughter, while the
years flowed on like water,
We've been doting on our daughter, me and my
lovely wife, Kathleen.
Checking debts and cash flow nightly, still I've
borne my burdens lightly,
Greeting each new day quite brightly, showing up
to work so keen,
Slavishly toiling, buried in debt, with mortgages
and multiple liens,
Hardest worker ever seen."

Stan attempts to clear his head, fighting back the
nausea and dread,
Fearing he will soon be dead yet angrier than he's
ever been.
Breathing so laboured he can't talk and so
confused he can barely walk,
He remains in total shock, feeling Jim's actions are
overly mean,
Hoping there might be someone somewhere,
someone who could intervene,

Some new savior yet unseen.

Stan refrains from taking more sips as the new
    coffee rhythmically drips,
Staring at Carrie's bluish lips, sensing the blade of
    the guillotine.
  Feeling overwhelming fatigue, he regards his
    murderous colleague,
Fully admiring this new intrigue he had not at all
    foreseen,
Wondering if an after-life might actually be more
    serene,
  Hoping for a savior yet unseen.

But there comes no passerby, no witness to watch
    these workers die,
Feeling the symptoms intensify they succumb,
    overdosed on codeine.
  Stan and Carrie slowly fall, collapsing by the
    lunchroom wall,
Far too weak to even crawl, no savior coming to
    intervene.
Wondering what they could've done, wondering
    what they might have been,
  Saddest workers ever seen.

"I am absolutely sure with you both gone my job's
    secure.
See my motives are actually pure; it's nothing
    personal or mean."
  Solemnly Jim watches them die without the hint
    of a tear in his eye
Saying as one not given to lie, "At least you've made
    the room quite clean.

Hoping to conceal nefarious misdeeds you've
　　completely scoured the canteen,
　Rendering the room totally pristine.

"I remember there was a time when we'd consider
　　murder a crime,
When the biggest struggle was overtime and
　　employment was much more routine.
　Now our values have really changed, morality's
　　been rearranged,
One-time friends are now estranged, and survival's
　　begun to contravene
Human decency," says Jim, "and now that work's a
　　different scene
　Keeping a job's become a tontine."

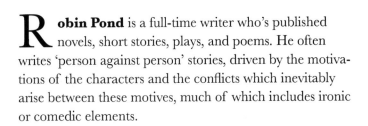

R　**obin Pond** is a full-time writer who's published
　　novels, short stories, plays, and poems. He often
writes 'person against person' stories, driven by the motiva-
tions of the characters and the conflicts which inevitably
arise between these motives, much of which includes ironic
or comedic elements.

A LINE OF CROWS

TC GRASSMAN

"Crows are the harbingers of doom," my grandmother would say. "Especially if one gets into the house." When the birds gather upon the line, their condemnation becomes clear. Woe to any who comes close to the marked one. Black eyes, feathers too, no color assigned but judgement. A murder of crows brings death.

And she was right.

When I was ten, the parlor window lay open to admit the cool breeze of late spring. A bird flew into the room, silent upon the almond-scented air from the purple heliotrope outside, and landed on top of the bust of some long dead poet laureate. The crow, that majestic bird so regal dressed in black, looked around the room as if holding court.

Not a sound did he make.

Until.

Grandmother came looking for me. As she bustled into the room, her taffeta skirts rustling, cawing in her high-pitched voice, cross at me for not being able to find me—I was there, in plain sight, just under the pie table—the bird responded in kind. Feathers ruffled, wings fluttered, the cry of agitation pierced through any semblance of misunderstanding.

My grandmother shrieked and grabbed the fire poker from the hearth. Brandishing it like a sword, she swung at the crow. He, that impressive beast, jumped into the air and took flight, cawing his way around the room. Grandmother screamed, ducked her head, and swung the poker wildly.

I found it most amusing.

The bird finally gave up his torment of her and flew out the window with a final *ca-caw!* My mother, as usual, came too late upon the scene to do much good. Grandmother laid the poker down and flung herself upon the pink cushioned chair, gasping for breath while my mother fixed her gaze upon me. Mother strode to the table and fair yanked me out from underneath it. Her grip tight upon my arm, I felt her nails digging in and the slight rattle of my brain as she shook me.

I hated her for that—amongst other things.

And wished her dead.

Two days later, I saw my wish come true.

It was a small funeral, to be sure. Only family and one or two friends—of my father's—not hers, as not many cared for her sneaky, venomous ways. I shed not one tear for she never acted the mother of my needs, only that of show for the neighbors and my father, who was the only one who wept.

Grandmother knew though.

That was a problem.

I liked her.

No fool, her, my grandmother. She kept a close eye on

me after that and I knew enough then not to bring attention to my activities. We got along fairly well for a few
more years, her and I, but as you've probably heard, these
things tend to come in threes.

When I was two and twenty, I wished to marry. The
man I chose was "Most unsuitable!" Grandmother said,
and since my father listened only to her, I was denied my
wish. My love wed another. On their wedding day, as I
walked through the graveyard to the church to give them
my well wishes on the happy occasion, I happened upon
the crows. All lined up on the headstone of one of the
defunct whose epitaph one could no longer read.

Three big, black beasts with eyes that stared right into
your soul. The clouds passed by, hiding the weak autumn
sun, and a mist appeared to rise out of the ground. No
sound did the birds make, nor I, transfixed as I was by their
gaze. The judgement was clear, and, I knew what had to be
done.

Funny how a little sugar goes a long way in making
peace, and, in covering the slight burnt almond taste in
cakes or biscuits for that matter. It helps if you have a good
hand in the art of bakery goods, knowing what flavor
palates to appease.

I do.

And it wasn't long before the bride was a bride no
longer.

We fair drowned in tears at the funeral. In fact, I found
it rather vulgar. But I was there, consoling my love, under
the ever-watchful eye of my grandmother. I didn't care. I
turned my chin up at her but quickly lowered my head,
daubing at my cheeks before turning my tear-welled eyes
upon him, whom I admired. He, that gentle soul, saw my
quivering lip, and shared his grief with me.

We wed in secret—after the appropriate waiting time. To the day.

Does the appropriate waiting time really matter, if it's in secret?

Grandmother weaseled her way into my childhood home, where upon my husband and I had no choice but to set up our own household. Would she never give up? Was I doomed to hear the rustle of taffeta, the reeking smell of liniment she used to oil her old joints, see that weathered face and beady eyes look at me knowingly?

I could no longer stand the sight of her or her high-pitched chattering. I had to do away with Grandmother, but she would not go quietly into that long sleep.

I plotted.

I planned.

Just as I'd done before.

I poisoned her tea. Well, her sugar, really. The sugar bowl only she used—it being an heirloom from her grand-mother's mother passed down to her. The little bowl, made of white porcelain, had dainty yellow flowers painted 'round the rim. Its lid, with a slot cut for the small spoon, also boasted the carnations. Tiny things, almost impercep-tible due to the dulling with age. They echoed how I felt—distain, rejection, and an almost imperceptible disappoint-ment that Grandmother wasn't as all-knowing as I'd once thought. Into this bowl went the granular sugar—now mingled with arsenic.

No one else used the bowl but her, that beady-eyed-black-clad-taffeta-wearing old crone. Within no time at all, she was dead. Oh, what a beautiful morning it had been too! All sunny, with a crow sitting on a branch of the heliotrope directly outside the open parlor window, his eyes so knowing as he looked upon the scene. Grandmother and I sat opposite one another. Our tea lay across the polished mahogany table.

With all grace and flourish, I poured—not one single drop did I spill! Although I was agog with nerves. My grandmother, that dame of all knowingness, sat there with her back straight as a poker—and as unyielding! However, I would not be daunted nor deterred from my task and I took comfort in the bird who observed my ministrations with his imposing countenance. Not one *ca-caw* sounded from him—only silent approval did I notice.

The tea poured, the doctored sugar spooned into her cup by her own hand, now dissolving nicely while we chatted. Briefly, I held my breath as she drank the ill brew. Would she notice a difference in taste, I wondered? Would she smell the almond upon the air and think it only that from the flowers of the heliotrope outside? Would this be the final dose—I'd been administering the poison for a week now and decided to up the amount of arsenic.

It had been different with my beloved's first betrothed. I'd made her favorite baked good, the almond cakes only she liked. The arsenic and sugar mixed in the batter and baked to perfect little treats she alone would eat. I'd wanted to be sure, so the concentration of poison had been high. So high in fact, it only took two to do the job. Since I couldn't have her round to our house, I'd gathered the treats in a diminutive basket lined with a tea towel and tied a ribbon around the handle. Humming, I'd walked the lane to my rival's house. Once arrived, I'd taken a breath before knocking and managed to keep a happy countenance when she exclaimed her surprise at seeing me and then adamantly invited me in for tea for two.

But that was then.

And now, the thing I wanted most happened.

Quite quietly too.

A widening of her eyes. A startled look at my face, then at the cup of tea in her hands. A quick *sniff* as she brought the cup up, then down to the saucer with a *clink!* A glance at the sugar bowl—a jerk of her hand, a spasm in her posture, a *gasp!* out of her lips—the final breath escaping her body as her head slumped forward, her body gone slack, her bowels let loose. Her corset, the only thing keeping her otherwise limp body upright in the chair.

Oh, how I savored the look of wide-eyed horror upon that leathery face! I sat, enjoying the rest of my tea, inhaling the scent of almonds as the breeze gently lifted the hair off the nape of my neck. I heard a rustling outside and turned to look.

A murder of crows sat upon the sill. Glaring at me with their black eyes—silent as death. They looked at me, one by one. I could hear their converse of condemnation. They sat there, resplendent as ever. Their judgement final. I was doomed.

Terrified, I slipped under the pie table as if I were ten years old again, trying to hide from them. But no use, as one by one the birds descended into the room. Black wings light upon the air. They settled silently. Not one sound nor ruffle of feather once they found a perch. Their beady black eyes narrowed at me, all of them! They surrounded me!

Judging.

Condemning.

Convicting. Until the authorities came to take me. That's when I and the birds flew away.

~

TC **Grassman** writes stories regardless of genre and isn't afraid to explore writing something they've never tried before. If, like TC, you're a fan of the best nation in the word—the imagination, check out their website and blog at TCGrassman.com or engage through social media via Facebook (TCGrassmanwordnerd) and Twitter (grassmantc).

THE HEART TELLS THE TALE

J.E.M. WILDFIRE

F ools! I see you hanging on every one of my nephew's self-serving words. You think he is a raving lunatic? No! He is unnerved by your presence but is as sane as you and I. His "disease" gives him hearing sharp enough to hear everything in heaven and hell. Judging by the way you converse with him, listen to him, dote on him, you accept his ego-centric viewpoint. Forget him. This is my story, not his. I'm the one. Who. Is. Dead. Let me tell you what really happened.

~🖤~

I hadn't seen him for over fifteen years when he arrived on my doorstep a few months ago, jobless, homeless, and destitute. He had worn out his welcome everywhere else after his father, my own brother, threw him out a year or so ago. For what? Who knows. Outraged that some had the nerve to call him insane to his face, he claimed everyone — his parents, roommates, landlords, and rooming house managers — all refused to accept his "illness."

Naturally, I assumed he embellished his account, as he had been histrionic from a young age. Tsch! My nephew was such an unlovable, annoying child. Nevertheless, with his tattered clothes, dirty fingernails, and noxious aroma, I saw he wasn't exaggerating his assertion he had been living rough. I took pity on him and welcomed him into my home. What did I know?

All I asked was that he assist me by keeping house. For longer than I cared to admit, I had been unable to do for myself, what with my blind eye and creaking bones. Agreeable at first, he undertook any task I set for him. Always bidding me to sit, have tea, while he bustled about, cooking, cleaning, washing clothes. He was assiduous with all his chores, refusing to pause to have tea and a chat with me. I began to think the insufferable child had grown into a tolerable young man.

You believe when he says he loved me? Hah! My dear nephew wasn't loving or particularly grateful for any generosity bestowed on him as a child and was even less so as an adult. No surprise, then, that he did not return my affection and gratitude for his thoughtfulness. Why, he never even thanked me for taking him in. What's worse is, he began to act odd, plying me with tea and a comfy chair one minute, shying away the next. The strangeness came on so gradually, I couldn't tell you when or how it began. It was little things. Almost unnoticeable.

For example, if I dozed in my easy chair after a meal, I would awaken to find him sitting directly across from me, staring at me. He always averted his eyes so quickly, I thought I had imagined it. But once, I awoke and remained motionless, controlling my breathing, so he would think I still slept. I peeked at him through the lashes of my good eye and watched him watching me. After a couple minutes, I yawned and stretched, so he wouldn't know I had watched him. He wasn't staring at me when I finally opened my eyes, but he never made eye contact with me again. In fact, he avoided me.

My nephew no longer took his meals with me and stopped preparing my dinner at noon. Instead, he brought tea early, sometimes as early as two thirty in the afternoon. And, when he would bring the tea and sandwiches, he flinched if my hand brushed his. He wouldn't set the pot and plate right in front of me, as you do. He put them scant centimeters away, making me reach. Every day, he set them a tiny bit closer to the middle of the table. I didn't notice at first. Who would?

I finally realized the lengths to which he had gone to evade my accidental touch when I had to raise myself out of the chair to reach my food. Grabbing his hand before he could retract it, I demanded that he put my food on my place mat. He said that's what he had been doing and insisted I had pushed it away. Told me I was crazy for thinking otherwise. Maybe so, I thought. I had to admit to him that, after I lost sight in the one eye, I wasn't able to judge distances very well. I even apologized for thinking poorly of him! The wretch.

After we had that little discussion, he seemed to return to his old self — calm, helpful, solicitous. My nephew resumed the routine started when he first came to live with me and introduced a surprising new habit: He awakened me each morning at dawn. Knowing I was fearful of burglars, he asked every day if I had slept well. The boy was a new man. I thought we had put the strangeness behind us. Until last night.

A noise jerked me awake. I thought the burglars had come through the shutters I had drawn tight before I slept. But, once awake, I heard nothing. I saw nothing. The closed shutters still blocked the entry of even a ray of light.

Trying to reassure myself that I must be alone if moonlight could not reach me, I sat in bed, swaddled in blankets, too afraid to investigate. Imagining what could have produced the racket that awakened me, if no person came through the window. Wondering if it might have been the house settling or a mouse or some other creature living in the walls. Maybe the wind. Terrified the inhuman sound would come again. I heard only silence, but I could feel the Presence of ... Something. Petrified, I waited in the dark, hugging my knees, rocking, listening, barely breathing, for what seemed like hours. Too frightened to lie down, to lay my head back on my pillow, to sleep.

A sliver of light from the doorway cut the dark. Where was it coming from? How was it there? I had left no light in the hall. There was no sound, only the unwavering light shining in my face. I was paralyzed with fear. Heart beating so hard, I thought it would break through my chest. The room so quiet I could hear every beat of my heart, louder and louder. I was panic-stricken that the Presence would hear it too and attack. Held my breath, hoping to quell the loud heartbeat. The light on my face never moved. Time never moved.

The door flew open.

Someone yelled, pulled me off the bed, and yanked the mattress onto me. Crushing. Squeezing the air from my lungs. I couldn't breathe. Darkness closed in. Silence.

I floated above. Watching him, watching me. He put his hand on my heart. After both hand and heart were motionless for several minutes, he left, returning with a cleaver and washtub. My nephew hefted my body into the basin. I could not look away as he severed my limbs from my torso. Witnessed as he cut off my head. He chuckled as he defiled the body of his uncle, my body, my corpse.

While my blood drained into the tub, he tore up three

floorboards, waiting to put my parts in until the blood flowed no more. He laughed full-throated after he finished, then dragged the tub away, closing the door softly behind him.

~ ❧ ~

Now you're here. Listening to him. Encouraging him. Mesmerized by his lies. You call yourselves police officers? Ignore him. Do your job. Investigate. Search. Find me. Find Me! Find. Me. Find. Me. Find. Me. Find. Me. Find. Me. Find. Me. Find. Me. Find. Me. Find. Me. Find. …

"'Villains!' he shrieks, 'dissemble no more! I admit the deed! — Tear up the planks! Here, Here! — It is the beating of his hideous heart!'"

∾

J**.E.M. Wildfire** writes speculative fiction and was inspired by a _StoryADay_ prompt to rewrite Edgar Allan Poe's "The Tell-tale Heart" from the old man's viewpoint after his murder.

THE BIRD WHISPERER

RICHARD ZWICKER

I first met Emmitt Griffin when we were cadets at West Point. I had a facility for elocution and my parents thought by enrolling in the academy, I could put it to patriotic use. I was not receptive to some of West Point's core creeds, however, and used my gift to talk myself out of punishments for dereliction. Emmitt's detachment made him even less suited to the campus. A gruff-voiced sergeant would demand to know why he remained immobile when everyone else was marching. After a few pregnant moments, a look of recognition floated to the surface of Emmitt's eyes. He'd say, "Oh, right," and hurry to catch up to the marching group.

He didn't fit in any better during the off-duty nights. While everyone else was drinking and chasing women, he stayed in his room and wrote desultory poetry about the fairer sex, to which, I'm not summarily opposed. However, they were generally of the deceased variety. I'm not an expert on verse, but the epic poetry I've read had people *doing* something before they climbed into their deathbeds. That's where Emmitt's poems usually *started*. As he had some ability as a lute player, he also tried his hand at writing songs. Most of them were thinly veiled critiques of the academy, such as "I Hate a Parade" and "We Are Our Own Best Targets." I asked him why he'd enrolled at West Point. He said his foster parents thought it would give him structure.

Alas, the only structure he gained was something to rebel against. After a year, Emmitt stopped reporting to classes and was dismissed from the academy, at which point I lost track of him. His absence put in clearer focus that I didn't belong there, either. It wasn't that I was unpatriotic, but I liked to talk things out, while my instructors wanted "people who would fall in line." Twelve months after Emmitt left, I resigned. My facility for conversation pushed me into the salesman trade. I drove a wagon full of coffee, sugar, clothes, medicine—whatever I thought I could make a profit from. This necessitated an inordinate amount of traveling, which over the years precluded me from settling down and starting a family. I had my mail forwarded to my sister's house and tried to stop there at least once a month. On the most recent of those stops, in the heat of July, I received this letter from Emmitt, our first communication in two decades.

Dearest Cornelius,

You probably don't remember me, though I now look on our misadventures at West Point as a highlight of my misbegotten life. I have done my best to make a living as a poet and writer of essays and reviews, but the wolf of poverty has never been far from my door. As a matter of fact, I would welcome a wolf at this point, because for the past month a raven has been perched on my statue of Pallas and stolen what little is left of my sanity. I am not long for this world and wish to thank you for our long-ago friendship before I shuffle off to the next world.

Yours in anguish,

Emmitt

Life was difficult, but I liked to think that after missteps and plans gone awry, everyone eventually found their way. That Emmitt was just as maladjusted today as two decades ago filled me with gloom. Up to now I'd used my gift of speech for superficial purposes, to avoid trouble and to convince people to buy things they may or may not have needed. Here was a chance for me to make a difference. I posted a letter to my suffering friend, telling him I would arrive for a visit seven days hence.

Emmitt lived above a tobacconist in a rundown building located in the center of a small western Massachusetts town. He had been born in Boston and never had a good thing to say about it, so I was surprised he'd returned to the state. I climbed the uneven stairway to the third floor and rapped three times. When he didn't answer, I knocked again, thinking he wasn't home. Finally, I yelled "Emmitt! It's Cornelius!"

I heard a slow procession of footsteps and the pulling back of a deadbolt. The open door revealed a man not greatly changed from his student days. If anything, Emmitt had lost a few pounds from his already thin frame. His hair was slightly longer and unruly, but Emmitt had always thought combs discouraged hair's individuality. The one difference was his eyes. If eyes were the windows to the soul, his were boarded up.

"Hi Cornelius," he said softly. "Sorry I took so long. I thought you were the wind and nothing more."

"I came as soon as I got your letter. You said something about a raven."

"Yes, it's still here. Come in."

He led me into his modest three-room apartment. His living room was lined with cheaply made bookcases, though some of them didn't have any books in them. A pink, rumpled couch had pride of place, clashing violently with the brown wallpaper. As the letter stated, a raven perched on a bust of Athena, which was set on top of one of the empty bookcases. I looked at it. In response, it turned its black head sideways and looked at me.

"Does it ever go out for food?" I asked.

"I've begun feeding it. The only thing worse than a raven stuck in your apartment all day is a starving raven."

"Have you tried to get rid of it?"

Emmitt emitted a full-bodied laugh, which unnerved me because I'd never heard him laugh before, except once when a cadet asked him what his favorite presentation-of-arms position was.

"Of course I've tried! What do you think this is? An aviary? It refuses to leave and all it says is 'Nevermore.'"

"It talks?"

"As I said, its vocabulary is limited, but go ahead. Strike up a conversation."

I was unsure of what to say to a raven, but I could talk to anyone. I questioned the reason for its unnatural behavior. Weren't some key needs being unmet? Why have wings and not use them? It remained mute, not even saying "Nevermore," but then, that response didn't fit any of my questions.

"Ask it when it's going to leave," said Emmitt.

I shrugged. "When are you going to leave?"

"Nevermore," it croaked.

"Why not?"

That got me nowhere.

"He's here because of Lenore," said Emmitt.

"Who's that?" I asked.

"A woman named by angels. She's dead." That seemed typical of the type of women Emmitt met.

"I assume you met her before she died."

"Of course," he said, with a trace of indignation.

"All right," I said. "We need to increase this bird's vocabulary, then we can better understand each other." I inched toward the raven. "People make assumptions based on vocabulary. Have you ever heard a foreigner with a poor grasp of English trying to talk in this country? He could have the brain of Michelangelo, but he'd still be ridiculed. So, let's try another word. How about 'exhilaration'?"

"No way," the bird croaked.

"That's progress. 'Empathy.'"

"Forget it."

"I'm still detecting a negative motif. How about 'altruistic'?"

"Not on your life."

I folded my arms. "Let's try a different tack. You've made your point. Staying here and beaking strategic 'nevermores' is overkill. And who does it hurt the most? You. Surely you have nests to build and worms to catch. There's a whole world out there that you're missing because of a misplaced obsession. Return to your avian brothers and sisters! Take these unused wings and relearn to fly!"

My exhortations were, like Athena, a bust. The raven stared at me in defiance. I met the stare and held it, feeling if I turned away, my friend would be lost. The ocular duel lasted minutes until finally, the raven squawked and flew out the window.

"Eureka!" I said, shutting the window, despite the heat from the summer sun. "You are free, Emmitt!"

Emmitt wore a frown like a full-body coat of paint. "I can still hear it."

In the ensuing days I tried to break my friend's mood by engaging in activities reminiscent of our younger days. I introduced him to women, encouraged him to keep a diary, and dragged him to nine-pin bowling, but it was too late. The raven had made its point and lodged it into Emmitt's soul. Flummoxed, I made a final offer: he could travel with me, meeting a variety of people and escaping his imposed prison. It was a chance for both of us.

I admit I was relieved when he declined, though it unnerved me that he did so by saying "Nevermore." As for Lenore, I learned nothing further, though I'm convinced she, as well as the raven, were secondary players in a life predisposed to isolation. Eventually, the last turning point lies too far behind us.

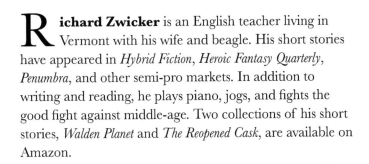

Richard Zwicker is an English teacher living in Vermont with his wife and beagle. His short stories have appeared in *Hybrid Fiction*, *Heroic Fantasy Quarterly*, *Penumbra*, and other semi-pro markets. In addition to writing and reading, he plays piano, jogs, and fights the good fight against middle-age. Two collections of his short stories, *Walden Planet* and *The Reopened Cask*, are available on Amazon.

TO HAVE AND TO HOLD

SHARMON GAZAWAY

A h, I remember you.

From behind the tattered merlot draperies I see you are as handsome, and kind, as I remember. But then, how could I forget? I, too, have an Usher malady. You do not remember me. No one still living does. My name is Marilla, sister to Roderick and Madeline Usher.

I imagine stepping into the room as you console Roderick, revealing myself to you. Would you gasp? Smile? But, no, I stay cloaked in curtains, staring through a moth hole. Like a ghost, among many, I haunt the House of Usher.

Madeline, Roderick's twin, drifts across the far end of the faded chamber, shadow-silent. Madeline will die soon. Roderick weeps as he tells you this. His only companion, they have never been parted. "Her malady is a mystery to physicians. A malaise, complicated by descents into catalepsy."

Awkward in the face of his outburst, you peruse the photographs on the table, lift one from the back and wipe away years of dust. It's a tintype of me. "And who is this golden-haired beauty?" you ask. You gaze steadfastly at my likeness.

Irritated, he says, "Oh, a relative, I was told. She is no longer with us." Dismissive of anything not concerning his ailments or moods.

Your spaniel eyes soften as you gaze at it, set it back on the table, but in front. My heart leaps. I cannot think of myself as a beauty, freckles scattered across pale cheeks, like dandelion seeds on snow. My pulse drums so loudly I fear Roderick will catch it with his preternatural hearing—his inherited torment. But he's plucking that infernal guitar, and you jest with him. I remain undetected.

I must, if I wish to stay in my ancestral home.

Thanks to our sire's philandering, I was injected with a hearty dose of peasant blood from my mother, a fetching milkmaid. Ma and I came after the wife and five-year-old twins. Father sent Ma away, and kept me, though not due to any paternal affliction. In the event his puling, legitimate offspring didn't survive to inherit, I was his recourse.

With a lingering glance at you, I recede into the hidden passageway between the walls. Intimate with each step, I love every damp stone in this decrepit pile of bones. The ghosts dissolve like sun on fog when I encounter them. They accept me as one of their own, sense that I too am restless, a phantom of who I could be.

That night I follow you and Roderick from afar, down, down to the dungeon vault, bearing Madeline's corpse in her coffin. You screw down its lid and slide her into a niche; it grates against cold stone. Roderick winces. The tarn's insidious waters penetrate from outside; a slow, seeping wound.

I long to trail after you, touch my bare feet where your steps have touched. But being this close to Roderick's acute hearing and his volatile temperament is dangerous. If exposed, I'll be turned out as an imposter, or worse.

I can never be parted from the House of Usher.

Shivering, I retreat to my chamber in the turret ruins, my home and prison. Before Father died, he put the grim valet Himmler in charge of me; so, you see why loneliness was my familiar playmate. I pored over the ancient tomes Himmler brought in towering stacks. I soon realized I had perfect photographic recall. All images—good, bad, or indifferent—were seared on my brain. My Usher malady.

Ravishing the tomes, I discovered the mansion's crumbling blueprint and its hidden, wartime passageways. Through them I escaped my prison and learned of my half-siblings, who, even as children were dull and selfish. I kept hidden.

Now Madeline lies in the deep dark, and I wonder if I will one day meet her in a hidden passage.

Except for the cryptic ghosts, I have been alone.

Until you came, my love.

Hunching into the down quilt, I count the hours till I dare see you again.

~⋅❧⋅~

A cold hand snuffs the still, autumn days, one by one. Unable to think with you so near, I toss aside a book on husbandry, and slink to your room. A mere wall between us, you pant softly as you pace. I remember when, still a youth, you arrived on an elegant bay to see Roderick. Broad-shouldered, you took the stairs two at a time and my breath caught, then as now. I used to watch for you, despaired when you no longer came. I dreamed I'd search for you, tell you all my heart, forsake Usher forever. But I couldn't. Could never.

I cup my hands against the wall as if to capture your breath, then press them, clenched, against my bosom and turn away.

The violent winds of a devil's-brew begin to shrill. Passing by Roderick's suite, familiar ghosts accost me, mouths gaping with silent screams, eyes black with warning. I hear Roderick groan and his hoarse words stop me cold.

"Madeline, how long will you torment me? I dare not let you out! Cease, I implore you!"

The blood dashes cold through my chest.

Dear God, is it possible Roderick entombed Madeline alive? Mistook a cataleptic coma for death?

We surely would have heard her screams, her struggle.

Her demise has unhinged him.

My heart flits like a panicked bird. No, we couldn't have heard—me, in my garret, and you, in your suite high above the vault. I envision her first scratchings, shredding the coffin's silk. Days of clawing, shrieking in claustrophobic terror.

We couldn't hear. But Roderick could.

Could hear each plank splinter, each fingernail ripping from flesh, her little white feet drumming till battered blue. Shrieks turning to sobs, sobs to begging, *please let me out.*

On slippery stone I race down to the vault.

The coffin's lid is askew. Her eyes are red-lit like some rabid, feral thing, her stench overpowering. And she is laughing.

I rip the splintered planks free and she scrabbles over the side like a crab from a pot. She flies past, emaciated, mangled hands dripping. Her white, blood-mottled gown billows behind her like an avenging spirit.

Had Roderick been *mistaken*?

I tear after her, knowing where she'll go; I fear she'll find you first. I care not if I'm exposed now.

I think only of you, love.

Ghosts reel 'round me, shrieking a dirge. The storm-pummeled house trembles beneath my feet and its bones begin to give.

Madeline reaches your suite a step before I do. You drop your book, affixed in horror.

Roderick stands, lips peeled back. With a guttural wail, Madeline leaps on Roderick, gnashing on him, teeth bared. She claws bloody stumps down his face—so like her own—and they crumple to the floor.

I swallow my scream, lest you think me one of their mad kind, and duck behind a suit of armor.

You bolt down the stairs, the storm invading the house when you plunge into the maelstrom.

Roderick's eyes stare, his face a rictus of fright—and guilt, perhaps. Madeline is truly gone this time. To a better place, I hope. This specter will never leave me.

The house shudders, cracks and groans, coming apart at the seams. Gusts whip my hair wildly about my face. Clinging to the banister, I slowly descend. The house is going. You are gone. I can choose the house and spend eternity here. Or I can follow you, my love, and hope.

~❦~

I find you beneath a blighted elm, your head gashed by a broken branch. I cradle your head in my lap and rain washes over us. It rouses you in time to see the vast, time-less hulk of Usher split asunder and tumble in on herself, in on the last of my kin.

And on Himmler, the last living person who knows of my illegitimacy.

"Who…who are you?"

"Shhh. Time for that later." I stroke a lock of hair from your spaniel eyes.

The tarn's greedy waters creep over the fallen stones of The House of Usher.

I wipe tear-mingled rain from my cheeks, smile down at you.

We will rebuild, my dear. With the same beloved stones, and the blueprint engraved on my brain, and heart. I am of hearty peasant stock, strong and determined. We'll drain the lurid tarn, and plant fruit trees there.

The halls will echo with the laughter of our children.

And the ghosts.

~

Sharmon Gazaway lives in the deep south of the U.S. and writes both speculative and literary work, published or forthcoming. A flash fiction is online at *Daily Science Fiction*, and a short story will be in the spring issue of *Breath and Shadow*. She sold a fantasy short to *Metaphorosis*, and has a science fiction short coming out in the fall in *New Myths*. A speculative piece was selected by Rhonda Parrish for the anthology *Dark Waters*, also released this fall. You can read her poetry in *Backchannels*, *micorverses.net: Octavos*, *The Society of Classical Poets*, *Welter*, *Tiny Spoon* and *Third Wednesday*.

THE FALL OF THE HOUSE OF POE

BY EVAN BAUGHFMAN

The front door, already ajar, invited Annabel inside.
She entered the ramshackle manor and, at first glance, saw only darkness. This encouraged her to keep the door open behind her.

The lantern in her grasp soon illuminated a rotted staircase and various decrepit furnishings bedecked in spiders' webs. To the right of the steps appeared a hallway draped in shadow.

Had she misread the address? Surely, no one of sound mind still lived here.

"Hello?" she called out, afraid of the answer she might receive. "I…I came as soon as I read your letter!"

Nothing.

Not a monster's growl. Not a phantom's voice.

Nor a friendly reply.

Merely the night's wind whistling around the building's brittle bones.

She turned back to the front door. She should flee.

Her friend would understand. Or perhaps he would not.

Either way, the setting for this engagement put her at great unease. Perhaps their relationship, like the house, was not worth the time to repair.

"Help me…"

The words whispered from darkness.

She recited a small prayer and then said, "Yes? Tell me where you are!"

"Help…"

The plea drew her toward the hallway's gloom.

The passage beyond was long and narrow. Many rooms joined together here.

Lantern's light was unable to reveal the hall's end.

"I am here," she offered.

The door to her left opened, creakily asking her to enter.

Before she could cross the threshold into the room, the lantern caught something gleaming.

A monstrous eye, wet with gore, held within the beak of a raven.

The bird stood atop a bloodstained floor, staring up at Annabel with its own beady gaze. Under the raven's feet, floorboards *thump-thump-thumped*, jostling the creature up and down, up and down, up and down, the sound marching nearly in sync with the rhythm of Annabel's own accelerating heartbeat.

The raven swallowed the eyeball whole.

"Dear Lord!" cried the young woman.

A hulking figure then stepped forward from behind the bird.

Annabel's trembling hand shined light upon an ape: an orangutan clutching a dripping straight razor in its massive palm. The animal had a rheumy glare and foaming lips.

Shrieking, Annabel pulled the door closed, more than ready now to leave the house of horror.

God save her friend if he was still in one piece!

Wait, what was this?

A wall…?

A wall!

"For the love of God!"

There was no wall here before! This is where she had come from!

How could a wall appear in a minute's time?

"Help me!" she cried. "Help!"

She pounded against the structure with a fist. Dust fell upon her head.

The entire house seemed to shake beneath each of her blows.

Beside her, the door she had closed opened again, revealing the orangutan's deadly grin.

Annabel ran from the terrible sight. The ape, triumphantly whooping, bounded after.

Under their footsteps, the building quaked.

Another door opened ahead.

Annabel stumbled into a second room, slamming shut the barrier between her and the murderous fiend.

In here, the lantern revealed more ghastly frights.

A man in a court jester costume was pinned to a broken bed. The poor soul was broken himself, his limbs crushed beneath piles of bricks.

A sea of red-eyed rats swarmed around and atop the mattress, feeding on the man as he screamed.

Only, the man's terror was not directed at the rodents.

His face was instead fixated on a giant pendulum's blade descending upon him from the ceiling at great speed.

Annabel screamed alongside the jester, not able to understand how any of this was possible.

The tide of ravenous rats drifted toward her.

She threw the lantern to the floor, creating a wall of flame between her and the vermin.

Still, determined beasts crawled through smoke and flame, eager to taste her flesh.

Annabel kicked away a few rodents, but one of the creatures climbed her dress, scurrying for her throat.

Flailing, she fell backward, through another wall, into an adjacent room.

She realized a hole had already been in place, formed after decades of neglect.

The rat was at her neck. Annabel grabbed the snapping thing and, standing, threw it back into the other room, into fire.

Growing flames lit up both rooms like a summer's day.

At Annabel's feet was an ax. She lifted it into her hands.

In the corner of the room was a black cat, yowling in fury.

The mangy feline had a single eye and clumps of spittle falling from its screeching maw.

Adding to the madness was the fact that the cat was perched atop a freshly severed head.

Annabel recoiled when she saw her own face affixed to the skull.

"Help me…" begged her impossible visage. "Help…"

Annabel raised a hand to ensure that her head was still attached. It was.

So, then, what was that impossibility on the floor? Why did it have her nose, her eyes, her lips?

The door to the room burst open, the orangutan crashing through with its blade.

A wave of vile rodents streamed through the hole in the wall.

The black cat leapt from Annabel's head.

The animals closed in.

Was there no escape from this horde?

No escape from this windowless room?

Unless…

Annabel turned to an unbroken wall and *hack-hack-hacked* with the steely ax.

The creatures attacked.

They bit. They clawed. They slashed.

Still, she swung the ax against the wall, praying for release.

The house groaned. It roared.

It collapsed.

The building fell all around her and onto the maniacal zoo.

As the manor opened up to the sky, an enormous wooden beam tumbled downward, striking the young woman across the torso, securing her to her fate.

Soon, the dust settled.

Annabel Lee died, peering up at an expanse of other-worldly stars.

~❦~

"Dr. Moran, is it over, sir?"

Moran looked to the other physician, a cherub-faced recruit less than one month out of medical school.

The men stood on either side of a bed at Washington College Hospital.

Between them was the body of Mr. Edgar Allan Poe.

The patient had been admitted days earlier in a state of delirium.

He eventually succumbed to a trance-like state, only occasionally speaking to persons and things unknown.

"You saw it just as I did," Moran said. "The light leaving this man's eyes as his mind fell apart."

The younger physician nodded. "The rabies finally ran a closing attack on his brain." He checked Poe's pulse. "Yes, sir, his heart has stopped, as well."

Moran studied the corpse.

"A mind like his," he said, "so full of wicked machinations, twisting in on itself in its final moments on Earth. To have witnessed the goings-on inside this man's head would have been a truly remarkable experience, indeed."

Evan Baughfman has found much of his writing success as a playwright, his original plays finding homes in theaters worldwide. A number of his scripts are published through Heuer Publishing, YouthPLAYS, Next Stage Press, and Drama Notebook.

He's also found success writing horror fiction, his work found most recently in anthologies by Black Hare Press, Blood Song Books, and Grinning Skull Press. Additionally, he's adapted a number of his short stories into screenplays, of which "The Tell-Tale Art," "A Perfect Circle," and "The Creaky Door" have won awards in various film festival competitions.

His first short story collection, *The Emaciated Man and Other Terrifying Tales from Poe Middle School*, is published through Thurston Howl Publications.

More information is available at www.amazon.com/author/evanbaughfman.

ISSUE 8: MIDWESTERN & SOUTHERN GOTHIC

LOVE LETTERS TO POE

BORMAN | BROCATO
NEWHOUSE | HANS

Volume 1, Issue 8 | May 2021
Edited by Sara Crocoll Smith

POISONED HONEY AND PICKLED PIGS' FEET

SHAWNA BORMAN

Her body's buried by the creek. But her tongue, that's sealed in a jar of pickled pigs' feet, encased in nearly a foot of cement, under the new barn out back. Just in case.

Mama never did like pigs' feet, pickled or otherwise. Said they was commoners' food. Still, every Monday, Daddy makes a fresh jar and, come Sunday, me and the boys feast on them like royalty. That's the kind of man Daddy is, someone who can make you feel like a princess even as you're slopping the pigs. Me and the boys never could figure out how he ended up with Mama. Every time we asked, he'd smile and say, "She has a voice like honey."

He was right. Her voice was sickly sweet as it oozed into every corner of the mind and slowly rotted it away. She spoke in words no one could *really* understand, luring people in with that thick, golden sweetness. Once they were trapped in her tones, inside the sweet nothings, her words became poison. It wasn't a quick death, either. She made her prey suffer, tearing their soul away piece by piece, eroding any chance of escape. And the world was none the wiser.

Daddy took the brunt of her sweet abuse, shielding me and the boys in his own quiet, laidback way. We were her blood, though, so she was deeper inside us than Daddy could ever know.

It was a bright spring day when it happened. Me and Mama was watching my youngest brother wade in the creek. His laughter could bring sunshine to anyone's day, but not Mama's. She only smiled in front of company, and then, only when they was praising her. They didn't see what we saw.

She pulled me close to whisper in my ear over the innocent laughter and burbling water. "You're going to be just like me when you get older. I can smell it on you."

"What're you talking about?" I asked, a butterfly stirring in the depths of my stomach.

"Any daughter of mine is definitely going to be a queen." The warmth of her breath against my skin made me want to run. "We're special, you and me. The boys are nothing more than drones, like your daddy."

"I think Daddy and the boys are good men."

She scoffed. "I got stuck with the first thing that came along. Don't make that mistake, baby. When you begin to flower, you'll attract many good men. I need you to wait for the great ones. Once you've got one of those, I'll teach you how to break him. You'll have everything you ever wanted and more."

I looked in Mama's eyes. They were as golden as her words and held a sinister glow. A shiver shot down my spine.

"I just want to be happy," I said, but I felt something wiggle in the back of my mind, as if to tell me I was a liar.

"You'll crave the misery of others, soon enough."

Mama smiled at me for the first time I could remember. It set a whole swarm of butterflies loose in my stomach. "You're almost ready to bloom."

A scream pierced the air. My littlest brother hobbled up to Mama, tears streaking down his cheeks almost as fast as the blood pouring from his knee. Mama stared at her crying child with a sneer.

"What do you expect me to do about it? Go find your daddy."

The expression on my brother's face before he toddled off would've been enough to break Lucifer's heart, but Mama just watched him go, disgusted.

"I don't want to be anything like you," I said. "Don't you see what your words do?"

"My words are my spell. They can build you up, then tear you down. Of course I know what they can do. You'll understand the power one day."

The butterflies surged up out of my throat along with a screech that turned the world red. I wasn't going to allow her to turn me into someone who could make a hurting child feel even worse. I wouldn't let her hurt anyone else, not anymore.

When I trudged into the house, covered in blood, and grabbed a knife, Daddy silently followed me to the mess I had made. He watched as I cut out her tongue, because that was the source of her power, then followed me back inside to the newest jar of pigs' feet, where I stuck it.

He buried her that night, then started the barn the next day. We haven't spoken of her in three months. Daddy and the boys are happier than I've ever seen them. Sometimes, her words echo in my ears, but they're getting weaker. Life goes on. And tonight, we'll feast on pickled pigs' feet.

∽

Shawna Borman holds an M.F.A. from the University of Southern Maine's Stonecoast program. Though she dabbles in all genres, her true love is horror. Whether dealing with your average socially awkward serial killer or an angel/demon/mortal hybrid entering the terrible teens, Shawna is most at ease visiting with the voices in her head. She resides in Texas with her father. For more information and links to her social media profiles, please visit www.snborman.com.

THE WALKING WIDOW

EMMA BROCATO

Rosemary peeled damp, stray curls off her face and sighed in frustration. She desperately waved her intricately carved fan in front of her face, trying to pretend the stagnant air wasn't full of mosquitoes dying to suck the blood from her exposed hands and face. It was another hot, sticky night in Galveston, and Rosemary was less than amused. She and her husband, Edward, had been living in Galveston for six months now. Having left all their family and friends behind, there wasn't much for her to do while Edward was gone all day. She was left alone to her thoughts – and, more recently, her nausea. The house was massive and gorgeous, but also lonely. Her only consolation was that the house came with a widow's walk, on which she was standing at this very moment.

The widow's walk allowed many things. It allowed her to escape the house and all the summer heat it trapped. It also allowed her to enjoy a view of the island from above. And, most importantly, it allowed her to see all the way to the ocean, so that she could tell whether or not Edward's ship was coming in. So far, it always had. But, of course, there was always the grim possibility the widow's walk would live up to its ominous namesake.

She paced back and forth, still feverishly swatting her fan through the thick air. Where was Edward's ship? This was later than usual. In fact, it was later than ever before. The last hints of pink dusk were fading, shaping an introduction for nightfall.

And that's when she saw it. Edward's ship arrived at the port, flooding Rosemary with relief – but only momentarily. Rosemary felt a twinge of concern upon realizing that no land crew appeared to greet the ship. As the minutes ticked by, no one — absolutely not a soul — approached the vessel. And no one got off the ship either. This ship was supposed to be full of sailors, but there were none in sight.

Rosemary glanced at her lantern, considering a venture to the port to investigate. That would be an awfully long walk to make all by herself. Unaccompanied women were not to be out at night, as she had been told many times. She was stuck between concern for her own safety and that of her husband.

Suddenly, the salty island air was pierced by song. Seamlessly intertwined with crying, the feminine voice issued forth a haunting melody but no recognizable lyrics. Her sobs were both graceful and aching. Entranced by the sound, Rosemary grabbed her lantern and descended from the widow's walk, into the empty house.

She tiptoed through her large and exquisite house, the interior of which was pitch black, save for the lantern's glow. Although Rosemary could still hear the singing from inside the house, it was clear that it was coming from outside. She followed the voice to her front porch and realized it came from the West. Carefully locking the door and holding her lantern in front of herself, Rosemary stepped into the street, determined to find the source. The hour was late, and the streets were empty of their usual horses, carriages and people. There was no one else in sight – it was just her and the voice.

Rosemary continued down Broadway Avenue, listening as the melancholic melody intensified with each step she took. It was unlike anything she had ever heard before, and yet, she knew it was calling her. The air was unusually still, without the slightest hint of an island breeze. Rosemary lifted her lantern to glance at the palm trees, noting that their fronds were motionless and undisturbed. This might have been the most walking she'd ever done. Her legs ached. When she arrived at the Broadway Cemetery, the voice stopped as suddenly as it had begun. It appeared that this was her destination.

In the absence of the voice that had guided her, Rosemary wasn't sure what to do. She entered through the gates, trying not to be alarmed that they were already open. A few stray frogs croaked softly, bouncing around in the grass that was freshly watered every day. Grand, ornate mausoleums — burial structures intended for use by entire families — towered over the plot of land like kings. Gingerly stepping around headstones and footstones, Rosemary wandered through the maze of graves, reading epitaphs and memorials for people she had never known. The air in the cemetery was noticeably thicker than it had been in the streets. A clinging mist crawled past her face and over her head, obscuring her vision. As she glanced to her right, her heart nearly sprung out of her chest.

Looming over her was a tall statue that certainly had not been there moments ago. The stern, imposing figure was carved out of smooth, white stone. It was an angel. The features did not match those of any of the named angels Rosemary had learned about in church scriptures.

Instead of a kind face that offered protection and guidance, this statue's face was quite serious, as if it were issuing a warning. But of what?

Rosemary crept past the angel, wanting to escape its ominous presence. A loud commotion disturbed the almost-silence of the cemetery. She heard waves crashing violently, punctuated by faint crashes of thunder, even though she was nowhere near the ocean. A cold breeze picked up. The air smelled distinctly of salt water. Confused, Rosemary looked around, seeing no visible signs of a storm. As she searched for a possible source of this noise, she saw a young lady kneeling at a gravesite.

"Come back! Please!" the woman begged.

Unsure of how to comfort the stranger, and unsure of whether approaching her in the darkness would even be advisable, Rosemary noticed that the grave was unmarked. In fact, several other graves appeared to be unmarked. Rows of weathered, inscribed headstones were interrupted by small handfuls of fresh stones, as if no one were buried there yet, but the places were reserved.

Suddenly, Rosemary noticed a sailor emerge from the fog. He was soon joined by others. As she looked around the cemetery, she saw several of them walking with purpose. Their faces expressionless, they didn't seem to notice Rosemary or the other young lady. She recognized some of them from when Edward had introduced them to her. The first sailor approached an unmarked grave and stepped right into it, his body slipping through the earth without a struggle. Although Rosemary's heart was clutched with panic, she watched in silent awe as the others did the same. One by one, each sailor arrived at his grave and entered it. The sounds of waves and thunder continued, yet the men were unfazed.

Edward appeared, his tall figure impossible to miss.

Like the others, he did not seem to notice Rosemary at all. She ran toward him and called out.

"Edward! Edward, it is me! Come back!" she pleaded as he walked right past her, staring straight ahead.

She raced after him, determined to catch his attention. Edward arrived at an unmarked grave and paused. Rosemary straightened her long skirts, which fit much tighter than they had seemingly weeks ago. She struggled to catch her breath.

"Edward, please! Do not leave!" she screamed.

It was too late. He was already stepping into the earth, his body swallowed up in one smooth motion. He was gone.

"Come back! Please, come back!" she sobbed, collapsing to the ground and leaning on the empty headstone.

Looking around, Rosemary witnessed dozens of other women like her, kneeling by the unmarked graves and pleading with their departing husbands through choked sobs in an eerie chorus reminiscent of the angel's song.

Her walk through the darkness that night had served to transform her into the widow she so feared becoming. Rosemary gently stroked her stomach, fondly acknowledging the child Edward would never meet.

∽

Emma Brocato is an emerging writer of multiple genres - journalism, fiction, essays, poetry, etc. She is currently working towards an MA in Science & Environmental Journalism. Her work has been published in *The Agriculturist*. She lives, works and writes in Arizona. "The Walking Widow" is her debut fiction publication.

THE WOUNDED AND THE DEAD

WADE NEWHOUSE

Do you believe in the Resurrection and the life? Do you believe in the blood of the lamb?

My new bride, golden-haired and dark-eyed, believes these things. She has not studied them in the seminary as I have, but she was raised to be studious and pious from girlhood, and she uses these words in her daily life the way a craftsman in Boston colors his personal life with the language of his shop. She has encouraged me to look back on the dark corners of my life and to be unafraid to name them.

I was in Petersburg when the war ended. We sat in mazes of trenches and rifle pits on the edge of the city and there were fires burning in the sky all midnight long. Every now and then they would come at us without warning, scarecrows of men barely alive screaming up out of the smoke and shadows.

I tried to rise up to fight them, but I couldn't make my arms move and they came down on us like locusts. And there was a boy—not more than fourteen, with a wild shock of yellow hair and his eyes glittering because he could not give up. He had a black spot here on his cheek, a mole or a sunspot or something, and he came right at me with his bayonet pointing, scrambling up the side of the pit where I was.

I remember thinking that I could smell—roses? I wondered how I could smell roses and I was thinking then all of roses, fat blooming petals and thorns and the smell choked me and I could not do anything else but smell roses. Then I saw something hit this boy square in his left eye. His eyesocket disappeared in a spray of blood and he fell in on me. He lay there with his remaining eye open to Heaven. His chest stopped heaving and, in an hour, when the fighting was over, he was cold and the smell of roses was gone.

In the morning when the smoke sank into the earth, the burial details came out and pulled some of the bodies away. Later the men in gray came at us again out of the black, fiery nighttime. Where did they come from? We killed them and we killed them and they fell in piles.

When I looked up there was a boy, with a shock of yellow hair and earth streaked down his face. He had a mole or something here—on his left cheek. I opened my mouth, not believing, like I might say something to him about how he could not be here. And I saw that his eye was gone and the shot-away space where it had been was open with dried blood. But he was there nonetheless, and a smell of roses was spilling up out of him and instead of asking him I stabbed him, here, with my bayonet and I watched him fall, still blind, into the pit. I stood over him, smelling smoke and roses, and I stabbed him again and then again until his chest was caving in. I passed out weeping, drowning, and then I was buried in the red earth and in my own blood.

Later I knew the feeling of being carried. I saw what the

city looked like upside down, while my head hung below the arms of the men who carried me. As I bobbed and shook, I saw fires burning downward instead of upward. At last, I knew the feeling of cooler, cleaner air when they laid me on the grass, and when the sun started to go down, I turned my head and saw a red-brick building with tall white columns and porches fronting. I heard the voices of women talking and moving between the wounded and the dead.

I remember candles and oil lamps and dark wooden floors. Men's heavy boots thudded back and forth under the smell of ether and blood and the sounds of crying and cutting and sawing. Behind all of that I heard the voices of the women and the sounds of water dripping in doorways. They put me in a dark room, and in the flickering of the light, I saw rustling, soiled skirts pass by my cot. I heard them say:

We'll take care of you now.

Other men were brought in. Some were stacked like firewood and were missing parts of themselves that they would have a hard time digging up come Judgment Day.

For many minutes I tried to talk but my mouth and throat were caked shut. I kept trying, moving in tiny spaces and swallows, and finally I was able to say, "I don't want to be dead."

You are not dead. You are saved. We'll take care of you.

Everything was upside down. I could not turn my head enough to see the shape of the room or the height of the walls or the color of the ceilings. "What is this place?"

This is a school.

I had a vision of desks all in a row, schoolmasters stalking past frightened children, and punishments being delivered with stern voices and the whip of a thin stick. But I also had visions of shells exploding and of arms and legs raining down on boys not much older than the ones who should be at their desks. I smelled women; I smelled blood and smoke.

Our school. We're taking care of you now. We will always take care of you.

There were soft hands on my forehead and holding up water to my burned lips. I slept and heard them whispering, talking like women do when they think we cannot hear them. If you have ever drowsed, happily, in some bed while mothers and sisters float by in the hallways, carrying flickering candles and sharing things, secret things, with one another, that we are not meant to know, then that is what it was like. Yet behind the soft voices, there were still the sounds of saws cutting back and forth, letting go of their shattered cargo in the next room.

More men were brought in. Others were carried out and wrapped in bloody sheets.

Stay asleep. You need your rest.

Then they brought in another body and laid it on the table beside me. I turned away because I knew that death carries over sometimes from one bed to the one beside it, and that the smell would find me and overcome me and drive me mad. But instead of death, I smelled roses.

I managed to turn my head to see, because it was impossible that there could be roses in this place. The boy on the table had a wild shock of yellow hair, and his eye was gone, the hole caked over with blood. His entire chest was hardened over with blood and sunken in.

I screamed.

Do you believe in the Resurrection and the Life?
Have you been saved by grace?
Do you know the power of the blood?
Have you been saved by the blood of the Lamb?

There were women all around me. One of them carried a bowl. Another, a razor.

"What are you doing?"

You need your rest. We will take care of you. It is for the Cause.

They cut me here, just a little, just so little that you cannot see the scar. They cut me while they sang. There is a scar that you can see and they took my blood in a bowl.

You need your rest. We will take care of you.

They made me sleep. As I was falling asleep, I saw them take the bowl to the boy with the yellow hair and no eye and a chest that I had caved in. They sang to him and gave him my blood. I slept. Shortly after midnight, I awoke to that boy rising up from my table and dragging himself toward the door of the school with the white pillars and the dark wooden floors, and I could smell roses.

I remained here after the war, never returning to my seminary in Boston. I have looked out of this window, watching the black gum and sweetbay trees wave in the wind, while I drowse in the hot summers lulled by singing, low, under these dark floors. My new bride, golden-haired and dark-eyed, comes to me in the night and touches me before she sets the bowl and the razor on the table. There is so much to rebuild now that the war is over, and when she takes my blood to give to the cold ones laid out on the tables, she tells me about the Resurrection and the Life, and she says:

I will take care of you. You are my favorite. You believe.

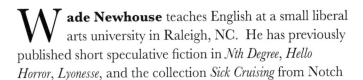

W ade Newhouse teaches English at a small liberal arts university in Raleigh, NC. He has previously published short speculative fiction in *Nth Degree*, *Hello Horror*, *Lyonesse*, and the collection *Sick Cruising* from Notch

Publishing House. A new story about theatre ghosts will be coming out in CORVID-19: The Second Wave, an anthology of short fiction that will be appearing soon to raise money for RavenCon after two years of cancellations. You can reach him at wnewhouse2 [at] gmail [dot] com.

TAKE THE FIRE FROM HER

BY SARAH HANS

F elicity's fire was merely a spark when she was a babe, a useful skill for a girl whose parents were settlers. They had no need of flint or tinder after her first birthday. They liked to show her off to the cowboys who passed through, painting her ability as a gift rather than a curse, especially when she could light blazing bonfires during the howling gales common in the Kansas spring.

True, she did sometimes set her clothes on fire, and once burned down the cabin, but the clothes were made from flour sacks anyway, and the cabin the family built to replace the original was far roomier and sturdier. And as she grew, Felicity was better able to control the fire, so there was no more worry about setting the grasslands ablaze by accident.

Mama and Papa had more children, but none of them possessed Felicity's gift with fire. They were relieved. One of her kind was enough for the family, thank you very much, and they'd been lucky it was an obedient girl-child. Could you imagine if her brother Jedediah had such a power? He could barely piss in the latrine hole without getting it all over his trousers.

Around the time she turned fourteen, Felicity woke in the night to her bed on fire. She ran outside and the family doused the burning bed with the bucket of water they kept in the bedroom for just such an occasion. Felicity burned for hours in the yard, her nightgown blackening and turning to ash. The fire had never hurt her before, but now it was like a thousand wasps stinging her all at once. She screamed and howled and rolled naked on the ground, desperate to make it stop.

Her family stood around her, throwing buckets of water and blankets over the flames, but the water evaporated and the blankets vaporized instantly in the heat of the six-foot-tall blue flames. They were reduced to putting out the small fires erupting in the grass nearby, waiting for Felicity to stop burning. For hours she wailed and cried and begged for them to help her.

Sometime in the mid-morning, the fire waned, the flames growing smaller until they finally went out, leaving behind a sobbing, soot-covered girl, thick gray smoke drifting up from her body, curled in the fetal position. All around her the earth was black, the grass seared away.

The poor girl was bald, right down to her eyelashes. The top layer of her skin was black and crispy to the touch. Over the next days and weeks, it would gradually peel away, revealing skin underneath as smooth and pink as a babe's. Her hair would grow back lustrous and golden. Her eyelashes returned longer and fuller. Even her gray eyes seemed bluer after that night.

The family built a special sleeping shed for Felicity after that, far from the main house, in an area cleared of grass. Just in case.

When cowboys and caravans of settlers visited the homestead, Felicity's gift was no longer what they noticed about her. Whispers began in town that Felicity was a witch. A carnival troupe passed through and offered ten whole dollars for her. Ten dollars was a lot, enough to feed the family for years, but Felicity's mother refused to sell. Her daughter was, after all, only a child, and she'd seen the look of lust on the ringleader's ugly face. She might be a witch, but she was still her mother's only daughter, and her first child.

One night, a cowboy snuck into Felicity's locked sleeping shed. She burned down the shed with him inside and would tell no one what had occurred, suddenly stricken with muteness. The local sheriff didn't know what to make of it. A posse of the cowboy's friends came for Felicity, but when they tried to grab her, she burst into blue flames. One tried to shoot her, but the bullets melted in the heat before they could touch her. Felicity burned and burned until the cowboys gave up.

After that, Felicity did as she pleased. She lived in the woods. Sometimes she would venture to the farmhouse with a skirt full of mushrooms or herbs and would eat dinner with her family. Other times they didn't see her for weeks. Some nights, her brother Jedediah would look out the window to see a bright blue spot glowing in the trees: his sister Felicity consumed by fire.

Desperate for help, Mama wrote to a faith healer advertised in the Farm & Feed catalogue.

Three months later, on a cold October day, Reverend Hightower stepped onto the farm. He was a tall man dressed in austere black, with a tall black hat and a huge black horse. He looked less like a faith healer, Mama thought, and more like a demon hunter.

Felicity emerged naked from the woods to greet him. Her lustrous hair was a matted tangle full of sticks and leaves. Her beautiful skin was caked with mud and criss-crossed with streaks of blood. But her eyes, her eyes were bright blue, fierce and full of fire.

Reverend Hightower promised he could take the fire from her. Mama wept with relief. Papa sent the other children to fetch buckets of water and soaked blankets, because he was a practical man. Felicity knelt before the Reverend, her head held high.

The Reverend walked around to her back and placed his hand against her skin. Flames erupted where he touched. He gritted his teeth and did not pull his hand away. The family watched in wonder as he burned while uttering a strange prayer in a language that sounded like Latin but wasn't Latin, not any Latin Papa had heard, and he'd spent his formative years in Catholic school.

When Reverend Hightower finally pulled his hand away, the fire came with it. Felicity screamed, long and low, the sound a cow makes when she loses her calf to wolves. The Reverend clenched his fist and the fire consumed his hand. He released a shout of agony as his skin blackened and peeled away down to the bone, but the fire died.

Felicity curled in on herself, collapsing to the ground. Mama ran to her, wrapping her arms around her precious baby girl and pleading with her not to die, yet Felicity breathed no more. The sound Mama made was so terrible the air seemed to waver and shrink back from her sorrow.

Papa's hands went to the Reverend's throat, but Reverend Hightower was gone. What stood in his place was a creature out of myth, a thing in the shape of a man, but with eyes of burning coal and a mouth full of needle-teeth. The thing disguised as Reverend Hightower laughed and executed a bizarre, boneless jig, mounting the horse that was now a skeletal nightmare. The sound of the demon's rasping, grating laughter hovered over the farm long after his silhouette had receded on the horizon.

The family buried Felicity in the forest. Every October, Mama and Papa woke in the night to see something bright in the trees. The ghost never came to the house, and she disappeared when Mama ran to her.

After Mama and Papa passed, it was Jedediah and his wife who saw the blue fire between the branches.

Jed wasn't surprised when one of his daughters had the spark.

Sarah Hans is an award-winning writer, editor, and teacher. Her short stories have appeared in over twenty publications, but she's best known for the multicultural steampunk anthology *Steampunk World*, which appeared on io9, Boing Boing, Entertainment Weekly Online, and Humble Bundle, and also won the 2015 Steampunk Chronicle Reader's Choice Award for Best Fiction. You can read more of Sarah's short stories in the collection *Dead Girls Don't Love*, published by Dragon's Roost Press, or on her Patreon for just $1/month. You can also find her on Twitter (steampunkpanda).

You can contact Sarah via email at sarah.hans [at] gmail [dot] com.

ISSUE 9: YOUR BODY IS A CANVAS

POE

LOVE LETTERS TO

VELENTZA | YORK
HUANG | BAKER

Volume 1, Issue 9 | June 2021
Edited by Sara Crocoll Smith

SMUDGE

CLIO VELENTZA

Lore paints her face on everything. There is nobody to stop her; Father is always away and Mother is now a kindly young poplar, growing from the headstone of her grave. The nursemaid is fond of little Lore's art and lets her fill the tablecloths, the walls, the floorboards with her scribbles. For her eighteenth birthday, Lore is given the keys to the house, the termination of nursemaid's duties and a dazzling array of oil paints and brushes.

Lore attempts to paint the garden pond, the beech trees by the canal, the lustrous crockery and the dim copper of the aspic molds. Her art, emboldened by a series of deferential tutors, is tolerable: the pond looks like a pond, and the kitchen pump looks every bit its massive, imperious self. She sends sketches to Father and he sends back his congratulations. He suggests that, now that his accomplished young lady has mastered this craft, perhaps she would consider mastering the old piano, or take up the patronage of *un vrai artiste*.

Lore writes back to thank him and sends her dutiful love, but when the letter leaves she takes her pruning shears and cuts every single one of the piano strings which snap, whipping her hands with vengeance at their release. Father's reply comes soon after. He has found a *bohéme* for her – an artist complete with secondhand gloves, debts to persons of ill-repute, and talent coming out of his thread-bare cuffs. He is sending the young man over, with his hopes that his daughter will seize the chance to refine her skills as a hostess and patroness.

Lore has only a few days left to be Lore who paints, Lore who cuts the piano strings, Lore unchecked. She unfurls a blank canvas and cuts and trims it to a portrait. She stares out of the window at the dove-gray hills and their treacherous green hollows, clutches her pencil and, as the light casts the outline of her head onto the easel, she draws that. She sketches herself from the back, half turned as if to someone calling her name.

She doesn't sleep, eat, take tea or answer calls. She piles paint on the canvas and scrapes it off again. Her hands are heavy and tired, but reckless with her tools. She paints her skin shadowy and warm, her hair thick and wild. The girl on the canvas has most of her face hidden, but the side of the mouth and the corner of the eye can be seen: they are Lore's own, watching over her shoulder with a defiant glare.

Finally, she takes in her work. Her tutors would have hated its obscure subject and misty lighting, the obvious likeness to its maker. It's ready, but she finds it too finished, too lifelike.

Driven by a half-superstitious, half-sensual urge, Lore leans in and kisses the portrait right on the visible side of its plump, dark mouth. The kiss leaves a smudge but she prefers it like this, incomplete.

In the morning, the portrait is gone. The study has been tidied, the paint has been scrubbed off the floor. Lore doesn't ask about it. She puts on her mother's jewels and makes herself ready for her guest.

The artist is a freckled young man, all knees and elbows, who has second and third helpings at dinner while she politely asks about his painting. He has brought some watercolors as a gift, and a portfolio of charcoal sketches of city life to show her.

Lore studies them. She is jealous of each one, but doesn't show it. He looks at her as if about to eat her up too, and she can feel his heavy, starved gaze on her skin.

"I paint a little myself," she says.

"I'm sure," he obliges her. He throws about phrases such as *accomplished beauty*, *gentle yet capable hands* and *feminine gifts*, and doesn't ask about her work.

Lore looks at his drawings and thinks of the medley of people who sat for him in bare rooms, of the richness of their hands and faces, the fluency of their gaze – and she feels a burning hatred. She wants to steal the life right out of him: all the streets that he walked, all the places he has seen. He mistakes her stony look for admiration, gets down on his knee and kisses her hand while she averts her eyes. If she would grace him so and sit for him, he begins, bashful, but she refuses and gets up to leave.

That night Lore is roused by the sound of feet shuffling outside her room. There are muffled voices, a door opening and closing, then silence. She falls back asleep.

During breakfast the artist stares at her and blushes so hard that his ears glow. He seems too embarrassed to bring a fork to his mouth. When she casually asks about his night he knocks his coffee cup over, apologizes profusely and flees the room.

In the afternoon they step out for a walk to look for paint-worthy vistas. As soon as they are out of sight of the house he pushes her against a tree and begins to kiss her. His hands gather up her skirts in clumsy, boyish gestures.

For a moment Lore is too stunned to resist but then tears herself away. The young man looks bewildered.

"I thought—" he stammers. "Last night—"

He swallows his words when he sees her pale, stern face and storms off in humiliation. Lore stays back, alone. She feels a failure as a hostess, a painter, a woman. They retire immediately after dinner, leaving the food untouched.

In the middle of the night she's woken up by the same shuffling, the same creaking door. She gets up and steps barefoot out into the dark corridor.

There is a sliver of light stealing out from under the guest bedroom door. Lore steps closer. She can hear thumping, creaking, the muted echo of sighs and grunts. She pushes the door quietly and peers in.

The artist is lying disheveled and flushed on the unmade bed. On top of him sits a naked woman, rocking back and forth. She has Lore's dark hair, Lore's breasts and soft belly. Her brown eyes are Lore's eyes, her blushing, sweaty neck is her neck. Only the mouth is different: the woman's is drawn and misshapen at one corner as if smudged, and it gives her face a fiendish air.

The man doesn't see Lore but the woman pins her eyes on her, and stares insolently as she continues to move, the man's fingers digging into her thighs. Lore retreats and stumbles back into her room.

The next morning the artist has dark circles under his eyes. He's watching Lore as she eats and twitches at her every move.

"Please," he whispers. "Please…"

Lore ignores him and butters her toast loudly. Tears brim in his honey-green eyes.

"Your charcoal," Lore says at last. She takes a sip of coffee. "It needs work."

His mouth trembles and his Adam's apple bobs up and down. He nods meekly and stares into his plate. This time, when they take their walk, he doesn't corner her, but lingers back obediently. At dinner Lore is lively: she talks, smiles and eats hungrily, while he stares and doesn't touch his food.

Lore sleeps peacefully that night. Even though the footsteps and the familiar sound of the door disturb her rest for a moment, she doesn't get up.

She wakes up refreshed, late into the day. There are unusual sounds of a commotion in the house, doors slamming, but she doesn't want to rush. She dresses lazily while shafts of light warm her skin. When she steps down for breakfast, the table has been laid for one. She takes her time to eat and read her letters, then walks back upstairs and into the guest bedroom.

The room is littered with the remnants of the artist's work. Every single sketch and painting has been torn up or fed into the fire. The carpet is strewn with ashes, the bed is still unmade. The air is thick with cloying, heady smells. Lore opens a window and takes deep breaths, and her eye is caught by a scrap of paper at her feet. She picks it up.

It is the quick, rough drawing of her face in the artist's hand. Only part of it is visible on the fragment: one dark eye and half of a clever, smiling mouth, its corner smudged over.

Lore laughs, kisses the drawing and rips it up. She tosses the scraps out of the window, and watches them dance as they are carried off wildly with the wind.

∾

Clio Velentza is a writer from Athens, Greece. She has studied Chemistry and has attended Postmodern Writing, Flash Fiction, and Creative Non-Fiction classes, as well as the 3rd Playwriting Studio of the Greek National Theatre. She is a winner of The Best Small Fictions 2016, Wigleaf's Top 50 2019 and Best Microfiction 2020, and a Pushcart Prize nominee. Her work has appeared in several literary journals, along with some anthologies in both English and Greek. She is currently working on a novel and a play.

TARANTISM

JESSICA ANN YORK

"Don't touch her." Silvestro's voice hits the starlight like a hiss of steam. "Not until after the dance. She'll spread it to you if she hasn't performed the Tarantella."

"But it's taking too long for Carmine to bring the instrument," my father says back to the priest. The glow from his lantern sways sporadically, like a trapped lightning bug, as he falls to his knees in front of me. "Concetta needs to be held down, her little body can't take much more."

"Let the girl move the venom out," Silvestro says. "The creature won't lose its hold on her otherwise."

In the white flames of moonlight, my fingers feel like charcoal when the seeds from the populus trees brush against them. The sweat on my skin easily captures the wind-tossed fluff, as if the sticky residue were barbed and sharp, and I think back to the wolf spider's own splintery hairs. I think I can see her eight eyes peek out of the fanged cypress trees that tower around me as another contortion overcomes my body.

The two oil lanterns a few feet away shudder with their holders, as the men fight to calm their spooked horses.

They stand around me at the edge of an olive tree field. My father's lantern comes closer, and when it does, I can better make out the glow in his wide eyes. I hadn't meant for him to be part of this moment, but I won't let his presence stop what I intend to do.

I am still on the ground, but my eyes have adjusted to the lanterns, and I can see the two figures more clearly. My father, in his dusty coat and breeches, is riddled by tears. Silvestro fumbles to document my every symptom on a parchment of ink-stained paper. He gazes around the cypress trees annoyed, hopeful a sharp rock or low branch isn't close enough for me to puncture myself on. It's the same look he's always given me, or rather it's the look he doesn'tgive me. A look I can get from every other man, single or married, in town buthim. The priest's morals won't let him. But I had everyone else captured. An ideal wife in just a few more years. An innocent, silk doll.

Even when I had set foot upon the cobble streets of Certaldo earlier today, the giant, black welt of the spider bite very visible on my wrist, and hysteria broke out—it was the giant mass of people tearing their clothes off with caterwauls of dance and fright screaming, "if pure little Concetta can be possessed we all will be" that caught the young priest's eyes first. Silvestro had calmed the mass madness of the town's folk by explaining they had to be touched by me to actually be possessed by the wicked wolf spider. But now he had to deal with the little nuisance herself.

In his eyes I was a squish-able pest who had retreated into the secluded olive fields from the chaos I had wrought. He couldn't foresee that I had intended for him to follow me there alone.

"Finally." My father's shout pulls me out of my head. "There. Do you see him?"

In between another convulsion I see Silvestro nod towards a distant lantern light that blinks between another olive field a little ways beyond us. The shadow of a man holding a guitar spins his way through the coiled trees behind the lantern's glow, and I think again to the eyes of the wolf spider when they had similarly crept out of the branches of one of my father's olive trees.

I had heard the warnings. Knew she would make me dance if I wanted to be released from her bile. That my body would shiver and moan in the release of the Tarantella if I were ever to be whole again. Sweet Concetta forced to quiver in unholy ways she shouldn't know how to in front of the town's typically preoccupied priest. I didn't hesitateto hold my wrist out to her. The venom discolors my skin and widens my eyes, but I am fine.

The guitar man finally arrives among the light of the other two lanterns, and I can hear my father complain that it's not a more noble instrument like a violin or a harp being used to cure his beloved little daughter, yet I keep going back to the beautiful wolf spider on the olive tree branch this red Tuscan afternoon. Envy coats me.

She had been swollen, bursting with tiny brown squirming life. Her children were wrapped around her round abdomen. More baby spiders than she knew what to do with. All wriggling like tiny chocolate diamonds caught in the light.

The guitar strums. I blink.

Carmine is beside my father with his instrument.

"Concetta, get up."

Silvestro's voice is still indifferent, but his eyes are on mine at last. After all, he is the town's priest. He *has* to watch and make sure that the wolf spider's evil is released.

"You have to dance now, the venom won't leave until you do."

I nod back at Silvestro, rise to do the Tarantella, but I know the venom will never leave. It's always been there.

I clutch at my sides and weave under the starlight that illuminates the olive trees around me. My spine twists and pops, until my muscles disconnect, shriveling out into black heat. The vibrating roar of my insides is like six extra pairs of legs tapping the night air. Pedipalps strumming web. I scream, and I can't tell if it's blood or venom that sprays from my mouth. My heart may burst from the excitement. Father and Carmine could be miles away now for all I care, all I can see are the trapped eyes of Silvestro. He is mine.

Jessica **Ann York** is working on her debut novel. You can find her other short stories at *PseudoPod*, *Vastarien*, and in three anthologies from Cemetery Gates Media, including *Places We Fear to Tread*, *Campfire Macabre*, and *Paranormal Contact*. She's also on Twitter (JessicaAnnYork1) and Instagram (jessiannyork).

SOUL INTENTIONALLY SOLD

ELLEN HUANG

in my dreams I choose to glow
radioactive from being bewitched,
pulsing outside for lack of heart within.

in my dreams I choose to dress pressed and tight
in a ball gown made from hourglass, sand
burying me alive, but ghosts never looked so fine.

in my dreams I choose the touch of smoke
taped over my mouth and materializing me away
rather than the sun in a friend's selfless open arms.

I stick to shadow enveloping me in nightly webs
and turn from love bathed in golden light
and I shrink back from human touch like
a hypnotized princess from a spinning wheel
    spindle,
turning from open embrace to secure clutches.

in my dreams, I choose to feed on existing where I
    am strangely useful
rather than be unnecessarily, unconditionally, freely
    loved
and like finding my dark hair, still attached, knotted
to the bed frame in the morning, a spider's web of
    thoughts
the question binds me up: why would I choose such
    chains?

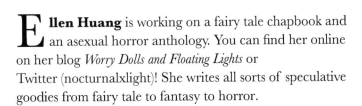

Ellen Huang is working on a fairy tale chapbook and an asexual horror anthology. You can find her online on her blog *Worry Dolls and Floating Lights* or Twitter (nocturnalxlight)! She writes all sorts of speculative goodies from fairy tale to fantasy to horror.

HER FONDEST WISH

BY JARED BAKER

I pen this final missive with no expectations – neither exoneration of my crimes, nor even belief on the reader's part. Such simple prospects are luxuries beyond my means, and time – that most precious of all treasures – soon will be. The hangman prepares his gallows even now.

In my years as a painter, I sought to depict the truth. I work in a lesser medium these last moments, but my aims remain unchanged. If the truths my words carry should see the coming sunrise that I never will, I shall be content with that hope.

That hope, and one other.

I met the widow Viscountess Belmont long before she wore either title. Despite our societal disparities, our families had some acquaintance, and we shared many triumphs and tragedies in youth. From my earliest years, I adored her. As time shaped her into a lady of esteem and myself into an impoverished artist, I learned we were not to be; her family's fallen fortunes demanded any romance consider coin as dearly as love. Though wealthy beyond measure with the one, I had precious little of the other.

She consequently married the Viscount, whose station soared above mine as the stars above the firmament. I passed most nights thereafter in delirium, drunk on sorrow or spirits. I *ached* to see her, to bask in the glow of her smile again. I thought myself destined for the madhouse; only my work brought me any comfort.

But one evening, as lightning lanced the sky and a deluge pelted my tiny garret window, I heard a knock. As if in dream, the lady Marian Belmont stood upon my threshold; pale loveliness and raven hair as I remembered, but a peculiar light burning in her eyes.

"Jonathan," she whispered, clutching a cloth sack to her breast. "Will you see me? I have no right to ask, but I must."

"V-Viscountess." I bowed her into my humble chamber.

"Burden me not with titles! We were *friends*, Jonathan." Thrill and despair cleft my heart at her words. "I have a favor to beg, and precious little time."

I blinked. "How might I serve you, milady?"

"A commission – a portrait!" Marian hefted her pack. "With these materials, this very night."

I objected – such a feat was impossible! – but she overrode me.

"*This night, Jonathan.*" Her liquid eyes held mine. "If ever you cared for me, please hear me now."

I did. She bore paints, brushes, and canvas, which I must employ for a portrait of the late Viscount. Both materials and time were crucial – the work demanded completion before the howling storm could break. As the sole painter of her acquaintance, no other could grant her this. When I questioned her, she would reply only that her eternal happiness depended upon it – upon *me*.

How was I to refuse? As a child, I could deny her nothing; I fared no better now.

The paints were far thicker than I preferred, and the brushes ancient relics. Rough, discolored fibers wove through the canvas, making fine work onerous. Yet I agreed to her terms – for I wished *so* to see her smile again!

Per Marian's pleading directives, I was to depict her husband where he had asked for her marriage-hand, overlooking the Thames at sunset. His clothing must be the finest, his expression joyful, his arm extended as if to embrace her. And yet, she was *not* to appear with him.

These and a thousand other details she insisted upon, and vetoed a dozen sketches as I failed to match her fierce vision. Despite my joy at seeing her, I grew irritated at her insistence on both speed and perfection; even more so at her refusal to answer any question I posed about her purpose or the need for such urgency.

"I cannot say," Marian rebuffed me each time. "Do not ask me, I beseech you!"

When the floor was carpeted with rejected drafts, when resentment soured my affection and my last dregs of patience fled, she pronounced my design acceptable. I began work on the canvas, blocking in the scene as she wished. The thick, curdling pigments fought me, but I forced them through their labors.

For her part, Marian monitored my progress on a continual pacing circuit of the room. This further frayed my nerves; at last, I suggested she might either peruse a volume from my shelves for distraction, or (I could scarce believe my temerity) claim an hour or two of rest upon my cot while I worked.

I expected a blush or a tongue-lashing. Neither came.

"I *cannot* rest, Jonathan," Marian's voice was bleak, sick

with despair I knew well. "I have not known true slumber since my husband's death. I fear I never will again."

"You loved him." It was agony to admit. "But he would never want grief to carry you after!"

Her blue gaze was glassy. "I can no longer know his wishes. But *my* fondest wish is to be with him again."

I flinched at this latest stab, but laid in the contours of the land, the water, the slinking shadows. As I brought forth the scarlet sunset, an equally-red haze crept over my vision. Why could she not have loved *me* with such fervor? My hands trembled, and Marian's gasps of dismay at each ill brush-stroke only fueled my gathering bitterness.

Yet I persevered, keeping the feverish pace she demanded. Long past midnight, I paused to wipe the sweat from my brow and evaluate my work. Marian wrung her hands ceaselessly, her worried gaze returning always to the window as her ears sought the next thunderclap. Limbs aching with fatigue, my temper flared.

"Marian, I shall rip the canvas apart!" I swore. "I am only human, not God to grant your impossible desires!"

"No, you must *not!*" Seizing me, her fingers dug into my flesh with the strength of near-madness. "This is my last chance, Jonathan!"

Confusion fanned my anger, and I did the unforgivable – I struck her. The crack was deafening, and she recoiled as if shot. Blood dripped from her lip, and the silence and guilt threatened to smother me. But her eyes held no recrimination; only the painting and the storm. That obsession, from which even my sinful violence could not distract her, pulled me from my stupor.

"Marian, I…" My voice was desperate. And weary, as was my body. "Only the final tints remain – the rest is done. I… I must clear my head, but I will return."

Her gaze darted to the painting, then to me. "It… it is finished?"

"Yes." *Yes, my love. All for you.*

Eyes welling with joyful tears, she flung her arms about me. "Thank you, Jonathan! I can never repay you for this kindness!"

I choked. "I… ask only your forgiveness."

"You have it. And my eternal gratitude." Still embracing me, she turned and regarded the painting as she might a saint's relic. "For this… and for being my truest friend."

Her final word was the final wound. With a cry, I tore free and fled into the night.

When I returned, only my furnishings, my easel, and the portrait remained. I cried out for Marian, and searched my rooms in vain.

Silence.

Thinking she had abandoned me once more, I snatched up the wretched work to cast it into the fire.

And there – *in the painting* – I found her.

Marian stood with the Viscount, watching the sunset. Nestled into his embrace, the happiest smile upon her lips.

Her *torn* lips. With a crimson smear along her jaw.

Impossible.

Numb, I tried to paint over the wound. But it would not be concealed. The blood rouged her cheek as a testament to my love and my shame.

I stared at her image – *at her* – until dawn.

Few had known of her journey to me, as discretion and decorum demanded. But at length I *was* questioned, for none had seen her since that storm-stricken night. With the evidence found in my studio – blood thickening the paints, skin woven into the canvas – there was no room for doubt. I would hang, they said.

Perhaps I should. For what is murder, if not removal from this world? It appears I *am* a murderer. Even if I know not how.

As I await the rope, questions still haunt me. Was our interlude real? Or did my years of alcohol-soaked longing curdle somehow into madness? *Could* I have plucked her from this life and wiped away my own memory of the deed?

I cannot answer.

When I began this testament, I spoke of hope. Though I hear the hangman's heavy-booted tread even now, though I shall never again lay eyes upon she whom I loved and who could not love me… perhaps hope is not yet beyond my grasp. Hope that these truths, however alien, will survive me. And hope that, whether by simple slaughter or unfathomable mystery, I have rendered my darling one final service.

For I have granted her fondest wish. How many – save, perhaps, the Devil himself – can truly claim the same?

~

Jared Baker's previous fiction has been published by Hellbound Books, LLC (in a quirky anthology called *The Toilet Zone*, with horror stories meant to be read in one "sitting") and Critical Blast Publishing (in another anthology called *The Devil You Know*, about people's experiences meeting the Father of Lies himself).

You can also find him on Twitter (**JaredKBaker1**).

ISSUE 10: WEEP FOR ME

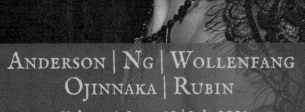

LOVE LETTERS TO POE

POE

ANDERSON | NG | WOLLENFANG
OJINNAKA | RUBIN

Volume 1, Issue 10 | July 2021
Edited by Sara Crocoll Smith

LADY OF THE BLEEDING HEART

COLLEEN ANDERSON

She stood between the willow trees in every season, gazing at animals and people as they came and went. Her gentle yet sophisticated compassion needed no words. She radiated peace by just being. Purity cloaked her, her head always covered, as if protecting her from the rain of tears that pewtered the sky. She never spoke to me but I knew she made me promises nonetheless; and she never rejected me.

I had only ever dared to touch the lady's cool hand once and was struck by her calm.

Every day I visited her, drawn as inevitably as a leaf is into a whirlpool, even though it dances carefree.

When I arrived through the great iron gates, I walked the undulating paths amongst the flowers, seeing her at a distance, sometimes coming close to stare at her, reluctant to engage. But I watched her, wondering. Her serene gaze held a hardness, a steadfastness as she tended the gardens through all these years. From time to time she wept.

The Lady opened her arms to all without judgment. I wanted her to acknowledge me, wrap those arms about me, yet I dreaded it. Did she ever truly see me? But to speak to her catered madness and a loneliness I dared not admit.

I had killed in the name of justice and democracy. It had been a brutal, bloody time and my soul bore scars. For this reason, I had come to the gardens for solace, and she never questioned, never criticized. She stood in shadows, always watching.

She made it easy, her calm descending like a monk's cowl to comfort me when the world grew too hectic in its new ways. As time crawled on, when no one else ventured into the gardens, I ranted to her as if she were my confessor.

I lie. My confessions never would have had such bare truth.

I wanted to believe that I had somehow thawed her firm resolve, that she favored me above others. Maybe she heard me, because of my resolute attendance, and then I worried that she had.

I walked to see her nearly every day. She offered me a relief from my pain, but I always refused her silent promises. Within her outstretched arms, I saw the blissful void, but I wondered if she gave the gift to anyone who acquiesced. I told myself not to fear, and proved it by attending her without ever committing.

Sometimes I lost myself in watching birds weave twigs into branches of trees, creating a nest, or the determined ants carrying away mysterious minutiae. At other times, I sat, pain throbbing through me like the thudding of mortar fire. At those times I wanted to beg her to hear me and give me something more, something like love.

I had known she could give, but I hadn't known she could take at the same time.

~🐝~

The ice storms came that year and coated everything in a snow queen's hell. My infirmaries kept me from navigating the silvery, slippery streets. Weeks later, muffled from the needles of cold air, I finally managed to totter with cane and a slow, but no longer stately pace, to where I knew the lady waited. I vowed to visit her no more after this. My infatuation did not bode well for my future.

In the white fog, I stood looking at her as my breath formed halos about my head. Isolated, we stood as if on an island untethered to any place or time. I may have said a few words as I stared at her sculpted beauty. Pale, vigilant, she lulled me as ever; the same calm gaze, the same offer. I bowed my head, trembling, knowing I would return yet again.

Months of daily visits and my denial grew even as my obsession strengthened. I began to truly fear what she offered and vowed again to stay away. I could feel her in my heart. I wanted her to step into my arms. The tombstones I passed began to resemble rows of hungry teeth. Each time, I swore never to return. The deadly attraction had rooted deep in me.

Then the day came, after an angry, thunder-cracking tempest. Hundred-year-old trees had toppled; tombstones and statuary in the cemetery shifted as if uneasy spirits woke. Leaves and branches lay like the wounded on the sidewalks. Cats skittered as if Hell chased them. The Lady of the Bleeding Heart waited, humble as ever. Someone had placed a blush of a rose upon her dark, marble shoulder.

I stood before her, looking for a clue, smelling the damp, raw earth. How could she draw me again and again? I had long come to dislike the company of others, except for the Lady. I still did not know if I wanted her compassion or her indifference. That she had never spoken to me in words had made it all easier. Yet I clung to life no matter the ills of my body, and she had never promised me health. Part of me loved her, had padded her in soft flesh and interest though she remained hard and immovable.

The wind scythed through me, and I didn't notice the unstable base she stood upon as I reached to touch her cold stone hand one last time. Then she fell into my arms, as if life had finally fired her marble core, and she took what I had so long denied her.

Now we are more different than before, my substance thin and ethereal to her corporeal, black marble. She has given me death, as I gave her my life. While I may rest within these gardens, we will never be together.

∾

Colleen Anderson is a Canadian author with a BFA in writing who has been nominated for the Pushcart Prize, Aurora, Rhysling and Dwarf Stars Awards in poetry, and longlisted for the Stoker Award in fiction. As a freelance editor, she has co-edited *Tesseracts 17* and Aurora nominated *Playground of Lost Toys.* She edited *Alice Unbound: Beyond Wonderland* (Exile Publishing) and guest edited *Eye to the Telescope.* She has served on both Stoker Award and British Fantasy Award juries, and received BC Arts Council and Canada Council grants for her writing.

Her works have seen print in numerous venues, including *Polu Texni, The Pulp Horror Book of Phobias, The Beauty of Death, HWA Poetry Showcases, and Cemetery Dance.* Her fiction collection, *A Body of Work* was published by Black Shuck Books, UK. Visit her website at www.colleenanderson.-wordpress.com.

THE HYPNOTIST

LENA NG

The bed was soaked in my sweat. *Burning—burning—burning*—my body ablaze in fever. Still he stared at me, standing too close to the bed, his face cut away in shadows, with glowing eyes, compelling eyes, eyes that commanded me to obey. The red and green fern leaf pattern of the wallpaper trembled and shivered around the room, with low hissing sounds, like snakes.

My hands twisted around the sheets. Even without speaking, he wanted me to leave this bed and follow him. For five weeks, I had resisted. On the stage, I had done everything he had told me. He had pointed at me in the audience, and like sleepwalking in a dream, I couldn't stop myself from going. His eyes enveloped me. As he counted down from ten, the hushed crowd of spectators disappeared from my consciousness until only the two of us remained. He whispered and my feet seemed to float. I pirouetted and sang and the audience laughed while I burned under his gaze. The stage spun until my eyes rolled back, and afterward, although I have no memory of how I returned home, I had to crawl into the bed from illness.

I had begged you not to leave. "Don't go," I cried. "I saw him! I saw him! You must believe he has returned." But business was more important to you, even on our honeymoon, and someone else wants to take your place.

The shadows receded. The face half-remembered emerged. The sharply chiselled nose. The sunken, dead eyes, black pinpoints in a pool of white. Looming shoulders like the hunch of a vulture. He spread his gaunt hands, pulled, and by invisible strings, I arose from the bed. I trembled in horror, but I couldn't stop myself from going. The lace on the hem of my nightgown swished against the stone floor. A veil appeared—the veil from our wedding—which was placed upon my head. Cold fingers brushed my shoulders, the light scratch of nails (talons?) grazing my skin.

I floated down from the window and into a carriage. He sat in the seat opposite to me, again hidden in the shadows, with burning eyes like dull coals. I know he'll take me far, far away. And no matter what he asks me to do, I'll obey.

~

Lena Ng has a mix of stories coming out this year, many of which can be read online at *Ghost Orchid Press*, *Dread Imaginings*, and *Zooscape* (animal stories). Her collection of short stories is called *Under an Autumn Moon* and can be found on Amazon.

ROUTES BEST LEFT UNTAKEN

NEMMA WOLLENFANG

"A taste o' oblivion," is what the filthy vagrant promised. "Best way t' hide forever."

Baring yellowing teeth in a rictus grin, he shook the bottle with a coaxing leer.

The tear-streaked lady stood before him in the darkness of the alley: her gossamer gown stained with blood, her willowy body assailed with shakes, the shouts of peelers at her back. Their boots tramped ever closer. Like the tolling of a bell counting down to her doom.

Nowhere to run. Nowhere to hide.

And that amber glass glinted so enticingly in his callus-roughened hand. Limned with shards of moonlight. Innocuous temptation. Deliverance from her sin. Abject salvation.

Evanesky: the drink of those who wished to be lost.

"One sip an' ye'll be gone," the vagrant wheezed, "one sip an' they'll never find ye."

A whistle shrieked, hounds barked, footsteps neared…

She snatched the bottle and drank.

The liquor did not burn, it froze. Icy tendrils swept

through her blood, crystallizing flesh and bone. She opened her mouth but birthed no cry as frost swept away her voice.

Numb sensations. Translucent fingers. The sound of his cackle fading fast…

It did not crack when it hit the ground.

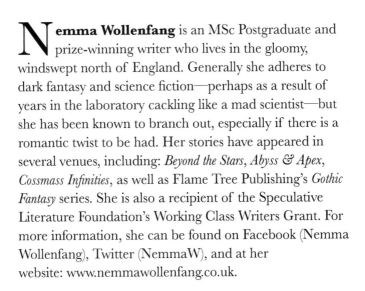

Nemma Wollenfang is an MSc Postgraduate and prize-winning writer who lives in the gloomy, windswept north of England. Generally she adheres to dark fantasy and science fiction—perhaps as a result of years in the laboratory cackling like a mad scientist—but she has been known to branch out, especially if there is a romantic twist to be had. Her stories have appeared in several venues, including: *Beyond the Stars*, *Abyss & Apex*, *Cossmass Infinities*, as well as Flame Tree Publishing's *Gothic Fantasy* series. She is also a recipient of the Speculative Literature Foundation's Working Class Writers Grant. For more information, she can be found on Facebook (Nemma Wollenfang), Twitter (NemmaW), and at her website: www.nemmawollenfang.co.uk.

DANCING DELILAH

ANNA OJINNAKA

As a little girl, I had all sorts of fancies of what married life would be like. I imagined waking up in the arms of my beloved in the brightness of the early morning, and then breakfasting in bed: buttered toast with jam and a glass of milk for me, porridge with cream and a black coffee for him. If I closed my eyes, I could smell this scene unfolding. I could even smell *him*, my dream lover, and his scent was wonderful indeed. It was the smell of pine trees, earth and rain. I thought of how simple and sweet our life would be in a small country house, perhaps even a cottage, away from the smoke and the noise of the city.

How foolish I was to think that life could be that idyllic.

I got married last July to a man I had known since my early childhood. I was surprised, but not unpleasantly so, when I learned that our family friend and doctor, Mr. Clayton Thorne, had asked for my hand in marriage. I found his amiable nature greatly appealing, and I thought he looked quite youthful for a man fast approaching forty. Our wedding took place on a particularly balmy day, and it had been a small yet charming affair. I didn't mind that he was almost twice my age, or that I wasn't his first wife. That honour went to his dear Delilah. They had been childhood sweethearts and had gotten married as soon as they could, but, in a twist of ill fate, she had died on their wedding night.

From the accounts I have heard, she died rather peacefully in her sleep, and the good doctor thought that she was still sleeping when he got out of bed to get them some tea. It was only when he returned that he realised that she was too still, too peaceful, and that something deeper than sleep had overcome her. It pains my heart to think of how devastated he must have been when he realised she was dead. What a cruel joke that he had been a bridegroom longer than he had been a husband. Nobody thought that he would ever marry again, and yet I had become his bride.

I now lie awake, cold as stone, in our marital bed. It is only the twilight hours of the morning, and yet my husband is not beside me, and I do not think he has left me recently, for his side of the bed is cool to the touch. This is not the first time he has left me alone. He has been escaping our bed in the middle of the night for some time now. Lord knows where he goes or what he does. I am too afraid to ask him for an explanation, for the answer might be worse still than my suspicions, and yet today I am compelled to see for myself what my husband is up to at this early hour. I rise out of bed as silently as I can and creep towards the door. I open it ever so slightly and take a peek outside.

It is dark in the hallway, but there is light emanating from the first floor. I skip across the hallway and descend the stairs, my heart pounding so hard that it's the only thing I hear. That is, until a shrill laugh escapes the drawing room. The sound is so unexpected and unfamiliar that I stop dead in my tracks and grasp onto the bannister as if it's the only thing tethering me to this earth. I wonder if I am going mad, because the laugh definitely does not belong to my husband. Feminine, it is high and sickly sweet, the voice of a young maiden, not the matronly maids under our employ. I decide to continue my journey down the stairs and make my way towards the drawing room. The door is slightly ajar and amber light floods out from the gap. Holding my breath, I dare to look at what's inside.

I would've screamed if the image before my eyes hadn't struck me dumb. I feel as if I've been submerged in an icy bath. My husband is inside–but he is not alone. There is a ghostly figure in his arms and they are waltzing across the room. I have never seen any pictures of my husband's first wife, but I sense it in my bones that it is she with whom he is dancing. A pang of jealousy hits me straight in the chest, melding with the fear in my heart, and the resulting feeling is so ugly that I want to purge it from my very core. Despite only being a phantom, she is unarguably lovely. Her skin glows pale like moonlight and her dark hair cascades down her back, swishing as they dance.

I watch transfixed and it strikes me that we share a resemblance, not uncanny, but undoubtedly there. Both of us are raven-haired and pale-skinned beauties, but somehow her deathly state has elevated her looks to an otherworldly level. She twirls and meets my gaze. A smile plays on her lips.

I gasp and take a step back. She has the gall to smile at me when she has been stealing more and more of my husband for herself! I turn and run back to the bedroom. I must be going mad, for there is no other explanation for Delilah's return. She is dead. She is buried. Death should've separated her and my husband for good. He is *mine* now, not hers. It is not my fault that she died, so why should I have to share him? No! I will not allow such an abhorrent arrangement. My husband is a good man, and he is mine alone. I would sooner see him dead than with her.

I climb back under the covers of the bed and feign sleep. I soon hear footsteps approaching and the door creaks open and then shut. I feel the weight of my husband beside me as he sinks into the mattress. He places his arms around my waist and is soon breathing deeply. I feel his warm breath tickling my neck. It's a pleasant feeling, and despite my anger at his disloyalty, I pull his arms even tighter around me. How am I to get rid of his phantom bride? Doing battle with ghosts was not part of my education. What I do know is that my husband still keeps a physical piece of Delilah in his study, perfectly preserved in a jar full of formalin amongst the other specimens that he likes to collect. I wonder what would happen if I were to throw her bleached heart straight into the flames of our hearth? I suppose I'll get my answer tomorrow night. God willing, she won't return.

$$\sim$$

Anna Ojinnaka is a full-time lab assistant who enjoys writing dark tales in her spare time. She also likes to paint.

THE WIDOW'S WALK

BY A.A. RUBIN

She wends her way around her walk,
And round and round she goes–
She does not speak, she does not talk,
As she wends her way around her walk,
And round and round she goes,
She goes,
And round and round she goes.

Her husband's dead, her husband's gone
He died, alack the day!
They will not let her into town,
They built a walk for her to round,
Because he's gone away,
Away,
Because he's gone away.

The widow wends her way around,
Round and round her home.
The children watch her as they play,
They make up stories every day

'Bout the witch who eats their bones,
Their bones,
She eats young children's bones.

Her husband does not know he's dead:
He follows round and round.
He whispers nothings in her ear,
He does not know she cannot hear,
He's buried in the ground,
The ground,
He's buried underground.

The widow wanders round and round
'Neath pale Hecate's moon.
She conjures spirits in the dark,
Up on her walk above the park,
In the night's dark inky gloom,
Its gloom,
In the night's dark inky gloom.

Are any of these stories true?
Forsooth, we cannot say.
We can't by any magic art,
Devine what's in her secret heart,
Her mind we can't assay,
Assay,
Her mind we can't assay.

But still we all do dream of her
Each and every night.
She sends us nightmares while we sleep,
Demons conjured from the deep,
In the moon's faint pale light,
Its light,

In the moon's faint pale light.

She wends her way around her walk
And round and round she goes—
She does not speak, she does not talk,
As she wends her way around her walk,
And round and round she goes,
She goes,
And round and round she goes.

&

A.A. Rubin surfs the cosmos on waves of dark energy. He writes in a variety of genres, from comics, to literary fiction; fantasy, to formal poetry, and almost everything in between. A winner of a *Writers Digest* award for Rhyming Poetry, his poems have appeared recently in journals and anthologies like *Poetica 2*, *Bards Annual*, and *Nassau County Voices* in verse. He can be reached across social media (TheSurrealAri), or through his website, www.aarubin.wordpress.com.

ISSUE 11: PARENTHOOD

LOVE LETTERS TO POE

BREWKA-CLARK | FRANCIS
MALENKY | DENTON

Volume 1, Issue 11 | August 2021
Edited by Sara Crocoll Smith

FAMILY PORTRAIT

NANCY BREWKA-CLARK

Wilfred Fellowes drew his handkerchief from the breast pocket of his mourning coat. "Come, come, Hildegarde, you mustn't make yourself ill." He proceeded to dab at his wife's eyes, all the while speaking briskly as one would to a distraught mare. "You're going to bear many healthy children."

Remembering how her impoverished father had given her hand in marriage to his oldest and richest friend, a three-time widower, promising him a fruitful union at long last, Hildegarde whispered, "But our precious Sarah lived only a few hours. What if it happens again?"

"Never dwell on the past." He beamed down at her. "Now, I have a surprise for you. I've hired a photographer to take a portrait of the three of us. Baby's all laid out nicely in the nursery. Bridget dressed her in her christening gown and bonnet. Out of bed with you and I'll ring for Bridget to put you in your loveliest frock."

Steeling herself to behave as her father would have wished, Hildegarde's hand moved to her belly. "It's odd, being slender again."

He smoothed his thick white mustache. "I will rectify that soon enough, my dear, I promise you."

~❦~

Months passed, but Hildegarde showed no signs of carrying another child.

"If things don't improve soon, I shall schedule an appointment with Dr. Farley for you." Wilfred scowled. "We'll see if a medical reason can be given for your barren state."

"Please don't use that word," Hildegarde quavered.

He pointed to the photograph hanging on the flocked red velvet wall of infant Sarah propped like a wax doll in her lap. "Then behave accordingly. Your duty is to preserve my line into posterity."

Remembering how the ancient mausoleum doors swallowed up the tiny white coffin, she murmured, "I swear that I will never forget, not even for a moment."

~❦~

Instead of insisting on endless bed rest, Dr. Farley had recommended that Hildegarde relax in the fresh air of springtime. Reveling in her good luck, she arranged the wicker chaise longue to face away from the old stone mansion and toward a double row of blooming lilacs. Behind their intertwining branches lay the graveyard where the Fellowes mausoleum rose like a miniature castle among the tombstones of lesser mortals.

Shutting her eyes, Hildegarde breathed in the sweet perfume and dozed.

"Mama?"

Hildegarde bolted upright.

A faint burst of giggles, light as soap bubbles, floated toward her. Bright against the lilac hedge stood four little girls, each taller than the last and all holding hands like paper dolls. Jaunty in their straw bonnets and white kid boots, they rose up, up, up, white skirts billowing.

"'Bye, Mama," the littlest cried.

"Sarah, my darling, precious Sarah," Hildegarde cried, "come back!"

But the children had vanished over the tops of the lilacs.

Where had her darling Sarah gone? And who were all her little friends? She ached to know. But how could she ever find out?

~ॐ~

In their massive mahogany bed that night, Hildegarde lay beneath her panting husband thinking of their little girl. Her endless grief had made Wilfred turn against her. If she could let the memory of Sarah go, surely all would be well. "I long for another daughter," she whispered.

"Don't say that," he growled, "or I will see to it that you will have nothing and be nothing. Nothing! Do you understand?"

His hands were at her neck, grasping and squeezing. "Wilfred," she choked, "you're hurting me."

After a terrifying moment, the deadly grip relaxed. "Concentrate," he told her, "on a son. Do you hear me? A son."

~ॐ~

As her maid helped her to dress the next morning, Hildegarde asked, "Bridget, am I like the others?"

The fingers stopped fastening the row of ivory buttons. "The other wives, I mean."

"Yes, madam." Once more the buttoning commenced. "How?"

Bridget shrugged. "Young. Pretty. Sweet."

Dead. The word echoed in her aching head. Wasn't that what *nothing* meant?

"I have to ask you." Hildegarde stopped, afraid to say what came next even though it had kept her awake all night. "Did—did the others—have a child? A daughter?"

A long silence filled the room. "Yes, madam, so they did. Each of 'em."

"And—and they all died?"

"Yes, madam." The maid cleared her throat. "Just as your bairn did. In their sleep." In a quick burst she added, "All in the old tomb out there, all four of 'em, three with their mothers."

"Bridget, how did their mothers die?"

"I can't say for sure, madam."

Hildegarde's hands shook as she reached toward the woman. "Please."

"It may have been something in their drink."

"And—and the babies?"

"Smothered in the crib. Doctor said it was the pillows. Too fluffy for wee bairns." Bridget's jaw worked grimly. "Now, madam, if you'll excuse me, I have work to do."

"Yes. Yes, of course."

Numbly, Hildegarde watched as the older woman walked slowly toward the door. Her heart lurched as Bridget turned back toward her. "I have a bit of money put by. If you want, madam, I can pack a valise. There's a train at 11:05. In the city, you can hire a detective. He'll get to the bottom of it all."

Hildegarde imagined four little girls, small and light

and bright as clouds dancing in a ring, and sent a fierce pledge to them all. The man who'd fathered them only to destroy them and their mothers would pay for his misdeeds. And, fortunately for posterity, there would be no male heir after all.

~

Nancy Brewka-Clark began her writing career at a daily newspaper chain on Boston's North Shore and went on to write short stories, poetry, creative nonfiction, and drama that have been published in the U.S. and abroad.

For two decades she also painted professionally under the name of Nascha, creating unique gilt bas reliefs that combined 18th century New England colonial japanning and Ukrainian folk motifs. That work was featured in *Yankee Magazine*, *The Boston Globe*, *The New York Times*, *People Magazine* and a host of other publications.

A lifetime devotee of Nathaniel Hawthorne, or more specifically his enigmatic older sister Elizabeth, she lives in Beverly, Massachusetts, with her husband Tom. Visit her Amazon author's page to see the full spectrum of her work.

DUST TO DUST

ROB FRANCIS

The long shadow of death cuts so deep into the room that Chiara can feel the bite of its moon-sharpened edge on her skin.

She avoids looking at the bed as she crosses the cool tiles to the window and opens the shutters. Alpine air sweeps in, painful against her wet cheeks.

"Mother." Giovanni's voice is faint now, little more than a moan.

Chiara moves to the bed and places a hand on her son's forehead. Cool. Giovanni appears peaceful, features calm, eyes closed.

"It's okay, Mother."

Chiara doubts that but smiles as best she can. "The doctor will be here in the morning. A specialist, they said. She'll know what to do."

Giovanni sighs distantly. "It'll be fine, Mother. I promise."

Voices drift in from the street, the sharp barks and laughs of teenage boys. Chiara closes her eyes and tries to breathe steadily until they are gone.

~❧~

Dr. Gallo arrives mid-morning and asks to see Giovanni without preamble. In the bedroom, Chiara draws back the bedclothes to expose her son's body for silent examination. The doctor pokes at the hard, grey flesh with a small steel pointer, her other hand worrying at a gold crucifix hung round her neck.

"Petrification. Well. There are a few records of human tissue mineralising in the archives at the National Library, though they are very rare. Mainly documented by priests, who ascribe it to periods of great stress or trauma. Has your son experienced any difficulties recently?"

Chiara thinks of the Conti brothers, the three boys always hounding Giovanni and getting bigger and bolder all the time.

"He won't say."

"I see." As if that is a failing on Giovanni's part. Or hers.

Chiara takes a deep breath. "So you'll take him to hospital? There is some treatment?" She can't keep her voice from breaking.

"I'm afraid not. There is nothing that can be done in such cases and moving him will just accelerate things. Take comfort in this: God is calling him home."

A flush of rage claws over Chiara's skin. "He can call all He wants. We won't answer."

Dr. Gallo offers a sad smile. "Sometimes innocents are chosen to bear great burdens. Their suffering is all the more meaningful, for being undeserved."

Chiara turns to the window and watches the pale sky in silence, until the doctor has gone.

While Giovanni sleeps, Chiara prays. But not to any god the good doctor would recognise.

Bread is all that Chiara can stomach. Leaving the little bakery in the square, a loaf clasped under her arm, she sees Tomasso Conti leaning by the fountain, smiling to himself. Until her hands are around his throat.

"What did you do to him? What did you do!"

He struggles, wide-eyed, thrashing; then is free and running across the square, people staring at them both.

The loaf lies forgotten on the cobblestones. Chiara's fingernails are streaked with crimson. She walks home carefully, so that the blood doesn't drip.

The bed is empty. Almost. Beneath the sheets are only fragments of powdery stone. Chiara runs her hands through the silt. Could a person, an entire life, have been reduced to this?

The town is quiet outside the open window. Probably she should weep for her son. Instead, she gathers handfuls of Giovanni's remains into a bowl before pouring herself a glass of Amarone and pulling a chair to the window.

As the daylight drains from the sky she sits, working the dust with her hands, Tomasso's blood still tacky on her skin.

She prays. Three times she casts the bloodied powder from the window into the evening air.

And three times, a shadowed breeze carries it high over the houses.

The little town is no longer quiet, its steady drone

punctuated by shouts of alarm that echo around the narrow lanes. Chiara sits, sipping wine and watching the glowering sky as it fades to darkness and back to light again. Sometimes she walks the room or rubs grains of stone from her son's bed between finger and thumb, watching them turn to dust.

As twilight comes once more, she looks from the window to see one of Giovanni's school friends passing the house.

"Francesca!" It feels odd to speak, as if she has spent an age in solitude.

The girl looks up in surprise. "Ms. Lombardi. How is Giovanni?"

"Resting. What's the news, Francesca? I haven't been out. But I hear things."

The girl's eyes widen. "You don't know? Two of the Conti brothers are dead. Carlo hanged himself from the old chapel bridge last night. Then this morning, Federico was found at Saint Peter's. He'd climbed the roof and fallen — or jumped — and his body was amongst the tombs, all smashed up. Imagine! Two of the Conti brothers, dying days apart."

Chiara grinds stone dust between her fingertips. Traces of dried blood still stain her skin and nails.

"How awful! Their poor mother must be suffering terribly. And how is young Tomasso taking it?"

"He's refusing to leave the house. Just hiding in the basement, scared half crazy. Isn't it dreadful?"

"It is." Chiara settles once more into her chair and pours another glass of wine.

~❧~

She watches the sky redden over the river, the smoke

climbing across the moon. Hears the anguished pealing of the church bells. All too late for poor Tomasso. All too late.

Something moves in the shadows behind her. The smell of smoke is sharp in the bedroom.

Chiara turns, but does not look. She crosses to the door, leaving the window open to the cold night and flickering sky.

She pauses at the threshold. "Goodbye, Giovanni."

The darkness maintains its silence. She closes and locks the bedroom door, then stands in the stillness of the hallway, a great emptiness held in her mind that permits no thinking or feeling. It is only when the dawn comes that she finally moves, crossing to the bathroom to try to wash the blood and smoke from her hands.

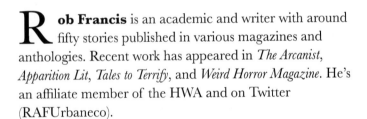

Rob Francis is an academic and writer with around fifty stories published in various magazines and anthologies. Recent work has appeared in *The Arcanist*, *Apparition Lit*, *Tales to Terrify*, and *Weird Horror Magazine*. He's an affiliate member of the HWA and on Twitter (RAFUrbaneco).

MRS. ANNA ENGLISH

AVITAL MALENKY

Ms. Ellie Wall, MSc, HCPC registered
December 1, 2018

She was the best, yet strangest student, I had in a while. My course, "Sensory Difficulties Children Diagnosed with ASD Face Daily, for Parents and Carers" was open to the public so I have seen my fair share of complicated people, but Mrs. English was a level above.

She wasn't disheveled or unclean, and her behavior was very polite; Mrs. English was a little old lady, a bit stiff maybe, a bit distanced when you interacted with her, but still just a cute, little old granny. It was the way she spoke that signaled the first different thing about her—she could turn a phrase that would catch you off guard and roll you down a hill. From her accent to her strange wording and cutting insights, Mrs. English was brilliant, almost scary in her genius.

She waited after every class to speak to me, having written everything I said down in her notebooks. During the lesson, she also found time to arrange a list of follow-up questions, requests for further bibliography, and several remarks that would surpass my knowledge and make my mind swirl. The first time we spoke, she left me in tears with a single one of these historic remarks.

"I ache for all the mothers who were far too late to join your miraculous course, Ms. Wall. Mothers who had to watch their sons wither and die in dark asylums just because they were born somewhat different. Far from being a Wall, my dear, you are a window and a doorway."

And gone, into the night, leaving me with a head full of questions. Leaving me shook up and pensive, smoking a lonely cigarette on a Tuesday night outside the old local school.

~☙~

Mr. Jacob Pane, Physician, St. Dymphna Abbey, House for the Insane
January 5, 1845

Having followed the accounts of young master English since his arrival at the abbey, I want to document them in writing for scientific and historic purposes. Beyond anything I will account for here, I am still a scientist and a physician. Whatever the 'powers' at work may be in this case, I cannot explain with reason and I bring them before you for you to judge.

Young English was brought to our care ten years ago with little to no chance of discharge. However, this past month he has been discharged to his family's care with my blessing–the only patient to leave St. Dymphna Abbey House for the Insane that I have ever seen in all my years working here.

At the age of ten young English was already a big lad,

and was brought in for violent and dangerous behavior to himself and his family. He had beaten the family servant girl bloody and was about to hit his own mother with a wooden cane. After this horrific incident, and being just barely restrained by the Father, young English was sent to the abbey to be admitted.

The first few months only the Father came to visit the boy. He had paid St. Dymphna a large sum of money each month for the boy's needs and came to make sure young English was well looked after. I asked if Mrs. English would visit as the boy seemed to miss her–he would often cry "Mamma", his only word, repeating it over and over until he would finally fall down, exhausted, and slept.

Mr. English commented he'd rather she not visit as she easily saddens herself. Since it was his decision to make, I did not press the matter.

There were a few months when no one came to supervise the boy at all and, later that year, it was only Mrs. English who came alone.

Mrs. Anna English had informed me coldly that her husband had died, leaving their entire fortune to young English and that she had been left his legal guardian. Supporting documents to verify her demands were presented. Mr. English, a well-known professor at our local university, disappeared from his lab one day and had been presumed dead. It had been quite the scandal and reported about in all the papers; foul play was suspected by the police as he vanished from his workplace without a trace.

Mrs. English, at her request, started seeing her son every day for several hours alone and largely unsupervised.

I secured a doubling of the payment made towards the abbey for young English and so happily approved her visits as a reward for the unhappy woman . The Bishop heard of my achievement and I was promoted, given a better room, and a ten pound raise to my annum.

~❧~

Ms. Ellie Wall, MSc, HCPC registered
August 3, 2019

It was just another Tuesday, smoking and talking to Mrs. English after class.

But it was the last night of the course and by then I was looking forward to talking to Mrs. English more than the actual classes. I knew it was going to be a goodbye—I just had no idea what kind of a goodbye it was going to be. I had already broken the law and many of my own rules for her.

At her request, I brought the full list of books and papers I used to write the course, including the same list from a dozen other courses I taught at other venues through the years. I made copies of everything I had and arranged it as easily as I could for her in a large black binder. Carefully packed was also a bag with as many Ritalin, Concerta or Adderall pills as I could buy on the black market in one week. Luckily I still had ties with "the guy" who sold me weed in college.

I did all this for her because the week before she finally told me who she was and why she joined my class. She confided in me why she asked so many questions and what she intended to do with all that knowledge and illegal pills. Smoking our little sinful cigarette, the wise silver-headed stranger I came to admire said to me:

"Imagine a woman, born some two hundred years ago. She is bright, brighter than anyone she knows, but she still can't help her son who was born, sadly, a little different.

Imagine this woman, after sadly losing her unloving husband, finally discovering one night the secret of time travel.

Imagine further her happiness, her absolute joy, when she finds her son might not be out of the ordinary at all, that in this fantastic future she found, she could learn how to diagnose and treat her only son, who she left behind in the past in an asylum, cuffed to a wall for his own safety, endlessly scared and alone.'

And if you can imagine all that, Ms. Wall, can you imagine why I must go back?"

I never saw her again, but I hope to science she was able to help her son.

For whoever may be who reads my words in the future, I hope a mother's love concurred all.

Signed,

Ellie

~❧~

Mrs. Anna English, St. Dymphna Abbey, House for the Insane
March 15, 1845

Upon my return, I seemed to have aged a decade overnight. Having lost my husband, and my only son a patient in St. Dymphna, probably indefinitely, I saw my aging as a sign of my unhappiness.

The visits I was so careful to keep each day were harming no one and so were allowed to carry on. It was two years before any change was visible in Emanuel but I was there that day it happened. That first day when he asked, with a single word, having never spoken it before, for water.

"Water" he said. I confess I didn't believe my ears at first. However, Emanuel said it again and again for about twenty minutes and would not rest until I brought him a drink of water. The next day it happened again. He has never asked me for anything in the past and would convey his hunger with moans or cries, beating objects continuously on the floors for the attention he didn't know he needed.

From that day, the changes in my son happened fairly quickly for a child with such communication difficulties. The staff's frustration with him dropped every day as he learned more words. The years passed and the child I once knew learned how to behave like a regular little boy, despite his age, leaving his noncommunicative qualities behind him. As Emanuel was becoming less violent in the process, discharge became a viable option.

As I kept on visiting, his hysterical episodes and tantrums, brought on by his frustration and unanswered needs, subsided and the boy he was started to come out for all to see.

It only took five years to get Emanuel to a position where his doctors agreed that it would be safe for me to continue to care for him in my home. Upon his discharge his physician took me to one side and said:

"Since the day I started practicing medicine, I have never seen anything like this. I believe with all my heart that I have seen a mother's love save a man from insanity."

Signed,

Anna

Avital **Malenky** is working on her debut novel, a time travel book about the plight of women throughout the centuries and the never ending fight for their rights. She lost two children in childbirth and her one living son has autism, She has lived with complex PTSD for 10 years now. Her family recently left Israel and moved to the UK and she's loving it.

DEAD MAN TALKING

BY ELLEN DENTON

Ayler opened his eyes and sat up in the center of a starlit field. There was no past and no future, just a rippling of bending grasses that murmured like harp strings in the wind. He could see bodies standing in the field all around him – dark, tattered forms that swayed like scarecrows in the singing breeze.

One by one, the eyes of those forlorn souls sprang open. There were pin pricks of starlight within the dark and otherwise lifeless pupils.

~ঽ▲~

He was moving through the field towards a town along with the others but had no memory of starting to walk. Ayler knew he was going forward because necklaces of woods to the left and right of him drifted slowly past, and the lights up ahead got fractionally larger with each step.

When they reached the outskirts of the town, as though sharing a single mind, they stopped, and he innately knew that they would now wait here. He could see the top of the clock tower in the town square. The moon sat over its shoulder spilling frozen, white light onto the surrounding housetops. That, along with the sound of dogs barking in the distance, was as meaningless to him as the earth beneath his feet.

~❧~

Daybreak came and the inert bodies jerked into motion. Ayler sensed an army of dead things rattling all around him like desiccated leaves in an autumn wind. He became aware of the ground beneath his own feet, then of the pressure of work boots against his ankles when he took a step. This sensation jolted him and he lurched sideways. He was so newly dead that things of the living, like a foot wriggling in a shoe, could still briefly enkindle something within him.

~❧~

Ayler and the others, stiff-legged, moved slowly but inexorably through the town. The stench of their decay heralded their arrival so that, like a match flame blown to extinction, all sound ceased as they approached. The dogs that had defensively howled through the night, now slunk shivering out of sight, while behind boarded up windows and doors, human survivors huddled quietly.

Many of the others, trudging in oblivion, stumbled and fell over half-eaten bodies strewn throughout the street and then lay face downward on top of the putrescent corpses. Those that couldn't regain their feet, simply buried their faces and mouths in the remaining juices of the decomposing dead, or licked the bones where only bones remained. Others rose and continued their march toward fresh, living meat.

Ayler, through some still-existing instinct, stepped around the dead and fallen as gnawing hunger within impelled him forward. He crossed a bridge, unconscious to the whoosh sound of rushing water and to the bloated bodies floating in swirling eddies downstream.

He passed three of his own kind fighting over the remaining carcass of a newly killed dog, even as they already held one or another of the creature's torn off limbs within their teeth. Ayler then approached what had once been a man, drinking green fluid out of the chest cavity of a rotting, human corpse.

He slowly came up beside him. The man-thing raised its head. The side of its face had a clouded over, milky-blue eye and white, pasty skin flaking off in places. It then turned fully toward Ayler. The other half of the face was a dripping, half-eaten nest of maggots, some from the corpse it was feasting on, some from eggs hatched in its own body.

For reasons he would nevermore understand, Ayler shuddered and backed away.

With no sense of time passing and no memory, it could have been either seconds or hours that had elapsed when he found himself alone on a narrow, cobblestone street. Ayler vaguely sensed the subterranean groans of the others scattered elsewhere through the town.

He'd been jarred into this murky awareness of his surroundings by the sound of frightened whispers coming from somewhere behind him, followed by the scampering of feet and a door slamming.

The pumping of living hearts so near to him were

thundering ocean waves in his ears, and the warm flesh smell flowed over him like honey. The black, relentless core of his hunger now exploded into a mindless, red frenzy.

Ayler spun around, almost tripping over his tangled-up feet, but with windmilling arms, righted himself before he hit the ground. He stumbled toward the fresh, living food source, drawn to it by the pungent magnet of its sweat. Two small children stood huddled together by a door that, in the basest moment of human terror, had been barricaded against them by strangers who would not risk their own lives or those of their family, by opening it for two street urchins.

Flesh-specked saliva containing bits of his own tongue, parts of it compulsively bitten off and swallowed in the throes of his hunger, dribbled down his chin at the sight of the children. One was a girl in a torn up, dirty dress, whimpering in terror, the other a boy who had his arms protectively around the girl, his own face white as a sheet.

Ayler, all blind appetite, lurched towards the children, aware of nothing beyond his all-consuming craving – not the panicked cries of the little girl nor the frightened, but defiant look of the boy, not the agonized shrieks from elsewhere in town as humans and animals were ripped to shreds while still alive and awake, and not the running footsteps that came up behind him. He didn't even register the out-of-breath gasps from the person who had stopped there until, like a dove flying out of a fog, a familiar voice said his name.

~☙~

"Ayler! Stop!"

He was leaning toward the children, but as though his legs were made of rock, they froze in place at the sound of the voice. His body, continuing its forward momentum, tilted forward like a listing sailboat, bringing his face inches away from those of the children, and then, supported by the inhumanly rigid strength of his legs, swayed back the other way, bringing him to an upright position again.

When he turned around, the woman who faced him was calm and had no fear in her eyes, only love and a pity beyond all words.

"Ayler. You could never hurt anyone. You won't hurt those children now, and I know that you won't hurt me. Even as you are, you still have a choice, and even as you are, I love you."

For Ayler, in the dark world he had come to inhabit, the air itself seemed to be made of black, spinning spiders and their webs. He thrashed through the clouded, sludgy heaviness of this purgatory in a struggle to see his wife clearly, as she stood before him now, one more time.

The air-spiders spun wheels within wheels of webs in a fabric made from shadows, decay, graveyards, dark, airless holes underground, the wails of the lost, and the murmured refrains of the dead. As though waking from the worst of all possible dreams, he saw her, but only with eyes that look inward. When he looked outward again, it was at an empty street; there never was anyone there. He turned and looked at the two children. They stood silently watching him, the girl clinging to her brother, who still protectively held her.

The last, clear, conscious thought Ayler would ever have was that, even in the limbo of hell's unending night, love still sits enthroned and inviolate in the heart. He held that love the way someone who moves through a dark house at night shelters a candle flame in their cupped hands. That love guided him back through the town and to the bridge where water still rushed headlong in wordless song, and there he stopped. A shattered statue lay in pieces at the entryway to it. With a strength born of all the good that resides in humankind, he lifted up the largest slab.

A few moments later, when he went backwards over the bridge into the water, the hundred-pound chunk of stone he held clutched to his chest would ensure he'd sink to the bottom, and rise no more.

~☙~

The bloated, blue bodies of the hapless victims of the holocaust that swirled on the surface of the water were eventually carried out to sea, to be mercifully eaten by whatever predators they encountered there. Only one still lays nestled in the silt of the riverbed, pinioned in place by a massive rock. It will be there for a long time, because even hungry fish will not feast on such tainted flesh. Eventually though, time and tide will erode it away.

For now, in the darkest part of night, when the sky is clear, you can stand on the bridge, look down through the rippling water, and see two pinpricks of reflected starlight shining back up at you.

～

Ellen Denton is a freelance writer living in the Rocky Mountains with her husband and three cats. Extended families of wildlife sometimes appear outside the windows of her house and exchange a meaningful look with her before moving on. Her writing has been published in over a hundred magazines and anthologies.

ISSUE 12: DON'T LOOK BEHIND YOU

LOVE LETTERS TO POE

DEVEAU | HOLLAWAY | WONDERLY
MATULICH-HALL | KNIGHT

Volume 1, Issue 12 | September 2021
Edited by Sara Crocoll Smith

DECAY

TRISTIN DEVEAU

The house was old. This had been true even when Abigail and her late husband, Henry, first saw it over 50 years earlier. The young couple had fallen in love with the Victorian relic, surrounded as it was by modernity. They dreamed of restoring its anachronistic beauty, already hidden from most observers by years of neglect. When Henry was still alive, the couple had managed to keep ahead of the constant decay of time. Since his death, both the house and its sole occupant had started to wither, and the once vibrant colours of youth had long since faded to a muted grey.

Any who have lived in an old house eventually become used to its particulars. Familiarity makes one deaf to the creaks and groans of its shifting bones, blind to the crooked walls that settle a little more each day, and immune to the signature, musty odor.

The summer had been hot and humid. For the past week, the air had been oppressive – threatening a storm that never came. Abigail, always a fitful sleeper, had been especially restless. She was lying wide awake atop the covers in her too-hot room; the sun was still hours away. Fatigue had crept into every bone, and the shallow, wet sounds of her breath disturbed her.

Abigail was suddenly aware of a smell lingering in the air. Not the expected scent of her decaying old house, but a different sort of rot; putrid yet horribly familiar. It had been twenty years, but she could never forget that smell.

"Henry?" Barely a whisper, Abigail's voice was swallowed by the vast emptiness of the house, the only reply its consistent creaking.

It was almost noon before Jimmy Classon's son, Duane, arrived. Seated in a worn wicker chair on the veranda, Abigail watched as the rusty pickup leisurely made its way down the street. Out the corner of her eye, Abigail could see a matching chair, long empty. She used to sit out here with Henry. They'd sit and chat as they drank their morning coffee, or perhaps read – Abigail, her romance novels; Henry, his westerns. Or, sometimes, they'd just sit in silence and watch the sun climb the horizon.

Abigail couldn't remember the last time she'd sat out here. She'd lost her taste for romances, and the warm rays of the sun offered no comfort from the cold she'd feel whenever her eyes fell on the empty chair. Still in her nightgown, she was certain that she looked every bit the crazed old woman the whole town whispered her to be. She'd been out here all morning. The thought of entering the house, of that smell…

The crunch of gravel signaled Duane's approach and Abigail, for decency rather than warmth, wrapped a tattered shawl around her shoulders. She'd been skeptical when Jimmy, insisting that he was too busy to come out himself, had told her that his son would take care of things. Duane had barely been talking the last time she had seen the boy, but it was a full-grown man who stood before her now. *Has it really been so long?*

She didn't follow him inside. For the two hours that Duane searched the house, inside and out, Abigail stood on her front lawn, which was overgrown and full of weeds. As the time crawled by, she wavered, lightheaded in the heat, and had to brace herself against the railing to ease the burden on her labouring lungs. Abigail appraised the building that had been her home for the last fifty years. Time had not been kind. *To either of us.*

"I'm sorry, Mrs. Renault. I couldn't find anything." The lad did look sorry. Embarrassed, even. "Maybe it was something from outside? Or some sewer gas?"

Jimmy had said as much when Abigail called him for help. "I know what I smelled, and I'm telling you, something has died inside that house."

A look danced across the young man's face, fleeting, but Abigail could read it plain as day. He was young, but not so young that he didn't know the stories. The gossip. Her lips tightened; she knew what they used to say about her. *Crazy Abigail Renault, as good as murdered poor old Henry.*

Even the smell of death was preferable to standing before that look. And so, with a brief thanks, she dismissed Duane and braced herself to re-enter her home. To her surprise, when Abigail stepped back inside, the only scent that greeted her was its familiar musk.

Alone, as she had been for the past twenty years, Abigail moved through the empty house which groaned along with each step, as if it shared the pain she felt in her own joints.

~❦~

It hadn't been the first time that Henry had stormed off after they fought. He had disappeared before, run off for a week or more before returning and slipping back into the quiet routine of their lives as if nothing had happened. How could she have known? She had heard his angry footsteps and the slam of the front door. *But it wasn't the front door, was it?*

He had survived a day at least. Maybe two. (*Didn't you hear him fall?*) *It's an old house.* (*Surely, he must have cried out.*) *It makes all sorts of noises.*

In the end, it was the smell that had led her to Henry.

~❧~

Lying on the bed she once shared with her husband, Abigail was drifting into an uneasy sleep when her breath caught sharply in her throat. *No.* The rank smell of putrescence, of death and rot, filled the air.

Some animal must have found its way in. Got stuck and died. Sliding out of bed, the stench made her feel faint. *Or the sewer has backed up.*

Abigail steadied herself against the wall as she left the bedroom, her hand sliding along the dull wainscotting. *All original*, a beaming Henry would proclaim to their guests.

Henry. Despite her own assurances, she knew exactly what the smell was. Nothing else had that particular sickly sweet scent. Abigail gasped for air, the odor intensifying as she crept downstairs. With each breath, came a fresh wave of nausea.

She had to get to the front door (*but it wasn't the front door, was it?*). She had to get out (*what did you hear?*), but she could not. Abigail had become a mere spectator in her own body – watching, rather than guiding, as she moved deeper into the house. The air, so thick with the smell of rot, felt as though she were walking underwater.

The cellar door was closed. Just as it did twenty years before, the rank air oozed through the gaps. Twenty years ago, she had felt no fear. Numb, Abigail knew exactly what waited for her on the other side *(Didn't you hear something?)*, crumpled at the bottom of the steps *(A crash? A cry?)*.

Tonight, Abigail trembled as she stood before the door, which seemed to swell, the miasma it held straining to burst free and spread foul decay to every corner of the old house. Abigail saw herself open the door. The air around her rushed in and washed over her like a wave, a receding tide pulling her into the deep dark ocean of the basement below.

In the blackness, the ancient steps creaked *(the house makes so many noises)*. The tainted air burned her lungs, she could taste the corruption as she breathed in and out. Her breath and the creaking of the steps the only sound.

(But wasn't there another sound? A crash?) Abigail lurched forward as a rotten board gave way under her weight. *(A cry?)* Her surprised shout barely left her lips before she felt the first, jarring impact. Brittle bones, weak with age, twisted and broke.

There was no pain, not at first, as she lay on the cold concrete at the base of the stairs. Just an overwhelming feeling of wrongness. Her breath, shallow, drew in the damp, stale air, so familiar to any who have lived in an old house. When the pain finally came, the house, shifting its own tired bones, echoed her cries.

Before the sun had risen, her cries had turned to whimpers, then faded to silence.

When Jimmy Classon stopped by the following week, the only sounds he heard were the familiar creaks and groans that every old house makes. It was the smell that led him to Abigail.

~

Tristin Deveau writes and direct short films. "Decay" is his first published short story. He's currently working on finishing a feature length science fiction screenplay called *Axiom,* along with developing a couple of new short films. You can learn more about his work at his website at www.tristindeveau.com.

THE HOUSE REGARDS

KEVIN HOLLAWAY

I am the House, and I regard

Aloft on the hill, the light seeks me
I can only absorb it, and feed the darkness

I am devoid of judgment
I do not discriminate
I welcome none, but allow all
Many have sought solace within
None dwell in peace

Have I no bones?
My columns support morbid actions
You dare say I have no skin?
My walls peel from unholy deeds

Have I not eyes?
My frosted panes tell no future
But swell with the past
Much I see, and do not relish the view

Do I not bleed?
My pipes seep of cursed life
I have no scars?
The ceilings are seared
They blister with aging sin
The floors are engraved with profane rage

I have no mind?
My attic seethes with shame
Motes dance amongst rotting beams, crooked from
    guilt
I do not breathe
But the decayed air echoes with stifled breaths

Yet, I still regard

I am the refuge of feats untoward
A sanctuary of evil, horror, and hell
My foundation cracks with buried intent
The bodies do not speak, but the dead do
Roaming the halls, yearning to confide, warn, and
    remind

Acts committed?
They cannot be numbered
Stories?
My rooms tell many

A planned execution upstairs
The curtains are still stained
A lonely girl, desolate and lost
The rope still swings from the rafters

A dark ritual, summoning an unbridled force

The ancient carvings still mark the floor
A lover's revenge on a cheating act
The holes still riddle the bed

A man on the run, looking to bury his guilt
The rumpled clothes lay charred in the boiler
A drifter just passing through
The perished food still rots in the kitchen

A remorseful leader bent with shame
The bath water still swirls red around the blade
Thieves fleeing the inevitable
The loot remains hidden in the basement

Yes, it all rests in me
Hate, disgust, desire, angst, rage
Remorse, sorrow, pain, grief, regret
And there is always room for more

As the dusk dissolves to night
The town still pretends
Yet I remain silent
I have long before, and will long after

I am the House on the hill
And I regard

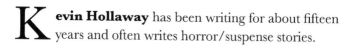

Kevin Hollaway has been writing for about fifteen years and often writes horror/suspense stories.

A FAMILY HEIRLOOM

JENNIFER WONDERLY

The place was a broken, bloody maw. Teeth were knocked out in the shattered windows and piano-key-crooked front steps, and no amount of flossing could ever scrape away the over one hundred years of decay and rot they left behind. Washed out paint bled through the gums of the foundation and the chimney was asphyxiated with cobwebs as thick as cotton. The iron fence resembled more of a busted bracket on braces than anything that could keep anyone out. But then, she thought, so did barbed wire at first glance. The door was a shade of coated tongue, cracked. It was with great trepidation that Rowan's fingers clasped the knob delicately and, fearful at the time that it might break, or worse, that the squeak of the door would awaken something that ought not to be disturbed, turned it.

As expected, inside it was ash-lung black, and despite the diminutive size, the darkness was cavernous. Miniature furniture jutted out like ominous stalagmites. She fiddled with a flashlight she had brought along for the inspection, and yet her nerves continued to quake with the rhythm of the jingling batteries even as light stretched across the room. It never quite reached far enough or illuminated everything. They never do. She didn't move further in but craned her neck, feeling like a fool peering into a crystal ball despite the dust therein. And no doubt looking more like the bird her old school mates often compared her to. She took in the dust-blanketed living room and breathed deep as her heart struggled between wanting something to happen—*to get it over with*—and nothing to move save for maybe a spider.

The truth of it was that Rowan wanted nothing to do with the house, but that was the uneven trade of death. Losing one priceless thing, usually, and in exchange getting an undertaker's worth of debt and junk that had been an amalgamation of what was once yours, in some capacity. Usually. Grandfather had kept it and, as the only remaining heir, so too was she tasked with its care. That was the how of things. The why was something that had continued to elude her, as he left no note or explanation. Even if he had, Rowan wasn't entirely sure it would have justified it. Perhaps he had done it out of some nostalgic love, or maybe more realistically, because he hadn't found a way to destroy it. Either way, Rowan could only speculate what she didn't know. What she *did* know did not a pretty picture paint.

The business was a harbinger of ruin, yet it did not start that way. Few did. Like a seed, it had been planted, and if left to its own devices maybe things would have turned out alright. Smothered before it could take root. However, the constant watering of the kind of isolating misery only a broken family could generate nursed that seed to a full, tragic bloom. Her great aunt Rose had been the unfortunate soul to be the soil.

The house had been a gift to Rose, and she had poured

her all into it, but forgot to leave some for herself. Rowan supposed that if the crumbs of stories had any substance of truth in them, she couldn't blame her great aunt. It was a scrap of salvation in what sounded like a hurricane, and if it kept her head above water all the better. The décor was picked with care and not a mite of dust was permitted life, no matter how small the cranny. Visitors were especially vetted before they were allowed in her sanctuary, never mind the more rigorous process residents went through. Hair was combed, clothes were pressed, and each had to be posed just so. Her dedication had been charming until slowly, the veil had been lifted to reveal its less welcome cousin, obsession.

Obsession is what kept Rose up in the witching hour, adjusting a frame here, repainting the living room there, and washing the dishes that were never dirtied. Broken wine bottles were repurposed for wall art, old clothes were sacrificed on the altar of the sewing machine for the sake of blankets, curtains, and rugs. It was when she heard voices that ought not to speak that people became worried. Yet like Cassandra's fierce prophecies, any concerns brought up went unheeded, smoothed over with platitudes that were as transparent and flimsy as Tupperware. There's a difference between a house and home and maybe the fact that hurt was pressed so firmly and so flatly in the pages of her psyche from a young age is what allowed the thorns to catch on her, like her namesake.

Rowan's flashlight stopped cold on an old stain splashed on the pine floor, the sort all humans instinctively recognize, an heirloom of knowledge our ancestors pass down to us. It sits on the shelf next to the horror of the unknown the dark conceals beneath its skin. The blood had crusted into the cracks and dyed the rug in front of the fireplace a light pink hue, and it was all Rowan could do to swallow. The beam of the flashlight stuttered to a start and Rowan swept it across the room, fast, then slow, undecided on whether she should yank the band-aid off and get it over with and go inside or peel it back slowly to get a better look. Still more caked the walls and if she didn't know better, Rowan would have thought a murder had taken place.

Consumption, the doctor had said, or so the story went, black bag in hand and shoulders slumped underneath the weight of the repetitive diagnosis, likely not knowing just how right and wrong he was. By the time the end came, the house had more life than Rose had. They tried to pry what was left of great aunt Rose from the floorboards, the shutters, the crevices of the fireplace bricks, and oh how she had screamed. To her dying day, Miss Muriel next door swore up and down the whole town heard it. That she could remember that but not her son's name said something Rowan didn't want to think about. Even as her earthly remains were carefully packaged away and packed down into the earth, her great aunt never left. Maybe if things had been different, if it had only stopped there, that would have been followed up with the teasing laughter and soft reassurances of cousins that never got to exist during late night sleepovers, told by the very flashlight she held.

Something scampered toward the kitchen. Warily, unthinking, Rowan stepped closer, broke the threshold in a way that shouldn't have been possible…and was only cognizant of it when her boots thudded hard against the welcome mat and the door slammed shut behind her. Spinning on her heel, she reached for a knob that wasn't there and her fingers dug into the edges of the exit only to find the entire thing may as well have been a painting. Scarlet painted her nails as she clawed and scraped uselessly. The flashlight fell dead to the floor in her panic, and with it, the light. It was only when it felt like stinging nettles had made a home beneath her skin that she stopped, turned, and slumped.

As she stood with her back to the door that would not open, Rowan hiccuped her breath and her vision fogged with tears. There was no one coming to save her, the others had already been taken, and for the first time in her life... she had no one to rely on but herself. Knowing she was the only one that could finish this and *knowing* she was the only one that could finish this were two different things. Footsteps fell like raindrops on the floor above, getting closer to running down the stairs like a downspout, and Rowan made a sound that her throat wasn't too sure of. Half hysteria, half gasp, her hand came up to cover her mouth as she tried to settle her breathing. Just tried to breathe, to not suffocate in this mausoleum. She scrubbed at her eyes stubbornly, and gathered as much courage as she could, though it continued to slip through her fingers like cards stuck to the floor.

In the darkness, a pearl-studded smile hovered at the landing, tarnished with that damnable color, and grinned down at her. Others materialized, curved knives in the night. Rowan sought aid from anything in herself and the room, courage, clues, hell, divine intervention from something she hadn't believed in for years. In the depths of her pocket, Rowan found her matches first and grit her teeth in determination. A light flickered to life in desperation, in defiance, and could be seen from the attic window of the antique dollhouse.

∽

Jennifer Wonderly often writes about new beginnings and is currently researching to write a story that marries the ghost story with a fairy tale, or fable.

LIKE ANY OTHER NIGHT

JUDE MATULICH-HALL

Her breath rose in small bursts of grey, dissipating quickly, becoming just another billow of fog forming about the dark, sleepy street. Lydia stopped abruptly, her heart quivering within her slight chest. Turning slowly, she gazed hard through the oppressive stillness, listening for what might be there – hoping that there was nothing.

Greeted by silence, she laughed, a small, sardonic sound, which rang hollow in the midnight air. Surely *it* would not come to this neighbourhood; how ridiculous to think such things. Yet, she continued cautiously, attempting to quiet the clatter of her shoes upon the red brick darkening from the settling mist, toward her destination: Safety.

The doorway engraved in her mind, though she could not yet see it across the courtyard. The street lanterns flickered through the haze like fireflies, unable to fend off the cloudy vapors with their illumination. She argued silently with herself, how silly for a lady to be walking home alone from the theatre. Yet, she had so many times before.

Besides, the beast only hunted in the lowly parts of the city; the docks, the redlight district, the slums, the opiate dens. It had for years. As *it* should, for those places marred this glorious city, making it dirty and unwholesome. Those in power had conjured it to take care of such riffraff. *Those that do not abide by the law shall be punished.* Bolstered in her piousness, Lydia slowed in her step.

A rage erupted… too close. She whirled around as the bewailing reached her ears, searching the deadly silence that settled in the call's wake. *It* was here!

She fumbled for her small pocket watch, tucked discreetly in her sleeve. Confusion encompassed her, for it was before the curfew. Her brow glowered as she held the fob to her ear. It was not ticking! Only a short distance, her steps quickened once more, their sound pulsing, echoing around her. Lydia gathered her dress and sprinted toward the doorway in which she would arrive any moment, any moment, now, there, within her sight. She would reach it in time. She must!

It was getting closer. Gaining quickly. Its ferocious snarls deafening. It was furious, cursing loudly. Its screams bellowed throughout the streets, claws raking the cobbles.

She reached the door and permitted herself a triumphant smile over her shoulder. As her hand wrapped around the latch, her thumb pressed… it was locked.

Its cold breath of decay washed across the back of her neck. She did not turn to face it. Sliding down into a crouch, huddling, Lydia made herself as small as she could; whimpering, pleading as its shadow covered her.

≈

Jude Matulich-Hall has a degree in Art and Creative Writing. She grew up in Colorado and New Mexico, but now lives in the hauntingly beautiful and grey Pacific Northwest with her hubby and son. When she isn't writing she teaches yoga and meditation for pain management, plays the violin in North Oregon Coast Symphony, and has a vegetable garden when it's nice outside.

She's preparing for her debut novel, *The Eversteam Chronicles – Small Demons,* to be published this October. You can subscribe to her channel on Youtube, follow her on Amazon, Twitter (HallMatulich), and other such places. Join her Facebook group – JMH Writers & Illustrators, and check out her website www.JudeMatulichHall.com.

THE DARKEST THOUGHTS

SAM KNIGHT

They come late at night, when there is no one to tell me how silly they are, when there is no sunlight to expose them for the shadows they are. I don't know why electric lights cannot dispel them as the sun does. I don't know why firelight makes them stronger. But I know, in the deepest of the nights, in the darkest of the hours, these thoughts take on a life of their own.

I can't remember how old I was the first time I noticed them. Maybe they have always been with me.

Sometimes I wonder if they are thoughts at all. Or if they are even mine.

In the twilight darkness, in the gloom of the room, I have watched the things that should not move, do things they should not.

Have you seen them too?

Dolls, toys, action figures, faces in paintings, patterns on the ceiling… Have you seen the way they move in the darkness? Some ever so slightly, so carefully, that you can't be sure you are seeing them at all. Others are bolder, reveling in knowing that you know but can do nothing about it.

The photograph of grandmother that winks at you. The stuffed animal that turns the other way when you aren't watching. The fish in the tank, barely visible in the reflections from the streetlight, that inexplicably stands on its tail, fins where its hips would be, if it had hips, and glares at you disapprovingly.

I know I'm not the only one who's seen them. They've told me I'm not. They whisper it in voices disguised to sound like house creaks, fan motors, rattling water pipes, distant trucks, and anything else they can think of that you, or I, could possibly explain away.

It's when they talk using the sound of distant dogs or coyotes that I hate it the most. They taunt me then. Taunt that maybe the dogs are real. Might be accomplices. That they are coming this time, finally coming here. Will tonight be the night the pact will be broken, the night something in the darkness will dare use the distraction, the arrival of beasts, to do the unthinkable? To do the forbidden.

To kill me.

They shouldn't even be able to touch me. But they have. And they get away with it. There's never proof they did it. Maybe a gust of wind did it. That's what knocked the curio off the shelf and onto my head. Or the vibrations from the washing machine on spin cycle, shaking the old wooden floor, rattling the whole house. That's what made the frame fall from the wall, sending shards of glass all over the room. Including onto my bed, five feet away—and three feet higher—than where it landed.

No proof.

A distraction might be enough for them to get away with more. I don't know what stops them. Some higher power that keeps them in check, maybe? But if the dogs get here, or the coyotes, if they got here, that distraction would be enough to let them get away with it.

I would drop my guard. I would be focused upon what seemed to be a real danger. And then they would strike.

Somehow.

Those things in the shadows. The things that the sunlight says are mine, would, under the cover of the night, claim me for their own.

And maybe not just me. Maybe others, too.

They've told me, in disguised voices, I'm not the only one who's seen them. And, I believe, anyone who has seen them is considered a threat. I don't understand why, but we are a threat to them, a threat that needs to be eliminated.

I've tried throwing some of them away. Giving some to charity. Selling others. But the threat isn't the things themselves. Whatever the threat is, it uses those things to come closer. To be close.

All the time.

To watch us. To mock us as we lay awake in the dark.

And then, eventually, to do more.

I feel the distraction coming, like a thunderstorm growing on the horizon. The tension is building in the air like an impending lightning strike, and the distant rumble is deep in the ground.

They are going to find a way to reach me soon. And now, I can tell, they are looking for a way to reach you, too. They are using me to get to you.

I am so sorry.

I didn't mean to.

Put this down now. Don't read any further. I pray you are reading this in the daylight. If you aren't, please forgive me.

These dark thoughts have escaped from me, forcing

their way out into the world. I no longer have control. They have already infected you.

Oh, God, why?

Why did I write this? Why did they publish it? How were they manipulated, compelled, to pass this on, to continue this curse? Didn't the editor feel it coming, as I did? As surely you must as well?

You can feel them looking at you, can't you? Feel it on the back of your neck. Feel them waiting for you...

Why didn't I have the strength to resist?

I should have allowed them what they wanted. Allowed them to kill me. I could have stopped this.

But I was weak.

They have won anyway. They have killed me in a different way. They have killed me through you. I can't live knowing what I have done to you.

What they will do to you.

Please. Why are you still reading? Put this down. Stay out of the darkness. Stay in the sunlight. Don't pass this on to anyone else. Destroy it!

Remember, firelight makes it worse.

Do you see them? Did something just move out of the corner of your eye? Oh, God. Is that moving when you don't look right at it? Was that a dog barking?

Please don't close your eyes. Don't get distracted.

I'm so sorry...

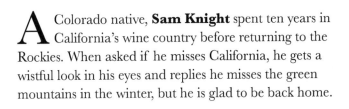

A Colorado native, **Sam Knight** spent ten years in California's wine country before returning to the Rockies. When asked if he misses California, he gets a wistful look in his eyes and replies he misses the green mountains in the winter, but he is glad to be back home.

As well as having worked for at least three publishing companies, Sam is author of six children's books, five short story collections, three novels, and over 75 stories, including three co-authored with Kevin J. Anderson, two of which were media-tie-ins: "Wayward Pines: Aberration" (Kindle Worlds, 2014) and "Of Monsters and Men", Planet of the Apes: Tales from the Forbidden Zone (Titan, 2016).

A stay-at-home father, Sam attempts to be a full-time writer, but there are only so many hours left in a day after kids. Once upon a time, he was known to quote books the way some people quote movies, but now he claims having a family has made him forgetful, as a survival adaptation. He can be found at SamKnight.com and contacted at sam [at] samknight [dot] com.

Free "The Masque of the Red Death" artwork when you sign up for the Love Letters to Poe newsletter!

Stay in the know on all things Poe when you sign up for the *Love Letters to Poe* newsletter.

Get your free "The Masque of the Red Death" printable artwork at www.LoveLetterstoPoe.com/Get-Red-Death-Printable.

LET US KNOW YOU WANT MORE!

A one or two sentence review can go a long way in spreading the word about *Love Letters to Poe* and all the amazing authors and poets published in this collection.

So if you've enjoyed the gothic stories and poems you just read, please consider leaving a quick review. Thank you so much—it means a lot!

ABOUT THE EDITOR

Sara Crocoll Smith is the publisher and editor-in-chief of *Love Letters to Poe*, a haven to celebrate the works of Edgar Allan Poe and encourage the creation of gothic fiction tapped from the vein of Poe. She also writes gothic horror, science fiction, and fantasy.

facebook.com/LoveLettersToPoe

twitter.com/LoveLettersPoe

instagram.com/LoveLettersToPoe

Made in the USA
Middletown, DE
14 September 2021